CHAPTER
36

6:30 p.m., Sunday

JEFFERY DEAVER

THE OCTOBER LIST

A Novel in Reverse
With Photographs by the Author

HODDER & STOUGHTON

Life can only be understood backwards; but it must be lived forwards.

– Søren Kierkegaard

She stood at the window of the Manhattan apartment, peering through a slit in the drapes. Her hands trembled.

'Do you see anyone?' the man across the room asked, voice edgy.

'I'm not sure. Maybe.' Her body pitched forward, tense, Gabriela tugged the thick sheets of cloth closer together, as if someone was scanning the windows with binoculars. Or a sniper rifle. 'Of course, I didn't see anybody earlier today, either. Until it was too late.' She muttered fiercely, 'I wish I had a gun now. I'd use it. If anybody's there, I swear to God I'd use it.'

Sam Easton asked, 'But who would it be?'

She turned to him, stepping away from the window fast. 'Who? It could be anyone. Everybody in the world, it seems, wants the goddamn October List!'

'How could they know you were here?'

Gabriela gave a bitter laugh. 'I don't seem to have any secrets anymore.' She hesitated, then, reluctantly, she looked out again. 'I just can't tell. I thought somebody was there. But then the next minute he was gone. I—' Then she whispered manically, 'The dead bolt!'

Sam stared, cocking his head.

Eyes wide in alarm, Gabriela asked, 'Did I lock it?' She walked quickly out of the living room around the corner to the hallway and then returned. 'No, it's okay. Everything's locked up.'

Sam now took her place at the window, looked out. 'I see shadows, I see some movement. But I can't tell for sure. Could be somebody, could be a tree blowing in the breeze. Damn streetlight's out, the one in front of the building.' He glanced at her. 'Was it working earlier?'

'I don't know,' she said. 'I think maybe it was. How could somebody shut out a streetlight?'

Sam didn't answer. He too stepped back from the slit between the drapes. He crossed the room and sat on a hassock near her. She'd noted earlier that he was in good shape but hadn't seen clearly how slim his waist was, how broad his shoulders. His muscles tested his suit jacket and white shirt.

Gabriela raged, 'Jesus, I hate this! . . . Sarah, what's she going through? What's she thinking? What—?' Her voice choked. Then she breathed in and out slowly. 'How soon, do you think, until we know?' Daniel and Andrew had left about a half hour ago to meet Joseph.

She wiped a dot of blood from her lower lip.

Sam said, 'Hard to say. Joseph's got his own agenda, you know. The . . . someone in his position pretty much has all the power.'

Gabriela could tell he was going to say 'the kidnapper' but didn't want to add that, maybe so that she didn't become more upset.

She exhaled slowly, pressed her rib cage. Gave a faint wince. 'I hate the waiting.'

Sam said awkwardly, 'They'll make it happen.'

'Will they?' she asked, in a whisper. 'Joseph's a crazy man. A wild card. I have no idea what he's going to do.'

A fog of silence filled the dim room, a silence engendered by two strangers who were waiting to hear a child's fate.

'When exactly did it happen?' Sam asked. His suit was unbuttoned, his tieless dress shirt starched smooth as Sheetrock.

'When did Joseph kidnap her?' Gabriela asked; she wasn't afraid to use the word. 'Saturday morning. Yesterday.'

Forever ago. That was the phrase that had occurred to her but she didn't use the expression with this man, whom she'd only known a few hours.

'And how old is Sarah?'

Gabriela responded, 'Six. She's only six.'

'Oh, Jesus.' His long, matte-dry face revealed disgust, a face older than that of most men in their mid-thirties. A jowl quivered.

She nodded, a token of thanks for the sympathy. After a pause: 'I hate Sundays.'

'I know what you mean.' Sam's eyes regarded her again: the new black jeans bought on the run while she and Daniel were being chased through the streets of New York. They fit poorly. A bulky, unbecoming navy-blue sweatshirt. He'd been noting her mussed auburn hair, and a gaunt face whose makeup had long ago been teared away. He scanned her lean hips too, her abundant breasts, but clearly had no romantic or lustful interest. She reflected, Whatever his circumstances or preferences, I'm sure I look pretty bad.

She rose and walked to the corner of the apartment. There sat a black backpack, from which the price tag still dangled. She unzipped it, then withdrew a smaller gym bag and, from that, a skein of yarn, some needles and the piece she'd been working on. The strands were deep green and blue . . .

Echoing a line from a song.

One of her favorites.

Eyes red, demeanor anxious, Gabriela sat once again in the shabby plush purple chair in the center of the living room. Though she clutched the yarn, she didn't begin the rhythmic, comforting motion, so familiar, with the red knitting needles yet. She touched her mouth with a tissue. Looked at the wad, which was white as fine linen, now blotched red. Her fingers were tipped with polish of a similar shade.

Then, *tap, tap*, Gabriela knitted five rows. She coughed several times, pressed her side, below her right breast, her eyes squinting shut momentarily. She tasted blood. Copper, salty, bitter.

Concern rippling his brow, Sam asked, 'If it's bleeding like that, shouldn't you go to the emergency room? It looks worse.'

Gabriela gave a brief laugh. 'That probably wouldn't be a good idea. Didn't Daniel tell you what happened this afternoon?'

'Oh. Sure. Wasn't thinking.'

'I'll live with it until I get Sarah back. Then I'll have things taken care of. In the prison hospital, most likely.' A cynical smirk accompanied this comment.

She studied the apartment once more. When she and Daniel had arrived two hours ago she'd been too preoccupied to notice much. In addition to being filled with beat-up furniture, and exuding a sense of the temporary, it was gloomy, particularly now in the oppressive dusk. She supposed this atmosphere was mostly due to the tall ceilings, small rooms, gray wallpaper flecked with tiny pale flowers. Her eyes went to the wrought-iron coffee table in the middle of the room. Its spiky edges looked like a weapon from a science fiction film.

Pain . . .

The table set her nerves aflame. But she thought yet again, as she'd done so often in the past two days: Your goal. All you should think about is your goal.

Sarah. Saving Sarah is your only goal. Remember that, remember that, remember that.

Gabriela asked, 'You work with Daniel much?'

Sam replied, 'We've had a relationship with him and The Norwalk Fund for close to seven years.'

'How many people've told him he looks like the actor?' She was thinking back to Friday night – could it really have been just two days ago? – meeting Daniel Reardon for the first time. Then later that evening: Recalling his damp brow, speckled with moisture, and beneath, his blue eyes, which were simultaneously easy and intense.

'A lot,' Sam said and again rubbed his bare, shiny scalp. 'I don't get that much: Are you this or that actor?' He was laughing. He had a sense of humor after all, maybe.

'And the head of your company, Andrew – what was his last name again?'

'Faraday.'

'He's a fascinating man,' she said. 'I've never heard of a specialty like his before.'

'Not many companies do what we do. He's made a name for himself. Travels all over the world. Flies a hundred thousand miles a year. Minimum.'

She knit another row of blue and green. *Tap, tap.*

'And *your* job, Sam?'

'I'm a behind-the-scenes guy. The operations chief for the company.'

'Like me,' she said. 'I run my company's office and . . .' Her voice faded and she gave a sour laugh. 'I *ran* the office. Before all this happened.' She sighed, dabbed at her mouth once more, examined the tissue and continued knitting, as if she were simply tired of receiving bad news. She gave him a wry look. 'Operations chief also has babysitter in the job description?'

He opened his mouth – a protest was coming – but then he said, with a grin, 'Was it that obvious?'

She continued, 'It doesn't make a lot of sense for you to be involved in this except for one reason: to make sure I stay out of their hair.'

'Daniel and Andrew are negotiating your daughter's release from a kidnapper. What would you do if you'd gone with them?'

She shrugged. 'Scratch Joseph's fucking eyes out.'

'That's what Daniel figured. Better for you to stay here.'

'And if I wanted to sneak off to the meeting, how were you going to stop me?'

'I'd probably beg.'

She laughed.

'What do you know about Joseph?' Sam asked.

The smile vanished like water in parched dirt. 'He's a monster, a sadist.' She cast a glance at the CVS drugstore bag, inside which they could see a bloodstain, paled by the white plastic.

Sam noted it too. 'Daniel told me about that. Unbelievable. Who'd do something like that?'

She closed her eyes momentarily, brow wrinkling. 'Joseph's big and intimidating. A bully, a thug. But you know what's worse? He's got this weird side to him. Like his haircut. He has real thick, blond curly hair and he greases it or something. It's eerie. He grins a lot. And he's got this, I don't know, this tone when he talks. You heard him on speaker-phone. Taunting. Giddy.'

'You know who he sounded like? That character from one of the Batman movies. Heath Ledger played him. Remember?'

'Yes, you're right. Exactly. The Joker.'

Suddenly Gabriela's fists closed around the knitting, as if she was going to rip the piece apart. A moment passed and she seemed to deflate, head forward, shoulders sagging. 'God, what a nightmare – this weekend.' A pathetic smile bent her lips. 'Two days ago I was a mother with a job I loved. I'd just met Daniel and, you know, things really clicked between us. And now? My daughter's been kidnapped. Daniel and your boss might be on their way to get shot. The police are after me and I've done some . . . I've done some terrible things today. Oh, Christ . . .'

She nodded toward the window. 'And apparently Joseph isn't the only one to worry about. The goddamn October List? Why did it end up in *my* lap?'

'It'll work out,' he said, though they both knew the reassurance was merely verbal filler.

After a moment she asked Sam, 'Why would Daniel do all of this for me? Anybody else would've been long gone.'

'Why? He's got an interest in what happens.'

'What?'

'You.'

'Me?'

Sam smiled. 'He likes you. That's what he told me . . . And told me not to tell you.'

She pictured Daniel's close-cropped black hair, his square jaw, his dancing blue eyes.

The actor . . .

She felt the rippling sensation, low in her belly. Had a memory of his lips on hers, his body close. His smells, his tastes. The moisture on his brow and on hers. 'I like him too.'

'Here's the thing,' Sam said, sitting forward on the leather hassock. 'No surprise: Daniel's good looking and he's rich and he's a nice guy. A lot of women see that and they think, Jackpot. But they don't care who he is, not inside. They don't connect. Daniel said you and he hit it off *before* you knew he had the boat and the fancy cars and the money.'

'Yeah, our meeting was *not* the most romantic experience in the history of relationships.' She gave Sam a careful gaze. 'Okay, he likes me. But he's also doing this because of what happened in New Hampshire. Right?'

'He told you?' Sam seemed surprised.

'He did, yes. Sounded pretty bad.'

A nod. 'Oh, yeah. Changed his whole outlook on life. And, true, probably that *is* one of the reasons he's helping you. Kind of giving back for what happened. That was tough. You know, with his kids involved and all.'

'Yes.'

'Daniel doesn't tell everybody about New Hampshire. In fact, hardly anyone.'

She stared at her knitting, the tangles of color. 'God, it's so risky, what he and Andrew're doing. They downplayed it, but . . .' She pulled her phone from the sweatshirt pouch, glanced at the screen, slipped it back.

'Anything?'

'Nothing.' A sigh. She rose, walked to the bar and poured some red wine. Lifted her eyebrow. Sam nodded. She filled a glass for him and returned to the couch, handed it off. They sipped. No tap of glasses or toast, of course. Not now.

Gabriela sat and started to sip, but eased the wine away from her lips. She exhaled audibly.

'Are you all right?' Sam asked.

Frowning broadly, she was staring at a newspaper on the *Alien* coffee table. Scooting forward.

'My God,' she said.

'What?'

She looked up, eyes wide as coins. 'I know what it is.'

He regarded her quizzically.

'The October List, Sam.' She slid the *New York Times* his way. He walked forward and picked it up. She continued, 'I know what it means! The clues were there all along. I just didn't put them together.' In a low voice, 'It's bad, Sam. What's going to happen is really bad.'

But before she could say anything there came a noise from the front hallway: a click, followed by the distinctive musical notes of the front door hinge, *O-oh*, high–low. Stale air moved.

Gabriela rose fast. Sam Easton, holding his wine in one hand and the newspaper in the other, turned to the hallway.

'Is my daughter all right?' she cried. 'Please tell me! Is my daughter all right?'

A man entered the room quickly. But it wasn't Daniel Reardon or Andrew Faraday, returning from their mission to save her daughter.

Joseph wore a black jacket and gloves and yellow-tinted aviator glasses. His glistening golden curly hair dangled to mid-ear.

In his gloved hand he held a pistol whose muzzle ended in a squat, brushed-metal silencer.

'No!' Gabriela gasped, looking toward Sam.

After scanning the room quickly, Joseph turned toward them, lifting the gun in a way that seemed almost playful.

CHAPTER
35

5:50 p.m., Sunday

40 minutes earlier

The warehouse was just as he'd left it on Friday, when he'd been here making preparations.

Damp, brick walls covered with scabby light green paint, redolent of cleanser fumes and oil and pesticide and rust, lit by unkind fluorescents. One began flickering and Joseph rose from the table where he'd been sitting, took a mop from the corner, the strands molded into a mass, sideways, like windswept hair, and with the tip of the handle shattered the offending tubular bulb. There was nothing sturdy enough to stand on to remove it. Shards fell, dust too. The crackle was satisfying.

This building was similar to the one where he'd done his little surgery last night, the warehouse west of Times Square. Here, in SoHo, there was a demand for industrial spaces to turn into private residences – at astronomical sums, of course. This particular building would probably never be converted. There were no windows. Bad for resale to chic-minded lawyers and brokers. Good for Joseph's purposes, though. In fact, he could just make out a faint spatter of dark brown dots on the floor. Several months ago those discolorations had been bright red. The man had finally told Joseph what he wanted to know.

Solid brick walls. They absorbed the screams well.

Before returning to the chair, he walked to the heater panel, turned the unit up. Mold-scented air slipped out of the vents. Warmish. Still, he kept on his gloves – thin, flesh-colored cloth. Not for the comfort, though. Force of professional habit. Joseph recalled many times in the heat of summer when he'd worn gloves like these.

He sat once more, in the chair on whose back his leather jacket was draped. Pulling off his baseball cap and rubbing his thick golden ringlets, Joseph reached into the bag he'd brought with him and extracted the distinctive green box of Dom Pérignon champagne. He then removed from his pocket two mobile phones – his own iPhone, and the one lifted from the same apartment where he'd taken the boxed wine. His phone he set on the table. The other he scrolled through – clumsily because of the gloves – and noted the phone numbers and texts.

He set the Samsung down then stretched out his legs, checking the time. He wouldn't have long to wait. That was good. He was tense. You always were on edge at times like this. You had to be. He'd known plenty of men who'd relaxed when they shouldn't have. They were dead or changed for the worse, much worse.

But adrenaline got you only so far.

He glanced toward a door at the back of the warehouse, secured with a thick dead bolt. It led to a small storeroom. From beneath the door warm yellow light flowed. You could hear the *Dora the Explorer* DVD.

'Hey, Boots! Let's go over there!'

Joseph looked once more at the box containing the champagne. It was marred with a bloodstain on the side. Six dots in a row, like part of the Morse code for S-O-S. He knew the prestige of Dom Pérignon, though he'd never had any. This reminded him that he had a thirst. He rose and, walking stiffly from the chill, went to a cupboard in the corner of the warehouse, where he'd stashed a bottle of his Special Brew. He twisted off the cap and thirstily drank down nearly half of the contents. Felt the rush, felt the comfort.

Slow down, he told himself.

But then slugged the rest.

He wiped his lips on his sleeve. He set the bottle on the table. He'd take it with him when he left, of course, after slicking the glass with his telltale DNA.

Then settling his heavy form back in the chair, Joseph winced at a sharp pain in his hip. He reached into the pocket of his jacket and removed the Glock 9mm pistol, dropped the mag and reloaded, replacing the two bullets he'd fired not long ago. He recalled the eyes of the victim staring at him in shock – too numb even to be afraid. Always curious, those moments just before the gun fired. People behaved in all sorts of mad ways. Heroic, pathetic, even blasé. He could write a book.

Joseph set the gun on the table and fished out the Gemtech silencer, checked to see that it was clear and then screwed it into the muzzle. Slipped the weapon into his waistband.

He glanced at his watch. The deadline was two minutes away. He wondered if—

A firm knocking resonated from the medieval door.

A glance through the peephole he'd installed yesterday. Daniel Reardon and a distinguished-looking businessman. Joseph tapped the grip of the pistol, to remind himself exactly where it hugged his body. Then undid the latch.

CHAPTER
34

4:00 p.m., Sunday

1 hour, 50 minutes earlier

In the living room of the apartment Daniel Reardon made introductions. 'This is Gabriela McKenzie.'

'Andrew Faraday,' said the older of the two who'd just entered. The other man offered, 'Sam Easton.'

Hands were shaken. Sam was tanned, balding and had a craggy face, quick eyes. Andrew, pocketing the keys to the apartment, was in his mid-sixties. He had thick white hair, streaked with black strands, swept back and razor-parted on the side. Businessman's hair. Politician's hair. Andrew was leaner than Sam and Daniel and not particularly muscular. No more than five-nine. But Gabriela's impression, an immediate one, was that he was more imposing than the others. And not because of the age.

A natural-born boss . . .

Daniel said, 'These are the people I was telling you about. I'm a client of theirs. Have been for years.'

Gabriela and Daniel sat down on the decades-old couch, which released a more intense version of the musty odor she'd tried to eradicate from the apartment with the kitchen trick not long before.

Funerals, she thought. Funerals . . .

Daniel poured some more of the red wine. He lifted the bottle to her again. She declined. Andrew and Sam both took glasses. They sipped.

'Daniel was telling us about the situation,' Andrew said. His voice was comforting, baritone.

She said with a frantic slope to her voice, 'I don't know what to do! It's a nightmare. The deadline's in two hours! Joseph said I have until six and no extensions this time. After that . . .' She inhaled, exhaled hard.

The men seemed troubled by these stirrings of hysteria, as if not sure how to reassure her. Finally Andrew Faraday said, 'Well, we have some thoughts.'

Sam deferred with his eyes to Andrew. He was secondary or tertiary in hierarchy, she saw at once. She assessed he was dependable and loyal.

Daniel eased against Gabriela on the couch and she felt the warmth of his thigh against hers. He gripped her arm briefly with his long fingers. And she felt the strength she'd noted earlier.

'May I call you Gabriela?' The question was from Andrew. He seemed the sort who would ask permission. Proper, old-school.

'Sure, yes.' She smoothed frazzled hair. Then stopped her busy hands.

Andrew continued, 'First, so I can understand, Gabriella: Just to get the facts. This man who's kidnapped your daughter – Joseph, you were saying. That's his name, right?'

'Yes.'

'He wants the document Daniel was telling me about. The October List?'

She nodded.

Andrew took in her hollow eyes. 'And Daniel said you don't know what it means.'

She shrugged. 'Names and addresses. Maybe criminals. All we really know is that people are willing to kill for it.'

Andrew said, 'And no idea what the word refers to, "October"?'

Gabriela glanced to Daniel, who offered, 'It could be something that happened in October, in the past: a meeting, an event. Or,' he added darkly, 'it's something that's *going* to happen – next month. Given what we've heard, it might be something pretty bad. But, on the other hand, it could be nothing more than a name. A company, even a person. Or maybe a code. Number ten – the tenth month.'

'Or,' Gabriela said, 'Daniel was considering anagrams.'

'You can find some interesting words in "October." "Reboot," "boot," "core," "rob." But out of context, we just don't know.'

'And there's this man named Gunther, who may want the list too. But we don't have a clue how he figures in.'

Andrew nodded, considering this. He leaned back and ran a single index finger through his hair. Gabriela now examined the newcomers' clothing: The men were in suits – coiffed Andrew's was dark blue, balding Sam's black, both conservative and expensive as hell. Dress shirts, blue and white respectively. No ties. Bruno Magli or Ferragamo shoes. The clothing and accessories were, as Gabriela's boss would say, 'primo.'

She said to them evenly, 'I know I should turn it in.'

'Turn it in?'

'If I had the courage, I would. I'd give it to the police, the FBI. They'd know what it means. That's the only moral thing to do. But I *can't*. The list is the only bargaining chip I have to save Sarah.' Her voice caught. 'I feel awful, but I have to give it to Joseph. I don't have any choice.'

Daniel said firmly, 'You didn't make this mess. Charles Prescott did.'

Andrew asked, 'Charles Prescott. Your boss, right?'

'Former boss now,' she muttered. And inhaled hard, coughed. 'Sarah.' She closed her eyes briefly. 'I can't imagine what she's going through.'

'It's a beautiful name,' Sam said, his first words since their greeting. There was a familiarity about him – the taut muscular physique, the casual angle at which he stood, calm eyes. Then Gabriela realized, with a shock, yes, the Professor! Though not familiar in life; at the funeral home, as he lay in the silk bedding of the coffin. And, of course, observed through the lens of tears – both then and now.

Andrew said, 'Beautiful name indeed. Now, Daniel was telling me Joseph wants not only the list but some money too?'

Gabriela touched her fingers to her eyes. They came away damp. 'That's right. A fee he paid to Charles.' She inhaled deeply and said, 'But I don't have that kind of money, a half million, even if I mortgaged my co-op. I . . .' She fell silent.

Daniel now turned his blue eyes her way, reassuringly. Sotto voce: 'It'll be okay, Mac.' The nickname was comforting too. Pressure of knee against knee, thigh against thigh, the pressure of fingers on her arm again. His hand retreated; his leg did not. She felt the strength and warmth of persistent muscle.

'So,' Andrew mused, 'Joseph wants the list and he wants money.' His illustrious face grew coy. 'Think about it, though: He's taking a huge risk, possibly going to prison for the rest of his life, getting shot by hostage rescue teams. That tells us there's more at work here than greed.'

'There is?'

Daniel filled in, 'Joseph's desperate. He may seem confident. But he's scared. I'd guess he owes money to someone. Or he has to work off some other debt. A significant debt. Somebody's got major leverage on him – to pay off something. Or maybe to deliver the list.'

'And that's good,' Andrew offered.

'Good?' Gabriela asked.

Daniel explained, 'It's always better to negotiate with desperate people.'

'He didn't *act* desperate,' she said darkly. 'He seemed pretty damn confident to me.'

'You've got the list?' Andrew asked.

'Not with us. It's safe, though. A friend of mine, Frank, has it in his apartment.'

Sam asked, 'And you trust Frank?'

'He's a little odd. But, yes, he's dependable . . . when it comes to me.' Her eyes avoided Daniel's. 'But I'm not sure where this is going. You said "negotiate." I just want to give him what he's asking for and get my daughter back. That's all.'

After a moment Andrew said, 'Well, Gabriela, I'm afraid it's not as simple as that.'

'Why not?'

'Did Daniel tell you what Sam and I do?'

'No.'

'I have an insurance company. Our specialty is writing high-risk policies. If you want to build a factory in a known hot spot – say, a transitional country like Libya or Myanmar – we'll underwrite your key executives and the facilities. One of our big money-makers is kidnap coverage. When a businessman is abducted in a foreign country sometimes his company or family members go to the police. But sometimes – when they can't or it's too risky to involve the authorities – they rely on companies like mine to negotiate a release and pay the ransom.

'And that's what I'm going to do with Joseph. Make sure he gets what he wants but under conditions that guarantee Sarah will be released unharmed.'

'You . . . you'd do that?'

Andrew smiled. 'It's all in a day's work for me. And, as odd as it sounds, it's really just like any other transaction. Kidnapping or bank loan or an acquisition or a joint venture, there's not a lot of difference when it comes down to consummating the deal. You always pay in installments. Never everything up front. If you were to give Joseph what he wants right away, then he has no incentive to . . . keep anyone alive.'

'I have the October List,' she said. 'But not the money.'

'Oh, you *do* have the money, Mac,' Daniel said.

Gabriela frowned.

Andrew explained, 'Daniel's providing the ransom and paying our fee.'

'*What?*' She spun to face him.

He nodded.

'I can't accept that from you.'

Daniel said solemnly, 'You can't afford not to. Not at this point. There're no options left. We're not going to find your boss's hidden treasure in time.'

'But . . .' She fell silent. Then turned and buried her face against his neck, sobbing. He gripped her hard. Even when she winced and gasped, he continued to hold her; in fact, he clutched her more tightly yet. Inhaled hard against her hair.

Andrew stirred and looked at the clock. 'It's four forty-five. We have an hour and fifteen minutes. How were you going to arrange to give him the list and money?'

'I was going to call him when I'd got the cash.'

'Okay. Here's what I want you to do. You'll call him and tell him you have everything he wants. But you're not going to meet him. You have a friend who's helping you with this.'

'You can tell him it's the man he met yesterday,' Daniel said. 'So he won't think it's a cop. Give him my name. He will've checked me out and knows I'm not a threat.'

Gabriela said firmly, 'No. It's *my* daughter who's been kidnapped. I'll do it.'

'Andrew and I'll go. Andrew because this's his business. Me because Joseph knows who I am, and that I'm connected with you.'

'It's too dangerous. I can't ask you to do that!'

Andrew added softly, 'It's not as dangerous as it seems. We have leverage. You're in possession of this list he's so desperate for, we have the money he wants.'

Daniel added, 'And we've got that.' His gaze slipped to the plastic CVS pharmacy bag in the corner of the room. Small but impossible to ignore. The dark stains inside were obvious. 'It'll have some evidence that can be traced back to him. He knows that.'

Andrew continued, 'Oh, yes, we've got some leverage. Not much, but enough, I think. Now, we'll meet Joseph at six. As for the money . . . We'll give him *some* of what he wants, a show of good faith. And part of the list – to prove we have it. And we'll insist on seeing your daughter. Not a video or a recording. See her in person.' A broad smile. 'Then we'll agree to have the exchange tomorrow in some public place – the full October List, the rest of the money and the evidence.' He lifted his palms. 'For your daughter.'

She nodded slowly.

Daniel said, 'Could you call your friend Frank, and get a few names on the list? Or do you still remember the ones you saw?'

'I remember them. Not the addresses, but the cities they're in.' She wrote these down and handed the slip to Daniel, who read and then pocketed it.

Andrew said, 'That's fine. Joseph'll check them out, verify they're real . . . Now, the money. We'll give him a portion tonight. Half of what he's asking is probably enough. It'll show we're willing to cooperate.'

Daniel said, 'It's easy enough to get two hundred fifty thousand together.'

Easy for some people, Gabriela reflected.

'Well, are we ready to give our friend Joseph a call?' Andrew asked.

Gabriela stared at the phone for a moment. Daniel leaned close. 'You can do it, Mac.'

She looked at him, inhaled and then found the number and dialed.

'Put it on speaker,' the older man instructed.

She hit the button.

A moment later Joseph's eerie voice came over the line. 'Gabriela! Hello, hello! I was worried. The deadline's getting closer, inching up. And I'm sure you remember what happens when you miss a deadline. Been on any good scavenger hunts recently? Found any good treasures behind Dumpsters?'

'That was the sickest thing anybody's ever done,' she snapped.

'Oh, I'll bet we can come up with a few nastier examples if we put our heads together, don't you agree? But it *was* delicious, wasn't it?' Another of his odd giggles.

Gabriela's jaw trembled. 'How's my daughter?'

'Well, truth be told, she's a little confused. "Where's Mommy, why doesn't Mommy call?" If it's any consolation she asks for you more than for Daddy Tim. Was he really that bad a husband?'

'Dammit! Answer my question! How's Sarah?'

'She's fine.'

'She isn't fine, and she'll never be fine thanks to you.'

Joseph said dismissively, 'People handle all sorts of trauma and are none the worse for wear. I'm a case in point.'

'I hate you so much.'

'Pity,' he said, that singsong tone again infusing his voice. 'If you got to know me, you'd feel different. Now, I notice we're on speaker. I imagine your good friend Mr Reardon's in the room with you now, or somebody else, but not the police because after the excitement this afternoon you're not going to be strolling into any station houses. At least not voluntarily. My, my, you sure made a name for yourself today, Gabriela. That was quite a mess . . . Glad you're not *my* office manager. Now, who's your *avatar?*' He laughed at this comment. '*Is* it Mr Reardon?'

Daniel leaned forward. 'That's right.'

'Aka J. P. Morgan. You're not a cowboy after all. You're a hotshot venture capitalist. I checked you out. The Norwalk Fund. The article in front of the name's a little pretentious, but it's an impressive outfit. Assets of two billion? If I had a retirement account, I'd let you handle it. And still you avoid fracking and unsustainable energy investments? How admirable. Surprised I'd do my homework?'

'Not really.'

Joseph asked, 'So, J. P., you're representing our Gabriela?'

'That's right.'

'Well, I guess the burden's on *you* to deliver the goods then, in a little over an hour. You told me you have the list. How're we coming with the cold, hard cash?'

Daniel explained their proposal, the partial payment and several entries from the October List so he could check them out, verify they were real. Then a public meeting for the complete exchange.

Joseph paused then said, 'I like dealing with Gabriela better. Let me think, let me think . . . I'm coming down on the side of no.' Offered cheerfully.

Gabriela started to speak, but Andrew calmly gestured her silent. Daniel asked, 'What's your counterproposal?'

'*All* the money now. Five hundred K.'

'Impossible!' Gabriela blurted.

'Let's ask little Sarah how she feels about impossibility, should we? Guess what I've been up to this afternoon? I've been trimming roses. Snip, snip. You know that it helps them grow to cut back nearly to the roots? Imagine that. It—'

'Stop it!' Gabriela turned to Daniel with terrified eyes. He nodded. Leaning forward slightly, he said into the speaker, 'Okay. Full payment tonight. Five hundred K. But only three names from the October List. And we see Sarah in person.'

'That'll work . . . Only, let me ask something first. Now, tell the truth, Gabriela, the list? You have it in your hot little hands?'

The foursome in the room glanced at one another. She said, 'We have it. Somewhere safe.'

'Do you now? I hope so. Because, let me say this, I'm a very bad person to cheat. If you try to trick me, in any way, or you hold out on me, there'll be consequences. I'm not going to threaten to kill your daughter because that wouldn't be helpful for anybody. But fuck with me and I *will* make sure she disappears into the underground adoption circuit, and you'll never see her again.'

'No!' she cried.

He continued, 'And that's not all, Ms Gabriela. I have to say I find you quite attractive – sorry, J. P. Morgan. Don't be jealous. She's a good-looking woman, right? I know you agree.'

Daniel's jaw clenched.

Joseph laughed, that giggling again. 'If things don't go just the way I want, I'll find you and I'll make sure we spend some *quality* time together. I have a house outside of the city. Very, very deserted. So, Gabriela, you understand what's at stake here?'

She nodded desperately, then realized Joseph couldn't hear her response. 'Nobody's going to cheat you! We'll do just what you want, I promise!'

'All right, J. P. Morgan, there's a place in SoHo . . . Elizabeth Street, two buildings north of Prince. On the east side of the street. A ware-house.' Joseph gave the address.

'I'll be there at six. With an associate.'

'Who?'

'My insurance man.'

'Ah, that makes sense. But any heroics and you heard the conse-quences. Sarah ends up in a trailer in West Virginia with a born-again mommy and daddy, and Gabriela and I commence dating.'

Daniel seemed to be using all his willpower to control his voice. 'Understood.'

The click of his disconnecting seemed like a gunshot.

Gabriela sank back on the couch. She looked too drained even to cry.

Andrew rose. 'All right. Let's get the money, Daniel. We don't have much time. Sam, you stay with Gabriela.'

Sam Easton nodded. 'Sure.'

Daniel turned to her and pulled her close. He whispered, 'We'll make it work, Mac. I promise.'

Then the two men were gone, the door closing with its distinctive two-note tone.

CHAPTER
33

3:30 p.m., Sunday

30 minutes earlier

Detectives Naresh Surani and Brad Kepler were sitting in yet another operations room in the NYPD Big Building, main headquarters. The third one in three days. Government. Fuck.

Third – and the worst. The view here was of a pitted wall of City Hall and a smooth wall of a bank, pigeons, a sliver of sky, pigeon shit. And whatever had been rotting away behind the file cabinets of the last room didn't come close to the chemical weapons here.

Kepler muttered to his partner, 'Are they ready?'

Surani hung up the phone. 'They're ready-ish.'

Which sounded flippant and wrong, given the circumstances, Kepler thought. You know, people's lives are at risk here.

Maybe Kepler's face revealed that he was pissed off; Surani seemed to understand. He added in a graver tone, 'They're assembled and staging. That's the last I heard. It's like they're too busy to talk to us.'

He was referring to the NYPD's tactical team, the Emergency Service Unit boys – and probably a girl or two as well. All the fancy weapons, machine guns, helmets, Nomex, boots.

Ready to swoop in nail the perps.

'Too busy to talk to us?' Kepler repeated, his voice gravel. 'The FCP Op didn't originate with them.'

The name of the operation had, in the past few hours, morphed from the official 'Charles Prescott Operation' down to 'the CP Op.'

Then, thanks to the complications that had surrounded the case, the inevitable modifier, commencing with the sixth letter of the alphabet, now preceded the name. Cops. Naturally.

FCP Op . . .

Kepler continued, 'It's *our* investigation. *We* should be all over it like . . . like . . .' His voice faded.

'Couldn't think of a good metaphor?' Surani offered.

Kepler rolled his eyes, grimacing. 'They're sure where Gabriela is?'

'Yeah, yeah, yeah. Don't worry. They're tracking her.'

Wait, Kepler thought: Like beetles on shit, like frat boys on kegs, like frat boys on coeds . . .

But too late.

'Call Surveillance again. Make sure there's a signal.'

Surani sighed. But he did as requested. Had a brief conversation. He disconnected and turned to Kepler. 'Yeah, they have a good signal on her. A humongous signal. A hard-on of a signal. Is it okay if I say that, or do *my* people not refer to erections?'

Kepler didn't even bother. 'Where *exactly*? Do they know *exactly*?'

'Yes, they know ex-act-tily. Which is where, like I said before, ESU is staging. They're ready to move in for the take-down as soon as we give the word.'

But, of course, it wasn't *we* who would give the word; it was *he*. Captain Barkley.

Kepler grumbled, 'I'd like to see pictures. I'd like to be on the ground. They have fucking cameras, ESU does. They should be beaming us pictures.'

'It's been hard enough to track her—'

'Tell me something I don't know.'

'—track her in the first place. You're not going to get high-def video, for Christ's sake. Oh, is it okay if someone of my persuasion says—'

'Enough with that.' Kepler noted the grimy windows, the clutter, the bile-green paint, the smell: food once more. But, unlike earlier, this time he was anything but hungry.

Surani glanced down and brushed at his brown suit jacket, which, Kepler thought again, clashed badly with the man's gray complexion. His own skin tone was a hard-earned tan, but his suit, unlike his partner's, was wrinkled and – he now noticed – bore an embarrassing stain on the sleeve. In the shape of Mickey Mouse ears.

He sat forward in the truly uncomfortable orange fiberglass chair, and thought: So is this how it ends? I'm balls-deep in an operation where people may get dead and no one knows exactly what's going on. And if it goes south, the brass'll need a scapegoat. Hello, Detectives Surani and Kepler.

There are of course a thousand different ways an operation can go bad, but in the end you don't need to worry about a thousand different ways because it only takes one to fuck everything up. And usually it's the one you never see coming.

The two men didn't jump to attention when Captain Paul Barkley strode into the room – NYPD detectives didn't jump at much of anything. But Kepler lifted his feet off a neighboring chair and Surani put down the coffee he was loudly slurping. For detectives with the kinds of lives they had and the cases they ran, this was about all they could muster in terms of respect.

Especially today, in the throes of the FCP Op.

'You have her location?'

Surani said, 'Yep. And she has no clue we're on to her. ESU's in position. They're assessing risk exposure.'

The captain uttered a snort. '"Risk exposure"? Forget bad cop movie – that sounds like something a banker'd say. Now, you seen the latest?' Barkley snapped, turning to a computer, logging in. 'I saw it ten minutes ago. Jesus.'

What was the old man referring to? Kepler had enough miles to show impatience with his boss and he did so now, though silently and in the form of a frown, his tan brow V'ing severely.

Kepler thought an official document or report or surveillance CCTV video was going to appear. But what they were looking at on the screen was the *New York Post* online edition, updated recently. Kepler sighed as he read the story, a follow-up of an earlier one. The first headline had included the word 'injured.' This one featured the verb 'died.'

Both articles included this sentence: 'Crushed beneath a delivery truck.'

Surani said, 'It's out of hand, I know.'

'And that's not acceptable. I want to move in. I want perps being processed in Central Booking *now*. It could turn into a bloodbath if we don't move fast.'

'It already is a bloodbath,' Surani muttered, looking at the photo of the body.

Gesturing angrily at the computer screen, Barkley muttered, 'Look at the press. Fucking mobile phone cameras. That's the problem nowadays. They're everywhere. Assholes with a Samsung or iPhone are on the scene faster than first responders. Shit. Crime Scene's on it?' he asked.

'Yeah, but they're not getting much.'

They all stared at the screen. Blood's pretty vivid in high definition.

'And Gabriela's with that guy?'

Surani said, 'Yeah.'

'That woman,' the captain intoned, 'has a lot to answer for.' The comments, devoid of obscenity, seemed particularly ominous. Barkley debated, or at least he cocked his head as if he was, and stared out the window.

Bank, City Hall, pigeon shit.

'Okay, I'm making the call. Send ESU in. Now.'

'That could fuck everything up,' Kepler said. 'I think we should wait, find out who the players are, what the risks are. What—'

'Send ESU in *now*,' Barkley growled, as if he wasn't used to repeating himself. Which, Kepler knew, he was not. 'We're not waiting any longer. Whatever else she's done in the last couple of days, if she ends up like –' A nod to the truck crush article. '– it's gonna be bad for a lot of people.'

Meaning him, meaning us, meaning the city.

Especially bad for Gabriela, too, Kepler wanted to say but refrained.

Surani snatched up the phone. He leaned forward, tense, as he said, 'It's Surani. Your teams're green-lighted. You can—' His gray-brown face froze. 'What? What?'

Kepler and Barkley stared at him. Barkley was hard to read, but undoubtedly what he felt was the same dismay Kepler was experiencing.

'*What?*'

The repetition was infuriating. If he said the word again, Kepler was going to grab him by the collar, take the phone away.

But Surani's next words were, 'Oh, shit.'

Kepler's eyes went wide and he lifted his palms. Meaning: Tell us the something fucking specific.

Surani was now nodding intensely. 'Sure, I'll put him on.'

'What?' Barkley asked, apparently not noticing he was echoing his detective.

Surani said, 'The ESU tac op commander has somebody he thinks you should talk to.'

'Who?'

'A Department of Sanitation driver.'

Barkley gave his deepest frown so far today. 'What the fuck does a garbage man have to do with the operation?'

'Here.' Surani handed him the phone as if it were a box of unstable ammunition.

The captain snatched the unit from his hand and spoke to the driver. He disconnected and sat back. Finally: 'We've got a problem.'

CHAPTER
32

3:15 p.m., Sunday

15 minutes earlier

'What happened back there, with that man,' Gabriela whispered, wiping tears. 'I . . . I don't know what to say.'

Daniel fell back into his waiting state: observing, not speaking. His eyes swept the overcast, afternoon streets of Midtown, east. 'Looks clear. Come on.'

They walked another block.

'There. That's the place, Mac. Let's get inside.' Daniel was pointing out a narrow dun-colored apartment building down a cul-de-sac on East 51st. It crested at four stories high and many windows were hooded as suspicious eyes.

'We'll be safe there.'

She gave a brutal laugh. Safe. Yeah, right.

Daniel squeezed her hand in response.

As they approached the structure, Gabriela looked around, scrutinizing shadows and windows and doorways. She saw no police. Or other threats. Daniel let them into the lobby, which was painted in several shades of blue and lit by brushed silver sconces. The decor was tasteful, though hardly elegant. A painting – by a Picasso wannabe, it seemed – of a ballerina, possibly, hung from the wall near the mailboxes. They took the stairs to the second floor, where there were doors to two apartments.

Daniel directed her to the left, which faced the front courtyard.

The key clicked, the hinge creaked. It made a funny sound, musical. The first two notes of 'The Star Spangled Banner.'

O-oh, say can you see . . .

After they'd entered the dark rooms, Daniel closed and double-locked the door, flicked on the overhead lights.

Gabriela dropped the new backpack, which contained her gym bag, on a battered coffee table in the living room. Daniel set his belongings beside it and sat heavily in a solid chair at the dining room table. He went online via his iPad and she walked to the window, looked out over the courtyard and cul-de-sac.

Gabriela found the smell of the rooms troubling. The aroma reminded her of a funeral parlor. Old, stale chemicals, though here they would just be cleansers, not preservatives for dead flesh. She recalled just such a smell from six years and two months ago. Her stomach twisted, hurt grew, anger grew. An image of the Professor arose.

Then she thought of her mantra.

Sarah.

Your goal. Focus on your goal.

Sarah.

It's just a random smell, she told herself, that's triggering hard memories. Still, she couldn't quite flick it away. She stepped into the kitchen and opened the refrigerator, which was mostly bare – a container of coffee, butter, a shriveled lemon, hard as horn. And in the crisper an onion. It too was past prime but not rotten. Green shoots were growing from the end, eerie. She thought of Joseph's unruly hair, slick, greasy. She found a knife, dull but sharp enough to slice the vegetable if she sawed with pressure. When she'd produced a small pile of rings, she found oil in the cupboard, which she poured into a dusty frying pan, without bothering to wipe it clean. She turned up the heat and cooked the rings and shoots, stirring them absently in a figure-eight motion with a wooden spoon.

The sweet scents rose and soon they'd mitigated the smells that had bothered her. The thoughts of past death faded.

Daniel Reardon walked to the doorway of the kitchen. She sensed him watching her closely. She glanced at his handsome face, felt that ping of attraction. Thought of Friday night, two days ago. A year, forever.

'Hungry?'

'Probably. But I don't want anything to eat. I'm just air freshening.'

'With onions?' A laugh. He had a wonderful laugh – just like the actor he so closely resembled.

Her voice shivered as she said, 'Every night when she's with me, Sarah and I cook. Well, not every night. But most. She likes to stir things. She's a great stirrer. We sometimes joke, we . . .' And she abruptly fell silent, inhaled deeply, looking away from him.

She touched her chest, wincing, and Daniel stepped close, taking a tissue and slowly wiping the blood from the corner of her mouth. Then he embraced her. His hand trailed down her spine, bumping over the strap of her bra beneath the thick sweatshirt and settling into her lower back. He pulled her close. She tensed and groaned slightly. He tilted her head back and, despite the residue of blood, kissed her hard on the lips. She groaned, frowning, and he released her.

'Sorry,' he whispered.

'Don't be.'

He pressed his face against hers once more, pulling her body into him. And then stepped back, as if forcing himself to. She shut off the stovetop gas and they returned to the living room.

She looked around the apartment. It was sterile, worn in the way of faded elegance, like rich folks downsizing, retiring. The bland furniture had been top quality ten, fifteen years ago but was dinged and scuffed. The cushions had suffered from too many asses, the carpet from too many leather heels.

Ugly, yes.

But it was quiet. And secluded.

Safe . . .

The decorations were largely nautical. Prints of ships in turbulent waves, as well as seafaring memorabilia and lanterns and fishing gear.

Gabriela regarded the wooden display rack of knots on the wall. 'Yours?'

'That's right. I tied them. A hobby.' He looked over the short pieces of rope bound into nautical knots, two dozen of them. 'They have names, each one.'

Another wall was devoted to photography. He spotted the direction of her eyes. 'Not as good as yours.'

'You've got an Edward Weston and an Imogen Cunningham, Stieglitz.'

'They're just reproductions, not originals.'

'Well-done, though. Quality work. And picking those pieces in particular. Weston was a groundbreaker. Cunningham too, though I think she needed more of an edge.'

'And there – something your daughter would appreciate.' On one wall was an antique riding crop and a pair of spurs.

An indelible image of Sarah came to mind.

Sarah . . .

She sensed Daniel was about to bring up a serious topic. She was right.

'Mac, I'm going to have some people help us.' He nodded toward his iPad, on which he'd presumably been sending and receiving emails.

'Help us?'

'They're good folks. And we need them.'

'I can't ask that.'

'You didn't ask.' Daniel smiled. 'Besides, I owe you big time. You're the one who came up with the Princeton Solution. I don't know what would've happened if you hadn't been there. It would've been a nightmare.'

'I'll bet you could've handled it.'

'No. You saved my life,' he told her.

Gabriela offered a modest smile. 'Who are they, these people?'

'A couple of guys I've worked with for years. Smart. We need smart.' Daniel regarded her ambling eyes. 'She'll be okay, Mac. I promise. Sarah will be okay.'

And Gabriela thought: *Promise*. What an odd verb. A word you can't trust. Or shouldn't.

Like the word *trust* itself.

Don't be so cynical, she thought.

But that was hard. Gabriela was cynical in the grain. She'd learned to be that way, because of the Professor.

She saw in her mind's eye his still face, waxy, surrounded by satin. A material she had come to despise.

'They'll be here soon.' He squinted, looking her way. 'What're you thinking? Something important. I can tell.'

In a soft voice. 'No.'

'No you're not thinking, or no you're not telling? It's got to be door number two because you can't not be thinking something. That's impossible.'

She tried to formulate the words so they didn't come out foolish. This wasn't easy. 'Too many people turn away when something bad's happening. They're afraid, they're worried about the inconvenience, worried about being embarrassed. But you're not willing to let Joseph get away with this and you're doing it for me, for somebody you've known for only a couple of days.'

Daniel Reardon wasn't able to blush, she assessed. But he was embarrassed by her words. 'You're giving me a complex.' He looked around and noted the bar. 'I need a drink. You? Wine? Anything stronger?'

'No. Just . . . not now.'

He opened a bottle of cabernet and poured the ruby liquid into a glass. A long sip seemed to exorcise her cloying gratitude. He had another. 'Now. We should think about our next steps. Andrew and Sam should be here soon. First, I guess we ought to call the complication. Make sure he's home.'

Complication . . .

She smiled at the word. Then scrolled through her phone until she found Frank Walsh's name and called. 'No answer.' She sent a text. 'But I'm sure the list is safe. There's no reason it wouldn't be.'

Daniel's face remained calm. Though of course he'd be thinking: *Without that list your daughter's dead. And the man who'd kill her, that prick Joseph, will be after you too before long.*

And he didn't need to add that Joseph would be looking for him too.

But then her phone buzzed and she glanced at the screen. A text had appeared. She smiled briefly. 'It's Frank. He's not going out tonight. Everything's fine.'

'That's one less worry we have. But I don't know how I feel about Mr Frank "Complication" Walsh on your speed-dial list. I'm thinking I'd rather take his place.'

'I could move you up to number two.'

'Only two?'

'Mom is first.'

'That's fair enough.'

Daniel walked to a tall glass-fronted mahogany entertainment enclosure, circa 1975, she guessed, though it contained newer components. He turned the radio on to a local station. After five minutes of bad music and worse commercials it was time for the news. She strode to the device and abruptly shut it off.

Daniel looked at her as she stared at the receiver. She told him, 'I don't want to hear about it. About what happened today – any of it! It has to be on the news. I'm all over the news!' Her voice had grown ragged again.

'It's okay, it's okay . . .'

She started at the buzz of the intercom. It seemed as loud as an alarm. 'Daniel?' came the tinny voice through the speaker. 'It's Andrew.'

Pressing the unlock button, Daniel nodded reassuringly to Gabriela, 'The cavalry's arrived.'

CHAPTER
31

2:15 p.m., Sunday

1 hour earlier

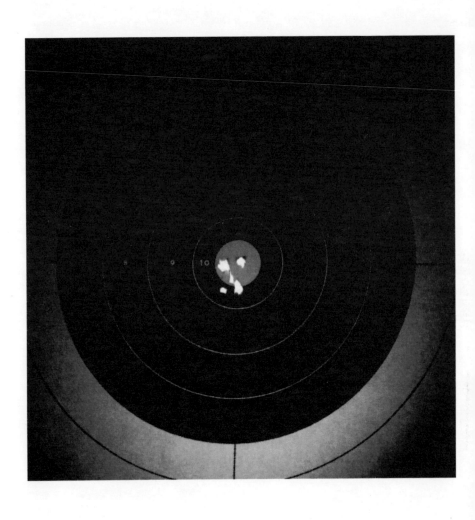

Detective Brad Kepler watched his boss read the media release once, twice, again.

Captain Paul Barkley looked up at the NYPD press officer, a wobbly young man with persistent acne, who sat before him in this hellhole of an operations room. Then, without saying a word, he looked down and read once more.

Barkley's stomach made a Harley-Davidson noise that everyone in the room pretended to ignore.

Kepler knew that most Sundays, this time of day Barkley was tucking away his wife's roast beef, along with – when she wasn't looking – massive forkfuls of buttered mashed potatoes. The detective was aware of this routine because he'd been invited to supper a few times. He had three repetitive memories of the occasions: Barkley telling the same quasi-blue jokes over and over. The roast beef being very good. And Kepler's spending the entire time trying to figure out if there was any possible scenario for telling Barkley's know-it-all college-student daughter to shut the fuck up. Which, of course, there was not.

Kepler himself read the release again.

Fred Stanford Chapman, 29, . . . wife, Elizabetta, 31, two children, Kyle and Sophie . . . Surgery to remove a bullet lodged near his heart is planned for later today . . . Investigations continue . . . Prognosis is not good . . .

Et cetera, et cetera, et cetera . . .

'How many calls?' Barkley asked the youngster.

'From the press? A hundred.'

Barkley snapped, 'That's an exaggeration.'

Kepler thought: Probably isn't. His partner, Naresh Surani, seemed to concur.

'I wanted to keep it quiet,' the captain said.

'A shooting?' From the PA youngster.

Public affairs. Crap.

'Yes, a shooting. In goddamn Manhattan. I wanted to keep it goddamn quiet. But I guess that didn't work out, did it? This was a leak the size of the *Titanic*.'

Kepler corrected, The *Titanic* wasn't a leak. The *Titanic* was a ship that got fucked *because of* a leak.

But, of course, the edit was tacit.

Barkley snatched up a pen and began to revise.

Which gave Kepler the chance to look around their new digs. This was the second room the Charles Prescott Operation – the CP Op – had been assigned to in the past two days. Sure, this happened to be a busy time for bad guys and little operations like the CP Op didn't mean very much, in terms of chalking up cred, so they had to take whatever room was free at the moment. But this one was the pits. The twenty-by-thirty-foot space did have a few high-def monitors, but they were off, and they didn't even seem hooked up. The walls were scuffed – nothing new there – and the government-issue furniture was cheap. Nearly a third of the floor space was devoted to storage. Something smelled off too, as if a take-out turkey sandwich had fallen behind one of the filing cabinets a long, long time ago.

At least it couldn't get any worse.

Barkley slid the press release back like an air hockey puck. 'Fix it. And by the way, no comment from me, other than the investigations continue. Stop at that. Nothing more.'

The press officer tried again. 'But a hundred calls, sir.'

'Why're you still here?' Barkley made a sound like a disagreeable transmission. This one came from his throat, not his belly.

'Yes, sir. Sorry, sir.' The Public Affairs officer scooted out.

Why the hell does that kid wear a sidearm? Kepler thought.

Barkley turned to the two detectives, sitting at a battered fiberboard table, and barked, 'Jesus.' He nodded toward Kepler's copy of the release.

Fred Stanford Chapman, 29, . . . gunshot wound . . .

Then the boss changed direction. 'Now, *her*.'

He didn't need to say Gabriela. There were no other women causing them so much anxiety at the moment.

'I told you yesterday I wanted her under surveillance. Twenty-four seven. What the hell happened? You were at her place, right? Cameras, microphones.'

Her.

Brad Kepler shrugged. 'She tipped to us. I don't know. And then started using evasive tactics.'

'The hell does that mean? Sounds like something from a bad cop movie.'

'But,' Kepler said, 'we're still on her.' A glance at his partner. 'Right?'

Surani called Surveillance, had a discussion, then clapped his hand over the mouthpiece and said to Barkley and Kepler, 'We've got officers close. It's righteous.'

Which sounded like something out of an even worse cop movie. *Righteous?*

The captain asked, 'How'd you manage the tail, if she slipped you at her place?'

Surani explained, 'Brad got a GPS on her.'

'How the hell you do that?' The captain gave one of his broad frowns that he used for emphasis, a gesture several of his detectives had developed pretty good imitations of, Brad Kepler included.

'She was distracted. It was chaos, weapons, screaming, diving for cover. I got the thing into her jacket pocket.'

Barkley was pleased, Kepler could tell, but his nature required him to ask, 'You think that was a safe idea?' The captain could never just say, Good job.

'Safe idea?' Kepler asked. He didn't know what that meant. 'I frankly didn't think about it. It was just something I had to do: Get the tracker onto her then back off.'

Surani, his gray complexion even grayer under the inhumane lights in the dismal operations room, said, 'It was pretty good, pretty smooth. She doesn't have a clue.'

'Microphone?' The captain brushed his trim, white hair – senior congressman's hair – twice, then a third time. He seemed to look Kepler up and down, as if approving of his impressive tan. Or disapproving.

'No, just a tracker. We lost her for a bit in the subway.'

The New York city metro system was huge and fast and efficient, and that meant it could transport Gabriela anywhere within a several-hundred-square-mile area. And GPS trackers wouldn't work there.

'But then she surfaced. CCTV got a facial recognition exiting a station in Midtown. The signal's been solid since then.'

'Unless she decides to hop on the A train again.'

'She can't live in the MTA,' Surani said. 'The food sucks down there. And the showers? Forget about it.' This drew a hard glance from Kepler because the joke was beyond stupid. It wasn't even a joke.

'And she was with the guy?'

'That's right.'

'Stay on her. But I want everybody tailing to be invisible. You follow me? If Surveillance gets made, then people could get killed. That's not happening on my watch.'

And why not? Kepler wondered, of the dramatic pronouncement. You can protect all the innocents in New York City, can you now, boss? A *lot* of people have died on your watch over the years, when you think about it.

But Surani said only, 'We've told the teams to stay back. They're near but not too close.'

One of the deputy chiefs stuck his head in the doorway. 'Hey, sorry, gentlemen. Need to commandeer this room.'

'What?' Barkley snapped. 'Move the op center? Again? You gotta be kidding me?'

The white-haired, rotund brass shrugged, looking only slightly contrite. 'Got a terrorist tip and we need an ISDN line. They're not up and running in the other rooms.'

'Terrorist. We get a thousand terrorist tips a year. Why's this one a big deal?

'Bureau's running it. Pretty serious, it seems. And could be going down in two, three weeks, so it's prioritized. Infrastructure target, that sort of thing. You got ten minutes to find new digs.' He disappeared. Kepler glanced at Surani and he knew that his partner was just barely refraining from giving the empty doorway the finger. They swapped smiles.

Sighing, Barkley looked over sheets of paper on the table. One was headed *Charles Prescott Investments*.

The other was another copy of the press release.

Surgery to remove a bullet lodged near his heart is planned for later today . . .

'We'll make this work. I know we will.' This flimsy reassurance came from Kepler.

Just then Surani got another call. He listened. He disconnected. 'Surveillance. Gabriella and Reardon're on the move again. Near

Forty-Eight and Seventh, moving west. There're a couple unmarkeds in the vicinity, but they're staying out of sight.'

Vi-cin-ty.

Jesus, Kepler thought.

Barkley slid the Prescott file away as if it reminded him of a bad medical diagnosis. He asked, 'Is the tracker a good one?'

Kepler said, 'Yeah. Battery lasts for days and it'll pinpoint the location down to six feet.'

Surani added proudly, 'And she'll never spot it. It's inside a Bic pen.'

CHAPTER
30

2:10 p.m., Sunday

5 minutes earlier

The sky had changed for the worse.

The spongy clouds, which had been floating so benign and frivolous in the azure sky, were gone. Taupe overcast stretched from horizon to horizon, as if the air itself were tethered to the raw edge of these past thirty hours. The harbor was choppy, the wind rude.

Gabriela and Daniel were emerging from the subway. After the screams, after the chaos on Second Avenue not long ago, the police had appeared in droves. She and Daniel had had no choice but to use the subway system to flee, despite the risk of getting spotted by Transit Authority police. But no one had noticed them and, on the streets now, they maneuvered through families, tourists, shoppers, and lovers, trying to find cover in the crowds – just as the two fugitives had lost themselves in the various subway lines for the past half hour. They'd ridden to Harlem from the Upper East Side, then headed crosstown and finally south to Midtown.

From here they'd walk to the apartment that Daniel had told her about – the one his company, The Norwalk Fund, kept for out-of-town clients. It was presently empty and they could hide out there.

He now looked around carefully. 'No police, no Joseph, no anybody else after us.'

Gabriela was solemn. 'All the blood, Daniel. Did you see it?'

Of course he had. He squeezed her hand tighter. The pressure seemed to have meaning. But what? She couldn't tell.

'Look!'

He too noted the blue-and-white patrol car speeding their way, the lights flashing urgently. Gabriela shucked the backpack off her shoulder and they veered, stepping closer to a store, putting a stream of passersby between them and the street.

The NYPD cruiser, though, sped quickly past, heading in the direction of the incident.

The blood . . .

Daniel directed her east. 'The apartment's that way. About eight, ten blocks. Not far.'

But before they started walking Gabriela took his arm and said, 'Wait. Let's ditch the hats and get some better camouflage.' She tapped the dark, logo-free baseball cap she was wearing. 'We need more than this to fool them.' Nodding at a discount clothing store up the block. 'Let's go shopping.'

Five minutes later they were out, wearing jeans – his blue, hers black – and sweatshirts and windbreakers, also dark. His top said, *NYU*. Hers was bare of type or images. The clothes they'd been wearing were in shopping bags.

She grimaced and clutched her ribcage, coughed. Then wiped a spot of blood from her lip.

'Mac!'

She said dismissingly, 'It's all right. I can handle it.'

They continued walking.

Her phone pinged, a text. She glanced at the screen. A smile, damp-ened by a wince, appeared.

'The Complication.'

'What did he say?'

'He got his present.' Gabriella decided not to tell him the rest that Frank Walsh had texted.

They were at the corner when a dark sedan sped by – it was clearly an unmarked police car. This one, unlike the squad cars a moment ago, slowed as it grew close. Then sped up and continued on, vanishing around the corner.

No other police cars or uniformed officers were in the area. 'I think it's clear,' Daniel said.

Into his backpack he stuffed the shopping bag containing the gray Canali suit and shirt he'd changed out of at the store. Gabriela exam-ined the contents of her bag and noticed spatters of blood on her sweater and windbreaker. 'I'm dumping these. Shit. I loved that sweater.'

She went through the pockets and kept only the money; everything else – receipts, bloody tissues and a Bic pen – she left in the bag. She looked around and noticed a Department of Sanitation truck, filled to the brim, en route to the processing facility on 14th Street at the Hudson River.

She slung the shopping bag into the back of the truck as the driver waited for the light to change.

Gabriela gripping his arm, Daniel set a good pace and they wove through the herds of pedestrians filling the streets on this blustery Sunday afternoon.

CHAPTER
29

1:40 p.m., Sunday

30 minutes earlier

Frank Walsh was standing in the tiny kitchen of his dim Greenwich Village apartment, thinking of the killing that morning.

It hadn't been easy.

Using a knife never was.

The problem was you generally couldn't *stab* somebody to death. You had to *slash*, go for the neck, the legs – the femoral arteries. The groin was good too. But stabbing? It took forever.

And add to the mix: If the person you were fighting was good at defense, as the victim that morning had been, you had to stay alert, you had to move, you had to be fast and you had to improvise; in knife fighting, advantages changed in seconds.

Solid – okay, *pudgy* – Frank pulled his Greek fisherman cap off and scratched his unruly red hair and the scalp beneath as he stood at the open cupboard door. With his left hand he absently pinched a roll of fat around his belly. He decided against the potato chips.

He continued to debate the food options. But was distracted.

Gabby was on his mind. As often she was.

Then his mind, his clever mind, slipped back to the fight that morning. Recalling the animal lust, the pure satisfaction – born somewhere, a shrink would probably say, out of revenge for the bullying he'd suffered as a teenager. He felt pride too at his skill with the blade.

He wished he could tell Gabby about the confrontation, though some things he knew it was best to keep from her. Felt a deep ping in his belly as he pictured her and thought of the present he'd just received. He wondered what she was wearing at the moment.

Then he turned his attention back to mealtime. His kitchen was a central hub of the apartment. The cabinets were white and the handles had actual release levers, as if the room were a galley on a ship that regularly sailed through gales. If the doors weren't secured, Doritos,

Tuna Helper and macaroni and cheese would fly to the floor in the swells.

Chips? No chips?

No chips, he decided. And continued to stare.

He took a breath and sensed something smelled off. Not spoiled food. What? He looked around. Noted the old scabby table, plumbed steady with folded Post-it notes under one leg. His hat sat on it. Was the hat gamy? He smelled it. Yep, that was it.

Did Greek fishermen really wear Greek fisherman hats? he wondered.

He'd have to wash it, he guessed. But would that take the good luck away? He'd worn it during the fight that morning. He slipped it into a Baggie until he decided.

Back to the *Titanic* cabinets and the fridge. No chips, but not doing the celery thing. Celery is evil.

An apple.

Frank snagged a shiny red McIntosh, huge, and a bag of Ruffles and loped back to his cluttered desk, snug in the corner of his bedroom. Just as he sat in the plush chair, he thought: Hell. Forgot the beverage. The. Beverage. He returned to the kitchen and got a Diet Coke from the chair beside the table, filled with magazines and books, piled high.

He glanced at the present Gabby had sent him. His heart stuttered. Man, he was in heaven.

Gabby . . .

How much have we lost? he wondered. Squeezing his belly. Six pounds in the past month. If he weighed himself *after* peeing.

He munched and sipped, wished the soda was cold. Should have fridged it. Why do I forget things? Frank Walsh knew he had trouble focusing, but he also took pride that it was a negative compensation for being so talented in other ways.

Like his knives.

He regarded his specimens of cutting-edge weapons, which took up two bookshelves.

When was the curved kukri going to arrive? He thought of the beautiful blade – the picture on eBay had depicted a classic Nepalese army knife.

Then he returned to reality.

All the fucking Post-it notes I keep buying. Have to remember to use them for more than propping up table legs.

Write: *Put the soda in the fridge.*

How hard was that?

He slowed down on the chips. Take your time. Write that down too. Don't eat another until you've masticated and swallowed the one you're working on. He noted that the soda – because it was frigging warm – had sprayed onto the Samsung monitor when he'd opened the can. He wiped the glass with an old T-shirt, aromatic with Windex he kept beside the computer. He'd have to wash the cloth soon. That was gamy too. Like the Maybe Greek Fisherman hat.

Write it down.

He would.

Frank didn't write it down and returned to the computer, unable to stop thinking of the knife fight again.

Oh, it was beautiful. Choreography. Dance. Beautiful.

His knife sweeping down then stopping halfway as his victim went into a defensive posture – which Frank had anticipated.

And he'd then spun around backward and whisked his steel blade along the exposed neck.

Blood flew and sprayed and danced into the sky.

Then fast – you never hesitated – he leapt to the right and slashed again on the other side of the neck.

And the dying eyes stared, motionless for a moment. Then closed slowly as the pool of blood spread.

Wait, Frank Walsh thought. Was that his phone? He grabbed for it. No.

He'd hoped Gabby would call.

Well, he *knew* she'd call. But he meant now. This moment. He stared at the phone, willing it to ring. It didn't.

He thought more about the coming Tuesday.

A brief fantasy played itself out: The doorman, Arthur, ringing on the intercom and saying, 'There's somebody here to see you. Her name's Gabriela.'

Frank Walsh would smile. 'Send her up.'

And he'd be waiting for her in his black jeans and black shirt – his best look, his thin look – teeth brushed and hair sprayed and body deodorized. His fisherman cap would be in a Baggie, if he hadn't washed it first, which probably wasn't going to happen.

He'd pull out the present she'd just had delivered today.

She'd turn her beautiful, piercing eyes on him. And they'd crinkle with fun and flirt. She'd say, 'I've never seen your bedroom, Frank.'

He looked at the note that accompanied the gift.

Dear Frank. Thinking of you . . .

Oh, man . . .

Then Frank revised the fantasy. In the remake, a slightly more risqué version, they sat on the couch, knees touching, and watched an old movie on cable, instead of going to the film festival. The present – he found himself actually stroking the box now – would play a role in this fantasy too. A central role.

They'd pick something noir to watch, of course. Maybe *The Asphalt Jungle*. Or *Pulp Fiction*. It would be like Travolta and Uma Thurman dancing. He *loved* that movie (though he always wondered: If Travolta was such a brilliant hit man, why the hell did he leave his machine gun *outside* the bathroom, for Bruce Willis to find it, when he went to take a dump?).

They could watch that, or *Reservoir Dogs* or *Inglourious Basterds*.

Or hell, they'd watch anything that Gabby wanted to watch.

They'd talk, they'd fuck. He pictured her crying with pleasure, maybe with a little pain.

And then they'd talk some more. She'd learn all about him, she'd learn who was the real Franklin Walsh.

He flopped down on the saggy bed and sent her a text. He thanked her for the present and then – he couldn't resist – described what he had in mind for their date next Tuesday. He included a few suggestions about apparel.

All very tasteful, he decided.

Then he replayed in his mind the knife fight. Once, twice, again and again. The blood, the screams, the body twitching.

Mostly the blood.

CHAPTER
28

1:00 p.m., Sunday

40 minutes earlier

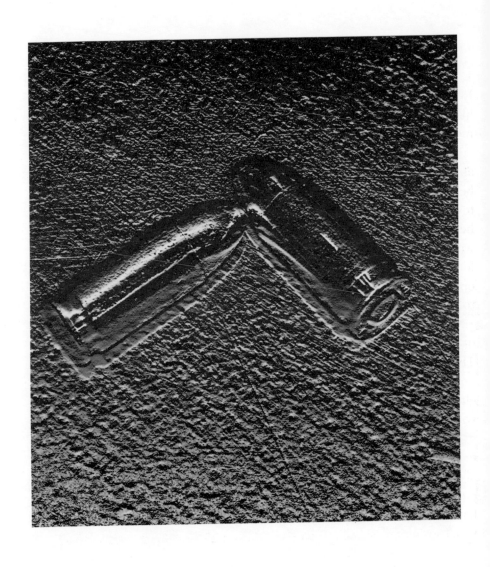

In his rhythmic, purposeful gait, Joseph Astor walked through the maze-like streets of this curious neighborhood like a tourist, eyes constantly moving.

He'd swapped the long black trench coat for black cargo pants, T-shirt and leather jacket. He was making his way back to the apartment he'd been to earlier this morning, though via a different route. This part of town was confusing. Avenues going every which-away. His GPS app was helpful but he wasn't moving in the most direct route, of course. He was taking his time, doubling back, striking through alleys and vacant lots. This confused the smartphone app girl Siri but there wasn't an option for picking routes to 'avoid spots where some asshole is waiting to put a bullet in my head.'

The air was chill and clouds ganged on the horizon sending bands of long, dim shadow over the sidewalks and streets and buildings here. The earlier sunlight was history. This was too bad because, believe it or not, bright light made witnesses' accounts less reliable than overcast; glare could be wonderfully obscuring. *Victims* too might not even see you or the gun when you approached.

He looked around once more. The residences were small, many of them red brick or dirt-brown stone that had once been white or light gray. A lot of soot and grime. He passed a bookstore for the gay-lesbian-transgendered crowd, a Laundromat, apartments with elaborate wrought-iron security bars. You could look right into the minuscule, street-level living rooms, which would fit no more than four or five people. Who'd live like that?

Plenty, Joseph reflected, to judge from the number of the cells he passed.

Manhattan . . .

In his mind once more, Joseph ran through the complex scheme he was orchestrating this weekend. Many parts, many challenges, many risks. But, being in a reflective mood, he was thinking that men are born to work. It didn't matter how difficult your job, how filthy your hands got – in all senses of phrase. It didn't matter if you were a poet or a carpenter or a scientist or whatever. God made us to get off our asses and go out into the world and do something with our time.

And Joseph was never happier than when he was working.

Even if, as he was about to do in a few minutes, that job was murder.

The silent GPS sent him around the corner and he paused. There was the brown brick building where his victim lived.

Thinking of how the night would unfold, Joseph again pictured Gabriela, her beautiful, heart-shaped face, her attractive figure, all of which jarred with the edgy voice. He thought too of the man with her, Daniel Reardon. He'd seemed smart and his eyes radiated confidence, which diminished only slightly when Joseph had displayed the butt of his pistol.

He thought too of the October List.

A complicated night lay ahead. But nothing he couldn't handle.

Now, no police in sight, he strode nonchalantly past the apartment building's door, glancing in. Yes, the doorman he'd seen earlier was still on duty. Joseph was a bit irritated at the old man's presence at the desk, which added a complication, but no matter. Anything could be worked around with enough determination and ingenuity. And Joseph was well fitted with both. He circled around to the back and counted windows, recalling the diagrams from the NYC Buildings Department of the structure's layout. Yes, his target was home. He could see movement and the flicker of light, as if from a TV or computer monitor. Shadows. A light spread out and a moment later shrank and went out; probably from a refrigerator door, since the glow came from the kitchen.

This reminded him he wanted a long sip or two from his Special Brew. But later. He was busy now.

Work to be done.

Joseph went to the service door. It was locked, naturally. Verifying that he couldn't be seen from any of the windows, he removed a screwdriver from his inside pocket and began to jimmy. This was all you needed 90 percent of the time; lock-picking tools were usually more trouble than they were worth.

He double-checked his pistol, then concentrated again on his task of cracking the lock, irritated that his target, Gabriela's friend Frank Walsh, lived on the sixth floor. His breath hissed out softly as he reflected that the last thing he needed right now was a climb up that many stairs.

CHAPTER
27

11:50 a.m., Sunday

1 hour, 10 minutes earlier

'I don't see him.'

Daniel Reardon was referring to the man who'd been following him and Gabriela from the chaos on Madison Avenue – the man in the rumpled gray suit and a bright yellow shirt, the man with the eyes of a hunting dog.

Gabriela said, 'Who the hell is he? I don't think he's a cop.'

'No. He would've called for backup. There'd be a thousand cars here if he was.'

They were moving quickly south on Second Avenue. The wind was now brisk, clouds were coagulating low in the sky. The cross streets were still in the high digits – fewer stores, more residences – so the sidewalks were less crowded than closer to Midtown. They looked behind once again. 'Maybe it was just a coincidence we saw him a couple of times.'

'You really think that?' Daniel asked.

'No,' she gasped. 'But, frankly, I don't know what to think anymore.' She winced as she held her side and stopped.

'Still hurts?'

'Does, yeah,' she said. She touched away a dot of blood on her cheek.

'Doctor?'

'No. The police might've contacted the emergency rooms. Let's just keep going.'

'If you broke a rib and pierced a lung,' he said, troubled, 'that could be a real problem.'

'I'll have to live with it,' she shot back. Then softer: 'Until we have Sarah. I'll live with it.'

They started again, making as much speed as they could away from the site of the incident just moments before. Daniel asked, 'What could he want? That man?'

'In the yellow shirt?'

'Yeah.'

Gabriela shrugged, as if it was obvious. 'If it *isn't* a coincidence, he wants the October List. What else? Joseph can't be the only one after it, I'm sure.'

Daniel was silent, head tilted. After another scan of the sidewalks behind them, he said, 'There's another possibility, about Yellow Shirt.'

'What's that, Daniel?'

'He's *working* for Charles Prescott.'

She frowned. 'Working for my boss? What do you mean?'

Daniel continued, 'Your boss sent this guy to track you down – to find out what you could have against him, information, evidence. To talk you out of testifying and going to the police.'

Gabriela shook her head. 'Charles would just call me up and talk to me.'

Daniel replied, 'The Charles Prescott you worked for, the Prescott you *thought* you knew might do that. But that's not the real Prescott. After what you've learned about him, don't you think he's capable of calling somebody up to do his dirty work for him?'

'Dirty work?' She clutched his arm. 'You don't think he'd hurt me?' Emphasis on the verb, as if it was too difficult to say 'kill.'

Daniel's voice was soft as he said, 'It's a possibility, Mac. We've got to consider it. You're the perfect witness. You can place Prescott at locations he doesn't want to be associated with. You know his girlfriend. You can testify about all kinds of things. And now – you found the October List.'

And when she said, 'No,' this time, though, her tone suggested even she didn't believe Charles Prescott was incapable of hurting her. Gabriela looked behind them, down the wide sidewalk. 'Yellow Shirt . . . where *is* he? I don't know where he *is*!' Her voice crackled with panic.

'It's all right. We lost him in the crowds. I'm—'

'No! There he is!'

Daniel's head swiveled too. 'Right.' Yellow Shirt was a block away, dodging around pedestrians, moving steadily forward.

'What are we going to do? If he stops us Sarah's gone. I can't let that happen.' Her wide eyes, rimmed red, stared toward Daniel.

'Just keep going. Faster.'

But, only two blocks later, she pulled up abruptly and arched her back, wincing and moaning. Her knees sagged and only Daniel's strong arm kept her from rolling onto the sidewalk. 'It hurts, Daniel. My chest hurts . . . I have to rest. Just for a minute.' She looked around. 'There. He won't see us there.'

Daniel helped her out of the crowds into the shadowy space she'd indicated, between two parked trucks. Noisy traffic zipped past. Daniel looked out, back in the direction where they'd last spotted the man. 'I don't see him.'

Gabriela leaned against the hood of the Mercedes truck, a Sprinter, and cradled her chest.

Another glance behind them. 'Nothing,' he assured. 'No cops either. We'll give it a minute then keep going. We'll get to the apartment. You can rest. Find out how badly you're hurt.'

'He's probably turned down a side street, don't you think? We tricked him.'

Daniel said, 'Could be.'

'Okay,' Gabriela whispered. 'Then let's go. I need to rest. I need to think.'

'There's a Lexington line station a block away. Can you make it?'

'Sure. I'm better now.'

They turned to the sidewalk.

'Wait!' a man's voice called. 'I want to talk to you!'

They swiveled around. Yellow Shirt had appeared from the traffic side of the gap between the trucks. The skin on his fat face was sweaty. He walked up fast, starting to speak and lifting his hands in an ambiguous way – could be a greeting, could be a threat.

Then he was reaching into his breast pocket.

Gabriela reacted fast. She stepped away from Daniel, placed both hands on the man's chest and shoved. As he stumbled back – into traffic – she said to Daniel, 'Let's go, run!'

But before they could start down the sidewalk, there came a squeal of brakes and a large delivery truck struck Yellow Shirt at close to forty-five mph. He tumbled beneath the wheels and a sickening, crumpled-box sound filled the air around them. No time for the driver to hit the horn, no time even for the man to scream.

Gabriela cried out, staring at the shattered figure. 'Oh, Jesus. No, no, no!' A thick wash of dark blood spread out behind the truck, which had slammed into a cab trying to avoid the man. 'No.'

Shouts, screams, people running toward the man's crushed body, people running away. Cell phones appearing for 911 calls . . . and for pictures.

Daniel Reardon took her arm. 'Mac! We have to leave. Now!'

'I didn't . . . I didn't mean to do it! I just reacted.' She stared, shaking.

'Listen to me!' Daniel gripped her face and turned it toward him, ignoring her wince of pain. 'We have to go.'

'But—'

'He was a threat. He *had* to be a threat. He wouldn't've followed us if he wasn't. You didn't have any choice. It looked like he was going to attack you. He was reaching into his pocket. Maybe he had a gun!'

'You don't know that! Look, he's still moving. His foot. It's moving!'

She stared at the blood, choked a cry.

Daniel's strong arm encircled her shoulders like a vise and he was walking her away. She half stumbled, half jogged beside him. It was as if she could barely remember how to walk.

His voice was tinted with panic too. 'I know you're upset. I know you're hurting, but we have to move, Mac.'

'I—' she began, shaking. 'I don't think—'

But Daniel interrupted. 'It's all about your daughter. Remember what you keep saying, "Focus." Well, focus on your daughter.'

'My . . .' she gasped.

'Sarah.' He said the name firmly. 'I'm sorry, Mac. It's a fucking shame this happened. But it did and we're not going to be able to help Sarah if you go to jail. There'll be a time to deal with it – later.'

Her face a pale mask, Gabriela nodded.

'Keep moving.'

She followed as if she were a toddler unsure how to walk.

Suddenly he froze. 'No, wait, go the other way. We'll circle around the block to the subway.'

'Why, what's wrong?'

'The way we were going, there's a meter maid at the corner.'

'Meter maid?' she asked. 'What difference does that make?'

Daniel leaned close and whispered, 'Gabriela, everybody in New York City, from dogcatchers to the FBI, is looking for you now.'

CHAPTER
26

11:35 a.m., Sunday

15 minutes earlier

In the trenches . . .

Think, figure this out, Hal Dixon told himself.

You work in the trenches. Improvise.

He looked around the streets, spotted someone he thought could help.

Dixon strode up to the hot dog vendor, who guided away the smoke of the coals warming chestnuts and pretzels in his cart with the wave of a hand. The smoke returned instantly.

The smell made Dixon hungry but he was on his mission and he ignored the sensation.

'Please, I need to ask you something,' he said to the skinny vendor in jeans and a Mets T-shirt. 'A couple came by here, a man and a woman. Just a few minutes ago.'

The man glanced at Dixon's wrinkled gray suit and bright yellow shirt and maybe came to some conclusion about the color combination. Then he was looking back at Dixon's sweaty face. 'Man and woman?' A faint lilt of accent.

Dixon described them.

The hot dog man was instantly uneasy. 'I didn't see anything. Nothing. No.'

'It's okay. I'm a deacon.' Trying to calm him.

'A . . . ?'

'In a church, Presbyterian,' the rumpled man said breathlessly. 'In New Jersey. A deacon.'

'Uhm,' said the street vendor, who seemed to be a Muslim and would probably have no idea what a deacon was but might appreciate devotion.

'Religious. I'm a religious person.'

'A priest?' the man asked, becoming confused. He was again regarding Dixon's old suit and yellow shirt.

'No. I'm just religious. A deacon's a layperson.'

'Oh.' The vendor looked around for somebody he could sell a hot dog to.

Mistake. Dixon said, 'I'm *like* a priest.'

'Oh.'

'A private person who helps the priest. Like helping the imam.'

'Imam?'

'Look.' Dixon reached into his breast pocket and took a small, black-bound Bible from it.

'Oh.' The man said this with some reverence.

'I was just on Madison Avenue.' He gestured broadly though the vendor would obviously know where Madison Avenue was.

'Yes.'

'And what happened was, I saw this woman commit a crime, a bad crime. The woman I just described.'

'A crime?'

'That's right.'

The vendor touched his chest with his fingertips, perhaps a form of prayer. Dixon noted his hands were filthy. He decided he'd never get a hot dog from a street vendor again. The man asked, 'All the sirens? Is that what's going on?'

'Yes, all the sirens. Lots of sirens.'

Dixon pulled a napkin out of the holder, then two more. He wiped his face.

'You want some water, Father? I call you "Father"? Is that what you say?'

'No, I'm not a reverend,' Dixon said. 'I don't want any water. A deacon. It's *like* a priest.'

'Okay, but if you do, just ask. A bottle. Or a soda.'

'Here's what I need—'

'You don't have a cell phone and you want to borrow mine?'

'No, no. I need to find out where they went – she and this other man, a friend of hers, I guess. I'm going to talk to them, help them give themselves up.'

The vendor blinked, waved at the smoke again.

Dixon repeated, 'She should surrender to the police. I'll help her. But she has to do it now. If they run, the police will think they're guilty and they may just shoot them down. They're panicked. I know they are.'

'You're . . . what do they call that, people in your bible? Who help other people?'

What? Oh. 'Samaritan,' Dixon said, wiping more sweat. The pits of his shirt were grayish yellow.

'Yeah, that's it.'

My bible . . .

'I guess I am. I don't know. They came this way.'

The vendor was more comfortable now. 'Yes, these people you're talking about? I saw them. A few minutes ago. I saw them because they were walking fast. And they were rude too.'

Dixon's heart beat a bit faster. 'Where did they go?'

'They went into that store there. Do you see it?'

'On the corner.'

'Next to the corner. The souvenir store.'

It was only forty or so feet away.

'Did you see them leave?'

'No, I think they're still in there. But I wasn't paying attention. They might've left.'

'Thank you. I think you've saved some lives.'

Dixon started across the street, then paused. The couple slipped from the store. They were wearing hats and she had a different bag, Dixon believed. But it was clearly them. They gazed up and down the street, spotted Dixon and froze for a moment. Then they vanished in the opposite direction. He noted the woman seemed to be limping.

Dixon started after them.

'Be careful,' the vendor said, his voice deflating, as if he wanted to append the word 'Father,' but was recalling that Dixon wasn't one. 'If they've done a crime they might not understand you want to help them. They might be desperate, dangerous.'

'I've made my peace with God,' Dixon called breathlessly as he broke into a trot, tapping his chest to make sure the small Bible was seated firmly in his pocket.

CHAPTER
25

11:10 a.m., Sunday

25 minutes earlier

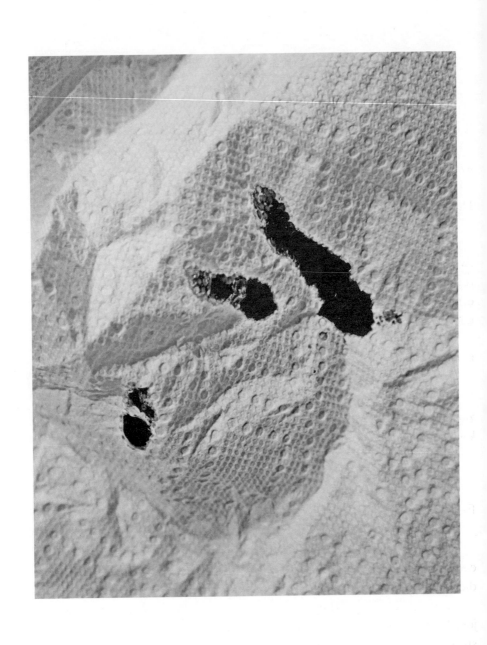

'The gun just went off,' Gabriela whispered, her voice the tone of hysteria. 'I didn't mean to do it.'

Daniel remained silent. He steered her quickly down the sidewalk away from the scene of the shooting.

She asked desperately, 'He didn't die, did he? What did you see, Daniel? What did you *see*?'

Still, no response.

Sirens filled the air around them as they headed east from Madison Avenue. There were lights too, piercing white and blue flashers. And reflections of white and blue flashers in windows. Lights seemed to be everywhere. Daniel and Gabriela kept their heads down. They didn't dare look up.

Then he directed her quickly to the side, a ninety-degree turn. She nearly stumbled but he held her firmly.

'What?' she gasped.

A car skidded to a stop, an unmarked police car. Two detectives in suits leapt out and headed into a crowded specialty food store, displaying their badges.

'Do they think we're in there?' she asked.

'Just keep walking.'

Manic, Gabriela asked, 'He didn't die, did he? He was so young! Please, tell me!' Her grip must have hurt. He frowned. She relented.

'I don't know, Mac. I'm sorry, but I don't know. It's possible.'

Walking as fast as they dared without drawing attention, they moved east, leaving the unmarked car behind. She glanced back. The officers didn't appear. She and Daniel hurried south, then east again.

To anyone else's eye, they resembled a typical couple. Not particularly jovial, not particularly conversational. Harried. A relationship limned by stress, money woes, child woes, sexual woes. Life in Manhattan, professionals. Yet every glance their way seemed tinted with suspicion.

But no one pointed, no one called out, no one seemed about to rip cell phones from holsters and speed-dial 911.

No one fled from the homicidal auburn-haired woman and her actor look-alike companion.

'I didn't think, Daniel. There was the gun. It was just there. I grabbed it! It went off. I've never even touched one before. I was just . . . Oh, Jesus. What've I done?'

A look behind revealed a half-dozen pedestrians, but no police. Still, Gabriela focused on a man in a suit – a rumpled gray one, of thin cloth, which seemed inadequate in the chill. He was walking in their direction. She noticed him because of his yellow shirt. His stride seemed purposeful though he wasn't paying particular attention to them.

Gabriela nudged Daniel. 'That guy? Yellow shirt? Look carefully.'

'Got it.'

'I've seen him before, I think. On Madison.'

'He followed us from the shooting?'

'I don't know—' Gabriela winced, gasped, then stopped abruptly, her hand on her side.

'It's bad?' he asked, gesturing down toward her ribs.

A nod.

'Can you walk?'

'Yes.' Though she frowned when they began again.

They kept their heads down, not looking anywhere but at the sidewalk. Suddenly Daniel took her arm and guided her quickly into a Korean deli, where they paused to examine the fresh-cut flowers and a tub of ice in which nested plastic bottles of orange and mango juice.

'What?' Gabriela asked in a whisper.

'Cops.'

A police cruiser sped past, silently, but its lights pierced as harshly as a siren.

Blue and white . . .

A moment later they took to the sidewalk again. They dodged through traffic and bicyclists and joggers and more pedestrians. When they hit the uptown–downtown street, another police car sped past.

She looked back and said urgently, 'I thought I saw him again. The yellow shirt guy.'

When they reached the next intersection, another police car sped past. It didn't slow, but the officers were looking around. He said, 'We need to get out of sight. There's a place we can stay.'

'Where?'

'The Norwalk Fund has an apartment, for out-of-town clients.'

'Norwalk . . . Oh, your company, right?'

He nodded. 'It's empty now. Off First Avenue in the Fifties.' He noted the cross street sign: 79th. 'It's a long walk,' he said. 'But I'm worried about cabs. They have that new video system, the TVs. Your picture might show up on the screen.'

'I can walk, sure.'

After five minutes, he paused and examined her. 'You can't walk.'

She sucked in a breath, then coughed. 'Subway, okay.' She leaned against him again. 'Is that man behind us, Yellow Shirt?'

'I don't see him.'

He took her arm and directed her east.

She inhaled again and let herself be led down the sidewalk. 'On Madison Avenue? He wasn't dead when we left. You saw that, right? He'll probably be okay, don't you think? He was so young.'

Daniel Reardon didn't speak for a moment. He said, 'I don't know, Gabriela. It depends on where you shot him.'

'He was married. He had a wedding ring on. Maybe he has children.'

'Gabriela . . .'

'I didn't *mean* to. I panicked. I didn't want to hurt anybody. But they were going to stop me and I couldn't let them. It was for Sarah . . . You understand. I had to do something.'

'People can get shot and still live.'

'The ambulance would be there soon, right? Probably minutes.'

At 74th and Lexington they dodged through traffic and paused at a light, next to a pushcart vendor, who called, 'You want hot dog? Pretzel?' He glanced at them with some curiosity. When they ignored him he turned to another customer and fished a frankfurter out of the gray frankfurter water.

The light changed and they crossed.

She said, 'People're looking at us, Daniel.'

'At you, Mac. Not us.'

'What?'

'Because you're beautiful.'

She gave a wan smile. She nodded at a souvenir shop. 'Hats,' she said, pointing to a rack.

'Good.'

They stepped inside.

She grabbed the first one she saw. But Daniel smiled and said, 'Maybe not.' It sported a Lady Gaga logo in glitter.

'Oh.' She picked a plain navy blue baseball cap. He picked a black one.

'Jackets?'

But all the store sold were brightly colored and sequined *I ♥ New York* gear, worse than the glitzy hat. Outer camo would have to wait.

They both also bought new luggage – small backpacks, hers black, his dark gray.

Daniel paid, cash, and they pulled on the caps and stuffed their gym bags into the new packs.

'Not much of a disguise but different enough.'

At the door Daniel gazed out, looking for police, looking for the man in the yellow shirt, looking for Joseph.

'Nothing.'

'But—'

She took his arm and grew serious. 'Listen, Daniel. This isn't right. It's time for you to leave. Get out now. I don't think they even saw you back there, when I shot him. Get away from me.' She choked. 'This isn't your problem.'

He bent forward fast and kissed her on the lips. 'Okay, that's it.'

She blinked in surprise.

'What?'

'Do you watch that show *CSI?*'

'I used to.'

'Well, now you've got my DNA on you. If they catch you, I'm going down too.'

She smiled. 'Oh, Daniel . . .'

'It'll be okay, Mac. I promise.'

'Mac?' She blinked, hearing him use this name.

'You're more of a Mac than a Gabriela. And come on, with a last name like McKenzie, don't tell me nobody's ever called you Mac?'

'True.'

Gabriela didn't tell him that she and her father used nicknames for one another, and the one he'd bestowed on his daughter was indeed 'Mac.'

'You mind?'

She smiled. 'I love it.'

'And I may just love you,' Daniel whispered.

She stiffened at the word, then let herself go and pressed against him, shoulders-to-thigh. And for a fleeting moment the horrors of the weekend vanished.

CHAPTER
24

10:00 a.m., Sunday

1 hour, 10 minutes earlier

Daniel and Gabriela had checked out and were sitting at a wobbly table in a coffee shop on the Upper East Side.

She nodded back to the hotel in which they'd spent the night. 'You always take girls to dives like that?'

'Only the ones I think can handle it. You passed the test.'

She gave a wry smile and turned back to her task. Dozens of documents sat in front of them, business records, letters, copies of emails.

She examined the last few in the pile. She leaned back. 'It looks like there's close to a million dollars in quote "miscellaneous assets" that my boss has. But there's no clue where they could be. It's so unfair! To know there's money out there, enough for the ransom, but not know where it is. How the hell'm I going to get Joseph his goddamn money?'

Daniel examined his half of the documents and he admitted that he had found nothing helpful either.

Gabriela's coffee sat untouched before her. Daniel was drinking tea. Two bags sat in the cup, dyeing the water ruddy brown. Not many people drank tea, she reflected. Her mother did. For the past six years, though, the woman mostly just stared at the cup of cooling English Breakfast on the table in the assisted-living home.

Forget that. Concentrate. This is important, this is vital.

Gabriela found herself sweating. She wiped her palms on her blue jeans. She'd peeled off the windbreaker, but the restaurant was hot and her wool sweater, which she'd knitted herself, was warm. The pale green garment was thick. She remembered picking out the yarn, searching online to find a good pattern for the collar and sleeves, an Irish chain.

She sipped coffee and picked at toast, for which she had no appetite. Then, with both hands, she gestured desperately at the documents and muttered, 'Where do we go from here? Safe-deposit boxes?'

'The police will've found them all, locked them down.'

They were silent, surrounded by the sound of the milk steamer, Muzak from CDs offered for sale, a little conversation and a lot of clattering keyboards. Looking out of the window, she noted the silhouette of the Queensboro Bridge, 59th Street. It was stark against an indifferent sky.

Gabriela had a sip of coffee, then another. It was bitter. She didn't mind. The sharp flavor made her alert.

'Did you find anything about this mysterious Gunther?' he asked.

'Nothing.'

'What about family property?'

'What do you mean?'

'Your boss's parents? Brothers and sisters? Someplace that was held in a different name than Prescott.'

Gabriela said quickly, 'Yes, yes! There is.' Her eyes grew wide. 'That could be it. When Charles's father died last year, he and his siblings were going to put the family home on the market but they decided they had to fix the place up first. Charles would go up there every few months to work on it. It's still being renovated.'

'Whose name was it under?'

'It was a trust the lawyers named something like One Oh Nine Bedford Road Trust.'

'The police might not have heard about it yet.'

She continued, 'I've seen pictures. It'd be perfect to hide money – it's old, two hundred years. And has dozens of rooms and a huge basement. How big is a million dollars?'

Daniel laughed. 'I wouldn't know. My clients use wire transfers. But it's probably not as big as you'd expect. Where *is* the house?' he asked.

'Near Ridgefield, Connecticut. In the western part of the state, near the New York border.'

'I know it. We could get up there and back in time before the deadline.' We can take my car. I garage it a couple blocks from here.' But then he frowned and asked, 'Is the phone up there still working?'

'I don't know. Why?'

'You better try it first, before we show up.'

'Why? You think Charles's hiding there? The police traced him to the Caribbean.'

'No,' Daniel said. 'I think the *police* might be there.'

'Oh. Of course.' She lifted her mobile.

But Daniel stopped her, pointing to a pay phone in the back of the shop.

'You think they're tracing incoming calls?' she asked.

'I'm way past paranoia at this point.'

She rose and walked to the phone, lifted the receiver and fed in some coins. Two minutes later she was back at the table, scooting the chair next to him.

She offered a rueful look. 'Good decision, Daniel.'

'Who answered?' he asked.

'Detective Holloway. Connecticut State Police. I said it was a wrong number and hung up.' Gabriela sighed and her body seemed to collapse in on itself. Daniel wasn't much taller than she was – maybe three inches – but she was so diminished at the moment that he seemed to tower over her. Her head was tilted downward. 'That was our last chance . . . Oh, Sarah . . .' she muttered. 'What am I going to do, Daniel? If we don't get that money . . .'

But then she fell silent and cocked her head. 'Wait, wait . . .' She plowed once more through the documents spread out before them.

'What? You look like a wolf going after a sheep.'

Her dark fingernail underlined some entries on a business form. 'These are accounts of non-deductible expenses that Charles had. Personal accounts. I never paid any attention to them before because they didn't have anything to do with the business.' Reading through the documents again, Gabriela pointed to some entries. 'He spent close to a hundred thousand at jewelry and department stores last year. Some of the items he had delivered to an address on Madison Avenue, a woman named Sonia Dietrich.'

'Who is she?'

'I never heard of her. I know Charles dated some but he never mentioned who he was seeing. No woman ever came by the office.' Perusing the balance sheets and ledgers again. 'Hell, he did more than buy her presents. He wrote dozens of checks to her too. A hundred thousand, a little more.'

'And maybe gave her some cash.'

'It could be,' she said excitedly. 'She might have the missing million.'

Daniel asked, 'Would she have left the country with him?'

Gabriela said, 'Considering he's a wanted man, Charles's probably the last person she'd want to be seen with. Women like her have a sixth sense. Survival, you know.'

He'd noted a certain tenor. 'Like *her*? I thought you didn't know her.'

'Intuition,' she said dryly.

'How should we handle it?' he asked.

'I could call and tell her . . .' She debated. 'No, how's this? I could tell her the police are looking for people connected with Charles. He wanted me to pick up anything he left with her, to keep her in the clear.'

'Including a large satchel of hundred-dollar bills? I don't think that'll work.'

'No, I suppose not. Well, how about *this*? I'll tell her if I don't get the money I'm going to the police and reporting that she's been hiding stolen money for him. What do they call that?'

'Bagman.'

'I'll tell those detectives she's a bagman. Well, bagwoman. I get the five hundred thousand and she doesn't go to jail.'

'I like that a lot better.'

Stuffing a crumpled napkin into his cup, Daniel asked, 'But what if she's not home?'

Gabriela thought for a moment. 'Then it's Plan B.'

'Which is?'

'I'll break into her fucking apartment and turn it inside out.'

They stood on the corner of 88th and Madison, two buildings away from the one Gabriela pointed at. 'That's it. That's where she lives, his girlfriend, or mistress, or accomplice. Whatever Ms Dietrich is.'

'"Slut" was the most recent job description, I thought,' Daniel reminded in a whisper.

Gabriela dug through the documents in her purse. She then placed a call and held the phone to her ear. After a few seconds she put the unit away. She said, 'Voice mail. I guess we assume she's not there.'

'As opposed to assuming she's not answering because she's busy cleaning her shotgun?' He looked boyish, he looked charming . . . and he seemed a bit charmed himself as he scanned her face.

'Okay. We go with the alternative.'

Plan B . . .

'Wait here a minute,' she told him and walked into the lobby of the elegant brownstone, looking over the mailboxes. She returned to Daniel. 'Brother, she's got the whole second floor.' They gazed at those windows, which were dark. The rooms seemed to be unoccupied.

'Come on,' she said.

They walked into the alleyway beside the building. All the windows on the ground floor were barred with elaborate, scrolly grates. The second-floor windows, however, were not protected, and one was partly open.

'Help me.'

They wheeled a Dumpster below it.

Gabriela then turned and walked back to the street, with Daniel following. She surveyed the scene. The sidewalk wasn't crowded. 'The alley's narrow,' she pointed out. 'There's no reason for anybody to look into it and see me.'

'You're really going to break in?'

'Yep. I sure as hell am.'

She noted a closed antiques store on the corner. In front were two massive Chinese lions, secured to the sidewalk with massive chains. Who on earth would steal them? she thought. How could you fence eight hundred pounds of ugly sculpture?

'You wait there and, I don't know – pretend to make a call. If you see anybody walk up to the building, call me.'

He gave her a quick kiss. 'Good luck.' He retreated ten feet and took out his mobile.

Gabriela started back to the alley. She had just reached the mouth when, with a staccato flutter of urgent, official lights, an unmarked police car, followed by a blue-and-white NYPD cruiser, skidded to a stop in front of the building.

Daniel started forward but Gabriela subtly gestured for him to stay where he was.

The two detectives who'd stopped the pair yesterday, Kepler and Surani, climbed out of the unmarked police car. A uniformed officer, blond and young, exited the cruiser.

None of them looked Daniel's way.

Kepler gestured toward where they stood on the sidewalk. 'Come on over here, Ms McKenzie.'

She didn't move.

'Please. Now.'

She hesitated then joined them.

'Tell us what're you doing.' Surani insisted, though politely.

'That's my business.'

'Well, explain what that business is and why it involves an alleyway.'

'I wasn't breaking any laws,' she shot back.

'No? Were you – just speculating here – thinking of maybe . . . breaking into somebody's apartment?' From Kepler, of course, and delivered frosted with sarcasm.

'That's ridiculous. A friend of my boss lives here.'

'"Friend"?' Kepler asked sarcastically.

'We know about Ms Dietrich,' Surani said.

Gabriela snapped, 'I have every right to talk to her.'

Kepler asked, 'About what?'

'And I have every right not to tell you that.'

Her eyes swiveled toward the antiques store, the massive lions. Daniel was standing behind some spectators, twenty feet away. He was close – he could hear the exchange, she could tell – but not so near that the cops noticed him. Her frown told him to stay there.

'What exactly were you going to do, whisper to Ms Dietrich from below the window?' Kepler looked at the Dumpster. 'Very Romeo and Juliet.'

'And what are *you* doing here?' she demanded.

Kepler laughed. 'You got quite the attitude – for a burglar. In answer to your question, since you haven't cooperated and since Charles Prescott is still wanted on suspicion of two dozen felonies, we're pursuing other leads in the case. One of 'em sent us here. Tell us what *you* know about Ms Dietrich.'

'Nothing. I was worried about Charles. I just wanted to ask her if she'd heard from him, how he's doing.'

'Again, I ask: through the window?' Kepler offered, and ignored her bitter glare. He added, 'They make these things called telephones, you know. But we'll have time to talk about it in detention.'

'What?'

'We searched your boss's office again. We checked the inventory and found some things missing. Gabriela McKenzie, you're under arrest for obstruction of justice.' He sounded as if he'd been looking forward to saying those words for some time.

She blurted, 'No!'

As if he couldn't resist himself, Kepler added, 'And we'll throw in an attempted burglary count just for the hell of it.' A glance into the alley. 'A Dumpster? Really.'

'You don't understand. My . . .' Her voice trailed off.

'Your what?' Surani asked.

'Please. I can't afford to go to jail right now.'

Kepler laughed. 'Sorry if it's inconvenient.' He turned away to jot some entries in a notebook and gestured to the uniformed officer. His name badge said *Patrolman Chapman*.

He stepped up to her. 'Set your bag down and turn around, put your hands behind your back.'

'Please!'

'Now. Turn around.' The officer reached for his cuffs, looking down to locate them. When he did, Gabriela lunged forward and ripped his automatic pistol from his holster.

The crowd gasped and scattered.

'Gabriela!' Kepler shouted. He moved in fast and gripped her arm. They grappled and Gabriela went down hard on her side, crying out in pain. But she broke free and swung the gun toward his face. He winced and ducked, waving his hand, as if to ward off the bullets.

'Now back off!' she screamed and aimed at the detectives. 'You two! Throw your guns away! Now! Under those cars!'

Surani called desperately, 'Don't do this! You—'

But she regarded them with a cold look. And they tossed their weapons where she'd indicated.

As her gaze was momentarily drawn by the tumbling guns, wincing as if afraid one would fire, the uniformed officer surged forward, trying to tackle her. Gabriela broke away and she stumbled. As she tried to right herself the gun discharged.

The young cop blinked, grabbed his chest and dropped to the pavement. 'Oh, fuck. Oh.'

Gabriela gasped.

Surani ignored both her and the pistol, which she still held, and ran to the fallen officer, whose arms were flailing, feet kicking. The detective bent over him and shouted over his shoulder, 'Call it in!'

Kepler said in a raspy growl, 'You fucking bitch! Shoot me if you want but I'm getting him help!' He pulled out his radio.

Sobbing, Gabriela backed away. Then turned and ran. At the corner she tossed the gun into a sewer grating. She joined Daniel, who was looking equally shocked. She started to sprint again. But he stopped her. 'Just walk. Look down and walk.'

'I—'

'Just walk. Slow. Walk.'

Gabriela nodded, inhaled deeply several times and took his arm.

They headed east.

Soon, only seconds later, the banshee call of sirens cut through the chill afternoon air from a dozen directions at once.

CHAPTER
23

9:45 a.m., Sunday

15 minutes earlier

'Okay,' Kepler said, looking up from his phone. 'The address is Madison at Eighty-Eight.'

'And what's that supposed to be?' Surani asked.

'Charles Prescott's girlfriend.' He looked down at a sheet of paper. 'Sonia Dietrich.'

'This is all very fucking complicated,' Surani griped.

'You've been cussing a lot lately,' Kepler said. 'Not like you.'

'Not like me? Because people of South Asian heritage – that's *Indian* to you, but not *your* kind of Indian – don't swear? People who work in call centers don't swear?'

'*That's* racist,' Kepler said indignantly. 'What do you mean, "*my* kind of Indian"? I don't go to the casinos.'

'*Casinos?*' Surani riposted. 'My point exactly. There you go.' His gray-complexioned face turned to his partner with a look of smug triumph. He took off his suit jacket and hung it over a chair.

Kepler was continually surprised at how his partner could be so slim, yet so muscular. The man played soccer most weekends. Cricket sometimes, a game Kepler simply couldn't get his head around.

Thinking he really should get serious about the golf, Kepler waved his hand, which meant the argument was over.

A figure appeared in the doorway of the operations room.

'Ah, it's Rookie Three-name,' Kepler said, eyeing the name badge.

'Fred Stanford Chapman reporting for duty,' the young blond officer said; *his* tone evidenced a bit of attitude, Kepler thought.

'And, if you're interested, for the record, *I* swear all the fucking time,' said the kid, who'd apparently overheard the conversation. 'Anyway, swearing isn't swearing anymore. It's different.'

Attitude . . .

Kepler gave him a *that's-not-funny-so-watch-yourself* look. Blondie shut up and decided not to offer what he'd been about to, whatever it was.

'All right, Fred Stanford Chapman—'

The rookie said, 'Why don't you call me Stosh? It's—'

'Naw, you're definitely a Fred Stanford Chapman,' Kepler said, like he was bestowing an honorary title.

'Definitely,' Surani echoed.

'Now. Listen up.' Kepler briefed the Patrol officer on the Charles Prescott Op and, even though he remained a little smart-ass around the eyes, the kid seemed to get it. And even made a few good suggestions.

Then Kepler said, 'Let's get some breakfast. Something big.'

'And expensive,' Surani added.

Kepler let drop, 'We'll charge it to Patrol. Our Viking warrior here'll sign for it.'

The kid was silent for a moment. He'd be thinking that even on stake-out operations he had to buy his own food. 'Me?'

'This case is so fucked up – excuse me, Gandhi,' Kepler said, with a look at Surani, who gave him the finger yet again, 'that we need some Bloody Marys too. Or, hell, Champagne.'

'Champagne?' The rookie was dying.

Kepler gave it a whole ten seconds. Then said, 'We're fucking with you, Fred Stanford Chapman.'

'Yeah.' And he tried to look as if he'd known that all along.

'We got time for coffee, that's it. We go to . . . What's the address again?'

'Madison and Eighty-Eight.' He added, to the new member of the team: 'That's where Prescott's concubine's supposed to be.'

The young officer said, 'A concubine is a woman who exists in a marriage-like relationship but's unable to marry her lover, usually because of a difference in social class. You wouldn't really have concubines in America. Fewer class issues, you know.'

Both the detectives stared at him.

The kid blushed. 'I'm just saying.'

'Jesus Christ,' Kepler muttered. 'Now you're definitely buying.'

Surani, the more-or-less voice of reason, said, 'Let's get a move on.'

The detectives waited, continuing to stare at the patrolman.

'What?' The kid's voice nearly broke.

Surani frowned. 'You weren't listening?'

'How's that?'

'The briefing. Just now.'

'I was, yeah.' But he looked uncertain, as if he maybe hadn't been listening as much as he ought to've been.

'Forget about that?' Kepler pointed to a bulletproof vest, sitting on a table near the door.

'I'll pass,' the young officer said. 'Sweat like a pig in one of those. Besides, what could go wrong?'

CHAPTER
22

9:30 a.m., Sunday

15 minutes earlier

They sat together on the edge of the unmade bed, sheets warm and twisted, concentric, like hurricane clouds seen from space.

Their legs touched.

'We should check out soon,' Daniel Reardon said. He was looking down at Lexington Avenue as if Joseph or a crew of other killers searching desperately for the October List were stationed outside. His bag was packed.

'All right,' Gabriela said absently. She rose and began gathering up her things, stuffing them back into the gym bag. Dark blue with a red Nike logo on the side. Did Nike still use that logo? she wondered. And the tag line:

Just do it . . .

She'd brought very little with her, apart from the files, and she was soon finished. She was aware of Daniel looking her over. Blue jeans and a V-neck green sweater over a cream-colored silk camisole. A light gray L.L. Bean windbreaker. Daniel was in a new outfit as well – a suit, like yesterday. Dark gray. Italian. It was perfectly pressed. He wore no tie, a concession of some sort to the weekend. The scent rising from the cloth was astringent – dry-cleaning chemicals – but she sensed a subtext of aftershave, lotion and musk. Shoe polish too. He was fastidious about his shoes. The combination was, for some reason, extremely arousing.

Yes, they should check out, Gabriela reflected. But she didn't want to. She wanted to stay here. Close to him.

Very close.

This was absurd under the circumstances. Yet, for the moment, the feeling of desire – and the possibility of a deeper, searingly hot connection – enveloped her.

It was then that he pulled her closer, his right hand easing like a silk scarf around her neck. She resisted but only for the briefest of moments.

Lips yielding and surging, tastes joining, heat rolling from skin to skin. The more she relaxed, the harder her gripped her.

And she sensed that irresistible uncoiling within her.

Another embrace, bordering on pain. Then he was backing away. 'I'm sorry. I shouldn't have done that.' Though he didn't seem the least bit contrite.

Despite virtually seeing the name Sarah emblazoned in her mind, Gabriela said softly, 'Yes, you should have.' And she kissed him once more.

'Let's get breakfast and keep going through our homework.' A glance at the documents. 'We've got a half million dollars to find.'

She nodded but found herself tempted once more to pull him down on the bed next to her. She easily pictured what would follow. Daniel was sensual, with a taut body – she'd seen and felt enough of it already. A firm, unyielding grip. Lips the right combination of firm and soft. He'd have a playful tongue and he'd use it frequently; he was a man who would enjoy taste as well as touch. He would press her down on the bed, pinioning her, which despite her obsession with control she curiously enjoyed – never been able to figure that one out – and then he'd devour her, one hand on her thigh, one on her breast. He'd be unrelenting, possessive, domineering.

And the warmth and pleasure, like drugs, would continue, growing and growing until the end would be pretty quick for her.

God, she wanted that.

A string of mismatched lovers stretched out behind her.

Mismatched and worse.

But, as tempted as she was, she forced the fantasy away and ignored the warm sheets, the scents of him, the memory of his hands and mouth.

Priorities.

Goals.

The name 'Sarah.'

CHAPTER
21

8:30 a.m., Sunday

1 hour earlier

He had a sense that somebody was watching him.

Frank Walsh was walking toward his apartment in the West Village, aware of a man in his forties, large, with curly blond hair sticking out from beneath a baseball cap, wearing a dark overcoat. The man was on the opposite side of Hudson Street, walking in the same direction. But it was odd, the way this guy was walking. Anybody else would have been looking down at his feet or ahead or at the windows to his left. This guy, though, was glancing pretty frequently at the sparse Sunday-morning traffic. Like he was worried about cars following him.

Worried why? That cops were after him, a mugger? A killer?

Or was Mr Overcoat studiously avoiding looking at his own target: Franklin Walsh himself?

The thirty-year-old knew about stalking up on prey, about fighting, about attacking. About survival.

About blood.

His instincts told him this guy was trouble.

A fast glance but the man seemed to anticipate this and looked away. Frank got only a look at a round face and that creepy hair – tight blond curls, slick. But this was the Village and weird was the order of the day.

Then Mr Overcoat paused to look in a window, head cocked with what seemed to be legitimate curiosity. So maybe he was just another local. Frank told himself to stop being paranoid. Besides, he knew how to take care of himself. He felt the knife in his pocket, tapped it for reassurance.

Soon his thoughts drifted away from Mr Overcoat. They even skipped over what was coming a half hour from now: the knife work he'd been obsessing over for days.

And they settled on . . . what else? Shit. The weekend visit with his mother. She'd overfed him. She'd made him take her shopping to the most crowded mall on Long Island. And there hadn't been much to talk about with her, of course – there never was – though the woman had managed to bring up Frank's sister's marriage at least a half-dozen times.

Part of that topic included the fact that Barbara and her husband would 'surely have a baby in the next year or so.'

Which involuntarily had conjured an unpleasant image of his sister having sex, which put him off dinner last night, at least until dessert.

'Brobbie and Steve want four, you know. Ideally one year apart.'

What was his mother's point? Did she think he could wave his wand (hmm, bad choice of word, that) and, poof, there was a wife popping out kids? Shit, didn't she know he was doing the best he could? His life wasn't like everybody else's. Who, for instance, would understand his obsession?

The knives, the fighting, the blood . . .

Also, another thing: the practicality. Given his line of work, he didn't meet many women.

Besides, he was holding out for one particular person.

Ah, Gabriela . . .

Tuesday, sure.

Her words, punctuated with a smile.

Frank was presently striding briskly back from Penn Station at Madison Square Garden. This was a pretty good walk, and guaranteed to burn off maybe a hundred calories, particularly in the chill autumn air. He'd purposefully taken off his jacket so his body would drop fat, burning calories in the chill – even though he didn't like looking at his round figure in the storefront windows as he passed them. He shouldn't have worn the knit shirt. It was clinging, revealing.

Well, don't look, he told himself.

But he did.

Still, he kept the jacket off. Cold weather made you burn up to 50 percent more calories than in the heat. In the Arctic you could eat whatever you wanted and still lose weight. He'd researched it. Six thousand calories a day. He should spend a year there.

Frank glanced around again and noted that Mr Overcoat was now on the same side of the street as he was, and the man's pace continued to match Frank's.

Stalking, attacking, killing . . .

Still, had to be paranoia.

What would this guy be interested in me for? And even if he is, how could he have found me here, on the street, striding south from Penn Station?

But, of course, Frank Walsh knew computers cold – the good side of machines, and the bad. He was well aware of phone tapping and datamining. He'd bought his ticket back to the city this morning with a credit card. He'd phoned his mother to tell her he'd made the train. If somebody wanted to, he could've found out what train Frank was on, when he'd be arriving at the station, even what he looked like – from the Motor Vehicle picture (even if the depiction was thirty pounds lighter than presently).

He then turned the corner onto his street in the Village and risked a fast look back, his hand on the knife in his pocket.

The curly haired guy was gone.

Frank continued up the block and approached his eight-story apartment building. As he got to the door he stepped in quickly and looked around but the quiet, tree-lined street was deserted of pedestrians.

He stepped into the lobby and finally relaxed.

'Hi, Arthur.'

The doorman was old and when he walked he shuffled and he smelled of Old Spice. 'Package for you, Mr Walsh.'

'FedEx?' He was expecting the knife, the kukri. Those Nepalese were far more deadly than people thought.

Cheery Sherpas, my ass.

'No, it was a hand delivery. Some Hispanic fellow dropped it off yesterday.'

It was a plastic bag containing something rectangular and heavy. He took it.

'Thanks.' He hadn't planned to give him a tip. Frank was plenty generous around Christmas. He looked into the bag and his heart thudded and he laughed as he read the note that accompanied it.

He handed Arthur five dollars.

The old man took it without thanks but with a raised hand that Frank chose to interpret as undying gratitude.

Frank unlocked his door and walked inside, tossing his jacket on his armchair in front of the big-screen TV.

The apartment, consisting of three rooms, was this: Dark and insanely cluttered, yet comforting – if claustrophobic at times, depending on his mood. A kitchenette with a two-burner gas stove and oven big enough for a TV dinner or two. His microwave sat atop a table, sharing the space with books and magazines. But back in the day, in this locale of glorious bohemian art, you created your poetry or paintings, you smoked pot, you slept with as many women as you could and you drank to oblivion; cooking was secondary, if not wholly unnecessary.

Frank walked to the window and looked out at Westbeth, the famous artists' community. He had a view of the very room where Diane Arbus had slashed her wrists in '71.

At least that was what the real estate broker, sensing a hooked fish, had said. As if it would make this dive more appealing to be able to look out over the space where a very weird photographer had offed herself.

Then he shifted his gaze and scanned for men in black overcoats.

Not a single *Matrix* killer with slick, curly blonde hair. He closed the curtain.

Frank then returned to the delivery he'd just received and, swollen with joy, lifted out the dark green box of Dom Pérignon champagne.

He peeled off the note.

Dear Frank. Thinking of you. We'll share this soon! Really looking forward to Tuesday. I'll call you! XOXO, Gabriela.

He felt like he'd just scratched off the last number in Lotto and won a million dollars. He laughed out loud with pleasure.

Champagne! And he didn't think this was the cheap stuff, either.

He pictured Gabby's slim waist, her high, spherical breasts, thick, straight, auburn hair that she seemed to wear up in buns or ponytails most of the time. But occasionally she wore it down, which Frank loved.

God, was she pretty.

He recalled seeing her in that yellow swimsuit, sunbathing in Central Park. He believed he'd seen a scar on her belly. He wondered if it was a C-section or from an accident.

He wondered how he could find out.

Ask her, dummy.

Their coffee on Friday had been great. He must've passed a test of sorts, because look at this! He regarded the green box again. Reread the note. Then again, and once more.

Hell, Dom Pérignon. He Googled.

Shit! A hundred fifty bucks!

Frank began to fantasize about when she came over on Tuesday. He'd have the place spick-and-span.

Vacuumed. And air-freshened; he sniffed and something smelled off. Clean sheets on the bed . . .

Frank glanced at his watch. Well, he'd have to think about their date later. Now it was time for the fight.

Time for death, time for blood.

His palms began to sweat.

In his musty bedroom Frank Walsh emptied his pockets onto his dresser: forty-three dollars in crumpled bills, coins, receipts, a Necco Wafer wrapper, a Kit Kat wrapper, and the knife he always carried, a two-inch Swiss Army model with magnifier, toothpick and scissors.

He opened the closet door. Inside were dozens of shoes, one suit, four combat jackets and a hat rack with a single piece of headgear, a Greek fisherman cap. This he grabbed and pulled over his ruddy hair. He sat down in his creaky office chair and booted up his computer, kicking his shoes off. Squinting at the computer screen, Frank moused up the volume, and music trilled, otherworldly music from a different dimension.

The familiar logo filled the screen, giving him comfort, like seeing the *Now Entering* sign of your hometown.

The Clans of Gravias Major
The Number One Online Role Playing Game

Frank clicked on *Resume Game* and motioned to life his avatar, a lean, handsome warrior whose appearance was similar to its owner only in hair color. He directed this figure to the armory to select the Daratian knife from his arsenal of weapons. Frank then flew the avatar, via a winged horse, into Prospecia Woods, where he would meet and fight an avatar manned by a young player in Taiwan.

They'd scheduled this one-on-one battle to settle a dispute between their respective clans, as the rules of the game allowed.

A few moments later he arrived at the Judgment Circle, which was already surrounded by several dozen avatars from both clans. The people behind those creatures – none of whom Frank had ever met in person, or even had a real conversation with – directed the warriors and wizards to applaud and leap up and down, offering cries of support. The other side, of course, did the same, encouraging *their* warrior.

After a moment the opposing avatar appeared, a bizarre-looking creature with a tentacle for a tail. He surveyed the fighting circle and stepped over the barrier.

Frank instructed his avatar to do the same. The two animated creations faced each other.

He had a brief memory of Mr Overcoat, but it faded quickly. He had a knife fight to win. He directed his avatar to crouch and, with the wicked blade forward, he advanced on his opponent, who dropped into a defensive position as its snaky face surveyed his enemy.

Frank feinted to the side and then leapt forward, knife swinging like an airplane propeller, and he clung to his strategy – pretending he was defending Gabby from being raped by the creature.

Blood flew and screams rose harrowingly, shooting from the Bose speakers, a month's pay.

Frank advanced again.

Stalking, attacking, killing . . .

CHAPTER
20

10:00 p.m., Saturday

10 hours, 30 minutes earlier

'Hal. Sorry to ruin your Saturday night.'

'Never a problem to see *you*, Pete.'

The men pumped hands vigorously. Both right wrists, coincidentally, were encircled by gold bracelets. One tasteful, one not.

'Well, sit down,' said Peter Karpankov, gesturing toward a chair across from the ornate but well-worn antique table he used for a desk, deep mahogany. 'Have a seat. Do you want a drink? You want some whisky? Is that your drink? You want something else?'

'Naw, but thanks.' Hal Dixon, body a bit stocky, suit a bit rumpled, but shirt pressed, even now at this hour of the evening.

They were on the top, the third floor, of the ancient building on Tenth Avenue that housed Karpankov's company.

The Russian poured some vodka and sipped it warm. He lifted his eyebrow. 'You sure?'

'Naw, really, Pete. I mean, you're right, yeah, I like whisky but nothing for me. The wife smells it on my breath I go home and it's all hell to pay. I can have a drink *with* her but not a drink *before* her. You know how it is.'

'Ah, women, women, women . . .' The lean man chuckled. He looked so much like Vladimir Putin that Dixon had wondered if he was somehow related to the Russian president. He had no accent but sometimes you imagined he did.

There was a rumble from the corner and Karpankov's large dog – whose breed Dixon didn't recognize – stretched and looked over the visitor slowly. Not exactly hostile, not exactly friendly. He flopped back down on his cushion and sighed. The thing had to weigh 150 pounds. The dog's brown eyes settled on Dixon and would not let go. Black and gray fur maybe naturally spiky, maybe rising, as in hackles.

As in just before the attack.

'He's a good boy,' Karpankov said affectionately.

'Big,' Dixon said.

'Things're going good for you, I hear.' Karpankov looked impressed. 'The new shopping mall project.'

'Sure,' Dixon said. And kept his eyes locked with the Russian's. 'We're making money hand over fist, even though I have no idea what the fuck that expression means.'

Karpankov blinked. Then laughed. 'Ha, that's true. I never thought about it. "Hand over fist." What's that mean? People are careless, what they say. Clichés, lazy speaking. Makes you sick, sometimes.'

'Sick.'

The view from Karpankov's office was of the Hudson River. Now, at night, the water was just a strip of black. What ebbed and flowed were lights, yellow, red, green, white, easing north and easing south.

Karpankov disconnected and then turned to Dixon, who regarded the man's eyes for as long as he could.

Those are some very weird pupils, he thought, looking away. Not fifty shades of gray. Two.

The Russian said, 'I'm thinking it's about time we should talk about that project in Newark. You and me.'

A joyous drumbeat tickled Dixon's gut. He said enthusiastically, 'That's going to be a ball buster, Pete. Eight figures, easy. Mid eight figures.' Then to himself: Calm the fuck down. You're talking like a tween gushing about Bieber.

'Eight, yeah, we're figuring.'

'You'll clean up with it,' Dixon said.

This was a joke because part of the project involved leases to a large dry-cleaning outfit. Dixon had been dying to participate.

Karpankov didn't seem to get the play on words, though.

Dixon kept his face still – you had to when dealing with people like Karpankov – but his pleasure was growing by the second. He'd been hoping for a year that Karpankov would bring him in on some project, any project. But Newark? Jesus. That was Boardwalk. That was Park Place.

'But I need a favor, Hal.'

For a piece of Newark, he'd definitely help Karpankov out. Whatever the task. He sat forward, frowning with pleasant anticipation.

'Anything.'

But details of the carrot, or stick, were delayed.

Karpankov's phone rang and he said a polite, 'Excuse me.'

'Go right ahead.' Dixon looked at the dog; the dog looked back. Dixon was the first to disengage.

He lifted one shoulder then the other, adjusting his gray suit jacket. It was tight and the cloth was thin wool, too thin for the day's chill. He'd realized this as soon as he'd left the house but didn't want to go back for his overcoat. The wife. His shirt was a pastel shade of blue that some people probably thought was too gaudy. Dixon didn't care. He wore bright shirts; they were his trademark. Yesterday pink, today blue. Tomorrow he'd wear yellow. The canary yellow. It was his favorite. And he always wore it on Sunday.

The Russian ended his call. Then, as always happened in discussions between men, Dixon knew, the mood changed, unmistakably, and it was time for serious horse trading. Karpankov put his fingers together, like he'd buried the pleasantries and tepeed dirt over their grave. 'Now, I'm aware of something.'

'Okay.'

Karpankov often said that. He was aware of something.

'Have you ever heard of the October List?'

'Not familiar. Nope. What is it?'

'I'm not exactly sure. But I do know this: It's a list of names of some people who're powerful. And dangerous. About thirty, maybe a few more. I've heard some of 'em I might've done business with in the past.'

'October List. Why's it called that?'

A shrug. 'Nobody I've talked to knows. A mystery. It could mean all hell's going to break loose in October.'

'Next month.'

'Next month. Or maybe it's that something big happened *last* October and there're plans in place as a result. Now, Hal, I want that list. I need the list. But I can't have my people do it – 'cause I may have a connection. Those people I've worked with. You don't have any connection.'

Because I'm smaller fucking potatoes, Dixon thought. But that didn't bother him. He nodded eagerly, like a dog. Well, a normal dog, not the big fucker in the corner.

The Russian continued, 'Now, here's the thing. I heard from Henry – you know Henry, my facilitator?'

'Right. I know Henry. Good man.'

'He is, yes. He heard that there's a woman lives in the city has the list or knows where it is. You get the list from her, then you and me, we'll go half and half on the Newark project.'

'*Fifty* percent?' Dixon blurted. 'That's very generous, Pete.'

The man waved off the gratitude. 'This woman's name is Gabriela McKenzie. She was the office manager of the prick who kept the list – he's skipped town.'

'You have her address?'

'Upper West Side but she's not there.' Karpankov tepeed his fingers. He leaned forward. 'She and some guy she's with're keeping low, but my sources say they're in the city somewhere. His name's Reardon. My people'll tell me they'll find out their location tonight or tomorrow and let me know.' His voice lowered further, and he put his hands flat on the table. 'Hal, I heard you were the go-to man when it came to life in the streets, you know what I mean? Life in the trenches.'

'I try,' Dixon said modestly. 'I know my way around.'

Karpankov cleared his throat. His eyes slid away to a model car on his desk, one of the six Fords. An Edsel. 'And you'd do whatever you need to, to get the list? You have no problem with that, do you? Even with this person being a woman. And innocent.'

'Not a problem at all.' Dixon meant this, though he didn't add he already found the task a turn-on.

'She's going to be skittish.'

'Girls get that way. Especially depending on the time of month.'

Karpankov smiled. 'I mean, she'll be cautious. I'm not the only one who wants the list. There're some other people after it.'

'Sure, you get me her location, and I'll take care of it.' Dixon frowned as he considered the job. 'So she knows people are looking for her?'

'That's right.'

'You know one thing I've done works pretty good especially with the ladies? I tell 'em I'm like a deacon in a church. It gets their guard down. I even carry a Bible around with me.' He fished the little black book out of his breast pocket.

'Smart, Hal.'

The man beamed. 'That'll let me get up close. Then I pull out my piece and get her into my car. Take her to one of the construction sites, and go to work on her. She'll tell me where the list is. And after? We're pouring concrete Monday at the shopping center. They'll never find the body.'

'Good.'

'And the guy with her? He connected?'

'No, just some businessman she's sleeping with, I think. I don't care about him. But . . .' A third tepee.

'I'll take care of him too. Probably better just to shoot him.'

An approving nod from the Russian. 'I'll call you as soon as my people find her.'

The men rose and shook hands again, even more energetically this time, and the gold links clinked dully. Seeing Dixon grip his master's hand so fervently, the dog stood. Dixon released and stepped back immediately.

'It's okay,' Karpankov said. 'He likes you.'

Yeah, Dixon thought, for a main course. He smiled at the dog, who was content to stand and stare.

In five minutes Hal Dixon was outside on the cool, windswept street, tugging his light suit around him. He was relaxing now that he was away from organized crime overlord Peter Karpankov and Godzilla. He began down the street with a jaunty bounce, wondering who he could sell the October List to once he made his own copy.

CHAPTER
19

8:30 p.m., Saturday

1 hour, 30 minutes earlier

'Horrible,' Gabriela whispered, her teeth set close.

She was quivering. Eyes closed, breathing heavily. 'How could he do that?' In the back of the taxi she leaned into Daniel and he put his arm around her shoulders. She wiped her eyes. 'How could somebody do something so despicable?' Looking at the CVS pharmacy plastic bag at their feet, Gabriela eased closer yet and he tightened his grip. He was strong. The nice suits he wore, the thick yet draping cloth, largely concealed his physique, but one touch of his arm left no doubt he was in good shape.

She thought again about meeting him Friday, yesterday.

And what had transpired.

Felt a low pop within her, at the memory of Daniel, so very close, wiping the moisture from her forehead – then, with the same handkerchief, from his.

Was it just twenty-four hours ago? It seemed ages.

The ping again, lower, warmer, pulsing. But she pushed the thought away. Now was hardly the time.

Sarah . . .

A half hour earlier their taxi had stopped at his loft in TriBeCa, and he'd picked up a gym bag containing toiletries and a change of clothing. They were now on the way to her apartment so she could do the same – and, most important, collect the file folders.

She told him, 'The documents might not have anything helpful but they're all we've got to save Sarah's life. I'm grasping at straws at this point.'

Now it was Daniel's gaze that settled on the plastic bag, crumpled like a tiny pale body. Despite what they'd been through, he had remained the epitome of calm – until, in that disgusting alley, he'd seen what tumbled from the sack. He'd jerked back, a more violent reaction than hers.

He'd hissed, 'Jesus . . .'

The shock was gone but in its place was a surfeit of anger and, perhaps, resolve.

'Why did you want to keep it?' she asked.

When they'd been in the alley Gabriela had flung the bag away fast, as if it were coated in acid. But Daniel, using his elegant silk handkerchief, had collected the sack, along with its contents.

He now said, 'Evidence. There'll be DNA on it' – a nod toward the bag – 'maybe even Joseph's fingerprints . . . if he got careless.'

'Sure. I hadn't thought about that. I was emotional.'

'Pretty understandable under the circumstances.'

They now drove in silence. When the cab breached Central Park and was nearing her apartment she glanced at the driver to see if he was listening but he was on the mobile speaking in some Middle Eastern language, lost in his conversation. She whispered to Daniel, 'The police'll be watching. Joseph could be too.'

So she directed the driver to the street one block north, behind the apartment building. The yellow cab parked on a dark side street. 'I'll just be a few minutes,' she told the driver.

But the waiting clock on the cab meter was running and he couldn't have cared less what his passengers were up to, what secret missions loomed. He resumed his staccato conversation.

Gabriela slipped from the cab and, walking close to the walls of the adjacent buildings, as if spies were after her, made her way to the service door of her apartment. The loading dock wasn't locked but the door leading into the basement was. Her front door key, however, let her in.

In five minutes she was in her apartment, which she kept dark. Working mostly by feel, she found and stuffed clothing and the business files she wanted into her nylon gym bag and then looked out of the door carefully, checking to make sure there were no neighbors or, of more concern, NYPD officers lurking in the halls. But no one was present.

She locked the door behind her.

Outside once more, she slipped quickly into the backseat and the driver eased away from the curb.

Daniel pressed her knee.

After several blocks: 'Sarah,' she said, a plaintive musing. 'I wonder what she's doing now, what's going through her mind.'

'Don't think about that,' Daniel whispered. She felt the enveloping sense of warmth as his arm encircled her shoulders again.

Winding through Saturday-evening traffic, which slowed with congestion around Lincoln Center, the cabbie steered south and east through Midtown. In ten minutes they were at the Waldorf Astoria. Daniel paid the driver and they stepped out onto the sidewalk on Park Avenue. Using a napkin again, he took the plastic bag, with its sick contents, and stuffed it into his gym bag.

'Be careful,' she said, numbly. 'The blood.'

As they walked into the lobby, she stopped and blinked. 'My God, it's beautiful.'

'You've never been to the Waldorf?'

'Not exactly in my financial genetics.'

'I generally just meet clients here, but I've stayed a few times. When I'm having work done on my place. This's old New York. That's what I like about it.'

Her head swiveled back and forth, taking in the rich wood, the massive clock in the center of the lobby, the soaring ceilings.

'Come on,' he said. 'We'll sightsee later.'

At the desk, they checked in, two rooms, Daniel using his credit card; he was worried that the police or someone else who might want the October List could track her here if she used hers. Datamining was all the rage nowadays, she'd read in *The New Yorker*.

They got out of the elevator. Their rooms weren't adjacent but were on the same floor, not far apart. As they walked down the corridor, Gabriela felt the seeds of attraction unfolding again – even greater than the feelings she'd sensed in the bar yesterday when they'd met.

Yes, she kept thinking, Sarah, Sarah. The name, however, didn't stop the stirrings deep within as she stole a glance at Daniel. But then: How can you *possibly* think of sleeping with him?

Still, she countered: Perhaps because you've been lonely for too many years.

And because Daniel Reardon is a little – maybe a lot – like you?

But she reminded: Stay focused.

Sarah, Sarah, Sarah . . .

In the hallway he said, 'Let's get something to eat. Or a drink at least.'

'Yes, I guess I need something.'

That morning's breakfast, which they'd shared, was a hazy memory.

After dropping the bags in their respective rooms, they met downstairs in the subdued, elegant lobby bar. They sat beside each other in a banquette, their knees touching. The server, a woman with severely bunned hair, approached and greeted them, sharing that her name was Liz. She inquired if they were in town on business or for a vacation. Gabriela let Daniel answer.

'Just seeing the sights,' he said amiably.

'Sorry the weather's not nicer. It was warm last week.'

They ordered: cheese and pâté and bread, and a bottle of Brunello.

Sipping the potent Tuscan wine, they talked about everything, free associating – everything, that is, except the October List and the kidnapping, much less the plastic bag. She'd brought to the table with her the files from her apartment, labeled *Prescott Investments – Open Items*. But she let them sit unopened, as if afraid they might not have the answers as to how they could save a kidnapped child.

She looked at her phone and sighed. 'From Rafael. He got out safe and made the delivery. So far, so good.'

Nodding at this bit of good news, Daniel slipped his jacket off and she caught a glimpse of a line of reddish flesh, a scar visible in the V where his shirt tugged open. It crossed from chest to shoulder. He caught her eyes and pulled his shirt closed again, self-consciously.

'Can I ask what happened?'

He seemed to be debating.

'Sorry, I didn't mean to pry.'

'No, I'll tell you. A few years ago I was driving with the kids up to New Hampshire and I was really tired. I shouldn't have pushed it. I fell asleep and went off the road.'

'Jesus.'

'The car went down an embankment into a river. The doors were wedged shut. It started to fill up with water.'

'Daniel, no!'

'God, it was cold. We'd gone to see the leaves. It was September but really frigid.'

'What happened?' she whispered.

'We would all've drowned but some local guy happened to drive by – looked like he was out of *Deliverance*, you know? A mountain man sort, a redneck. He drove his pickup down the embankment, grabbed an ax and jumped in after us, even though the water had to be about thirty-five degrees. He just swam to the car and kept smacking away at the back window until he got us out. I got cut on a piece of metal after I shoved the boys out.'

'Oh, how terrible.'

Daniel gave a brief laugh. 'And, you know what? As soon as we were on the shore, he waved goodbye and left. Wouldn't take any money, wouldn't give me his name even. He just acted like, hell, who *wouldn't* risk freezing to death to save somebody? Like it was the most natural thing in the world.'

'It hurts still?' A nod toward his chest.

'No, no. That was five years ago. Stiff sometimes, in the damp. But that's all.' He grew quiet. 'I was stupid and nearly got my sons killed. It was like that guy gave me a second chance. I don't really think I deserved it. But there he was.'

She lowered her hand on his arm and pressed. She wanted so badly to kiss him but, with some effort, refrained. They returned to the wine and both fell silent.

Daniel signed the check and, at her suggestion, they divided up the files. They would spend the remaining hours of the evening, until exhaustion struck, looking for any leads to cash that Charles Prescott might have hidden. They walked to the elevators. When they exited the car he accompanied her to her door.

She hugged him. 'Daniel, I—'

'Don't know how to thank me?'

Her response was to grip him harder and surrender to sobbing.

'She'll be okay,' he said. 'Your daughter'll be all right.'

Gabriela wiped her eyes and, stepping away, breathed deeply. Controlled herself.

A few seconds passed; they remained immobile, listening to voices laughing a few rooms away, a TV rumbling with an action flick.

She opened her door and stepped inside, turned back to him. Daniel eased closer.

Would he kiss her? she wondered.

She wondered too how she would respond.

But instead he offered the most chaste of embraces, murmured, 'Good night,' and, holding his stack of folders, he stepped back into the hall. The door swung shut and she was alone.

CHAPTER
18

5:55 p.m., Saturday

2 hours, 35 minutes earlier

They walked along a northbound street on the East Side, dodging trash and tourists and early diners, night-shift workers, dog walkers and homeless men and women . . . or perhaps just locals who appeared homeless – scruffy, inattentive to hair and beard and laundry.

Their mission, which was proving difficult, was to find a cab to take them to her co-op apartment. Gabriela muttered angrily, 'What they did back there, those assholes, it set us back an hour! And the deadline's in minutes!'

'At least you're not in jail,' he said.

She didn't respond to this tepid reassurance. 'Jesus, Daniel, it's hopeless. I knew we couldn't get the money in time but at least we could've found some concrete lead before the deadline. Something to reassure Joseph that we'd have the cash soon. But now . . . shit.' Desperation crimped her voice. She jerked her head to the east and south, where they'd just come from. 'They're fucking sadists, those two.'

'And where the hell are all the cabs?' he muttered.

Several sped by, either occupied or off-duty. Daniel waved his wallet at one of the latter but the driver just kept going.

They turned up a street that was grubby, darker and more pungent than in tourist-land, less congested, in hopes of finding a taxi. They passed stores in which dusty displays of DVDs or lace and buttons or used books or hardware sat faded behind greasy glass, a sad porn shop lit with bile-green fluorescents, Chinese and Mexican take-out restaurants that could not possibly have passed city inspection. In front of several of these establishments sat slight, dark-complexioned men, smoking and speaking in hushed tones or making mobile calls.

Gabriela's cell phone rang. She looked at her watch. 'Deadline time.' They paused and stepped to the brick wall of a building, so no one else could hear the conversation.

She took a deep breath, hit *Accept* and activated the speaker so Daniel could hear.

'Joseph?'

'Ah, Gabriela. I've been looking at the phone. Staring. It didn't ring.'

'It's just six. I was going to call you! I swear. Listen—'

'You have my money?'

'I've found the October List!'

'Have you now?' That teasing voice again. 'Cause for celebration! What does it look like? Is it thick, is it thin, is it printed on construction paper?'

She blurted, in a guttural tone, 'Tell me – how's my daughter? *Tell me!*'

'She's a little . . . troubled.' As if Joseph was pouting.

'What? What do you mean?'

'I told her I hadn't heard any good news from you. So there might not be any good news for her.'

'You told her that?' Gabriela whispered.

'Now, what do you think? Would it be in my interest to make your daughter feel any more panicky? Honestly, I can't even joke with you. You need to relax a bit. Okay, the money?' he asked, his tone suddenly blasé.

'I've got the *list.*'

'Heard that part. But saying that tells me you *don't* have the money. And since you dodged the question about describing the list, I'm a little skeptical of that too.'

'No, no! I swear!'

'Ever notice,' Joseph offered, 'when people say things like "I swear" and "you've got to believe me," they are invariably lying?'

'I'm not lying! I have it. It's in a place for safekeeping. I didn't want to walk around with it.'

'Not much need for that. Proportionately there're less muggings in New York than Portland, Maine. So, fine. You've found the list. *Wunderbar!* Let's get back to money.'

'I've been running around town all day trying to do what you asked,' she cried. 'Please, just a little more time. It's taken longer than I thought. I'm sorry!'

'Racked with guilt, are you?'

Daniel stiffened with anger. His face grew dark. But he remained silent.

She leaned close to the phone. 'Please, it's been a nightmare. The police are everywhere! I can't just sneak into the garden behind Charles's town house and start digging for treasure, can I?' Her voice caught. Then she muttered angrily, 'Tell me right now! How is my daughter?'

'She's alive.'

'*Alive?* But is she okay?'

'Pretty much.'

'She must be terrified.'

'And I'm afraid of heights. Snakes aren't my favorite either. But we cope. Now, money makes the world go 'round. That was the deal we made.' He seemed again to be pouting. 'You've breached it. You've broken our agreement.'

'I'll get your money,' she snapped. 'I just need more time! I'm doing everything I can.'

'More time, more time.' His voice was taunting.

'Just a little.'

'Could be, you know, that you've found the money and you're stalling, trying to figure out a way to keep it *and* get your daughter back.'

'No! Why would I do that?'

'Because you're out of a job, remember?'

She began to tremble. Daniel put his arm around her.

Joseph said, 'You were Charles Prescott's office manager.'

'Yes,' she whispered.

'So you know something about business?'

She hesitated. 'What?'

'You know about business?' he repeated petulantly.

'I . . . I know some things. What are you asking?'

'You familiar with the concept of penalties?' Joseph's voice was completely flat. The smarmy tone was gone. 'Like you don't pay your taxes on time, there's a penalty? Well, you didn't pay *me* on time. You missed the deadline.'

'I *tried*.'

'"Try" is a non-word. Either you do something or you don't. It's impossible to try to do something. So. New deadline. Six p.m. tomorrow—'

'Thank you! I—'

'I'm not through. Six p.m. tomorrow – you deliver the October List. And, now, *five* hundred thousand.'

'No! You can't do that.'

'Is that what you say to the IRS? "I'm so sorry. I *can't* pay what you want. No penalty for me!" Look at me as the Excuse Nazi.' Giddy once more. His laugh was nearly a giggle.

'Why not just a fucking million?' she raged. 'Or ten million?' Daniel squeezed her arm. She said to Joseph, 'I'm doing the best I can.'

'Ah, just like "trying." There's no "best" or "worst." There's keeping up your half of our agreement or not.'

'We don't *have* an agreement! You're extorting me, you kidnap—'

'Hello! Didn't we have a conversation about movie dialogue? Now, consequences, I was saying: First, the penalty, the extra hundred K. Then, second, you have to go on a scavenger hunt.'

'A what?'

'A scavenger hunt.'

'I don't understand,' Gabriela said, her voice choked.

'What's not to understand? It'll be easy. I'll bet it won't take you more than thirty minutes to find the prize.'

'You're insane!'

'Well, now, that's all relative, isn't it? Go to Times Square. Behind a Dumpster in the alley at Forty-Eighth and Seventh. West side of the intersection.'

'What's there?' she asked in a high, shaky voice.

But Joseph's response was to disconnect.

They didn't need a cab.

The prize Joseph had sent them to find was only four or so blocks away. They plunged into Times Square, a disorienting world of brilliant lights, massive high-def monitors, overlapping tracks of pulsing music, hawkers, street musicians, impatient traffic, mad bicyclists, tourists, tourists, tourists . . . The crowds were denser now, more boisterous, anticipating plays and concerts and meals and movies.

In ten minutes they'd come to the intersection that Joseph had described. She said, 'There! That's the Dumpster.' And started forward.

'Wait,' Daniel said.

'No,' she said firmly.

He tried to stop her. But she pulled away and dropped to her knees, looking behind the battered, dark green disposal unit.

Gabriela fished out the CVS pharmacy bag and looked inside. She choked. 'It's Sarah's sweatshirt!' The pink garment was wadded up tightly. She started to lift it out and froze. 'Blood, Daniel!' The streaks, largely dried to brown, were obvious. There was something primitive about them, like paint on the face of ancient warriors.

Gabriela gingerly lifted out the shirt, which was tied with a gingham hair ribbon. As she did, the garment unfurled and something fell from the inner folds to the grim floor of the alley. The colors were the pink of flesh and red of blood, and the shape was that of a small finger.

Daniel got to her just before her head hit the cobblestones.

CHAPTER
17

5:30 p.m., Saturday

25 minutes earlier

The only good is what furthers his interest . . .

Joseph Astor recited this to himself as he carried his shopping bag toward a warehouse on the far west side of Manhattan, in the Forties. Traffic on the streets was noisy; on the Hudson River, silent.

His large form blustered over the sidewalk, and people glanced at his bulk and his dead eyes and his curly blond hair and they got out of his way. Joseph paid them no mind, after noting that none of them was a cop or other threat.

An impressive view of the *Intrepid* aircraft carrier before him, Joseph turned down a side street and approached the one-story warehouse. He undid the heavy Master padlock and muscled the door open, stepped in and slammed it shut. He flicked on the lights. The warehouse was mostly empty, though there were two vans parked inside, one completely useless, and sagging boxes stacked in one corner, molding into an unpleasant mass on the floor. The place was little used and typical of a thousand such buildings, two thousand, three, throughout the New York area. Small, solid structures, always in need of paint and fumigation, either windowless or with glass panes so grimy they were virtually blacked out. Most of these buildings were legitimate. But some were used by men, *mostly* men, who needed safe houses for certain activities – away from the public, away from the police. Long-term leases, paid in advance. Utilities paid by fake companies.

Tonight would be the last time he'd use this warehouse; he'd abandon it forever and move to the other one, similar, in SoHo, for the rest of the job, which he might have called the Gabriela Job or the Prescott Job but instead had – with some perverse humor – taken to calling Sarah's Sleep-Away.

He took his jacket off but left on the beige cloth gloves – always the gloves. He strode to the corner of the place, a workbench. In the center of it was the windbreaker he'd showed Gabriela earlier in the day, along with a pink sweatshirt, on which *Sarah* was stitched across the chest. To the right were a dozen old tools and from the pile he found a large pair of clippers, like the sort used for cutting branches or flower stems. The edge was rusty, but sharp enough.

The only good . . .

From the shopping bag he extracted the fiberglass hand of a clothing store mannequin. He'd stolen the plastic appendage from an open loading dock behind a showroom in the Fashion District earlier that afternoon, after he'd been tailing Reardon and Gabriela near the building with the *Prescott Investments* sign on the front.

Gripping the clippers firmly, he cut into the dummy's little finger at the second knuckle. This he rested in the middle of the sweatshirt and lifted out the last item in the bag, a beef tenderloin, sealed in thick cellophane. He used the clippers to snip a hole in the end of the bag and let the blood dribble onto the plastic digit and the sweatshirt. There was more liquid than expected; the result was suitably gory.

Excellent.

He bundled the shirt up with a gingham hair ribbon.

Seeing the beef blood spread, he thought: How lovely, how *delicious* . . . A line he would remember to share with Gabriela later. As he worked, he opened a bottle of his favorite beverage in the world. His Special Brew. It was virtually all he drank. Sustaining, comforting. He drank deeply.

A bottle a day . . .

After tidying up and putting the steak into the refrigerator in a tiny kitchen area of the warehouse, he put his handiwork into a CVS drugstore plastic bag.

He returned to the table and sat, sipping his beloved Hawaiian Punch – the original flavor, red.

Joseph wondered what the reaction would be to the memento inside the bag.

Another glance at his watch. The deadline was looming. He was thinking about Gabriela and the October List and Daniel Reardon. Joseph had met him only about six hours ago, on the street with Gabriela, and already disliked him intensely.

Then his thoughts segued to Gabriela's friend, Frank Walsh, whom he did not know, but had only followed around and, of course, datamined. Joseph always did his homework before he went out to ply his craft.

Pudgy Frank Walsh. Nerdy Frank Walsh.

Joseph didn't have any particular dislike for Mr Walsh; he considered him to be a rather stupid, naive man. Pathetic.

He reflected that it was a shame Frank was going to spend his last night on earth with his mother, and not getting laid. At least, Joseph thought, sipping the sweet drink, he *assumed* not. Ick.

The September cold seeped in and, even though he had plenty of natural insulation on him, he shivered. Joseph was eager to get this part of the job over with and return home to Queens, where several new Netflix movies awaited, snug in their little red envelopes. Most people would probably be surprised that a man like him, who had killed twenty-two people in his life – men, women and, though only out of necessity or accidentally, children – would enjoy movies. And yet, why not? Killers were people too. In fact, he'd learned some things about his line of work from movies and TV.

The Long Good Friday, *The Professional*, *Eastern Promises*, others. *The Sopranos* not so much. Although he liked the acting, he wasn't quite sure why Tony and the crew – none of them particularly clever – hadn't been arrested and thrown in the slammer halfway through the first season.

Luck, he guessed.

No, scriptwriters.

He turned his jacket collar up and contemplated, with pleasure, returning home, sitting in front of the Sony by himself, well, with his Maine coon cat, Antonioni, and watching the latest disks. He wondered if he should take the tenderloin with him for dinner.

No, he'd do a Lean Cuisine tonight. Save the calories.

Joseph glanced at his watch. He took the CVS bag, stepped outside and locked the warehouse door.

CHAPTER
16

4:50 p.m., Saturday

40 minutes earlier

'I never thought we'd find it,' Gabriela said breathlessly. 'The October List.'

They were on Third Avenue, walking fast away from the office building.

Daniel Reardon said, 'I didn't get a look at it. What could you tell?'

'I just glanced at the first page. Names and places and numbers. Maybe accounts, maybe dollar amounts. I don't know what they mean. And I didn't recognize anybody.'

They continued in silence for a few minutes before he said, 'In the list, did you see anything about "October"?'

'No.'

'I wonder what it means. An anagram, a name?'

'Maybe,' Gabriela suggested, 'it means something's going to happen next month. Something really bad.' She sighed, as if feeling all the more guilty about not turning the list in.

'How long?' she asked. 'Until Joseph's deadline?'

A pause, and Daniel said, 'About an hour and ten minutes.'

'No! It's *that* late?' Gabriela tugged her jacket closer. The wind was brisk and filled with autumn chill. 'There's no way we can find the money in time! We don't have any leads.'

Daniel agreed. 'I don't see how.'

'We have the list, though!'

He hesitated then said, 'That's not what he wanted by six. He wanted the money.'

'But it's the most important thing to him. Didn't you get that impression? If he's reasonable, he'll take it and let Sarah go.'

'I'm sorry, Gabriela, but I don't think he *is* a very reasonable man.'

She stared at him and there was hysteria in her voice. 'But it's all I've got!'

'Still,' he persisted, 'we've got to try to find his money. Or at least a place where it *might* be, so we can tell him we're getting close. That could be enough – if we can give him something specific – to buy more time.'

Her shoulders slumped and she nodded back at the building. 'If there's nothing in the office, then I don't know where else we could find any clues to—' She abruptly stopped speaking.

'What?'

Frowning, Gabriela said, 'Last night, when I met you?'

He smiled. 'I remember.'

'I'd left work early for that meeting about negotiating the warehouse lease in Bankers' Square? The rush job? I had some files with me.'

'Right. I was thinking you were quite the workaholic. What's in them?'

'Open items for the accountant. Some business, but some personal of Charles's. If I find something in them, we can at least tell Joseph we've got a lead.'

'Then let's get to your place. Fast. We don't have much time.'

They hurried toward the uptown street, to catch a cab.

Daniel was lifting his arm to flag one down when a voice from behind them barked, 'Hold it right there.'

They stopped, exchanged surprised glances, then turned around.

Gabriela blinked and looked at the two detectives with unbridled anger. She whispered to Daniel, 'No, we can't wait! We have to get to my place now!'

She regarded the cops. 'Detective Kepler and . . .' She looked toward the other one, smaller, his grayish complexion.

'Surani.'

Kepler gestured the cab to keep going.

'No!' Gabriela barked.

The driver hesitated and then, responding to the detective's angry glare, sped off to pick up another fare.

Surani asked, 'Have you heard from your boss?'

'No. I don't know anything more about where he's gone. I would've called you if I found out anything.'

'Would you?' Kepler asked. 'You weren't too busy?'

'What's that supposed to mean?' Her voice was flint.

'Hanging out in your apartment, watching TV?' the detective shot back. 'Who knows what you've been up to?'

She asked, 'How did you find me here? You've been following me?'

'We were at Prescott Investments. Someone fitting your description was spotted walking away from the place. We thought we'd take a stroll around this beautiful neighborhood. And see if you happened to be here. After committing a felony.'

The more relaxed of the two, Surani, said, 'There was a report that somebody maybe broke into the Prescott office just now.'

'What?' she asked, frowning.

Kepler regarded her closely – and cynically. 'Was it you?'

'I—'

'Don't lie.'

'No,' Daniel said firmly.

Gabriela turned to look at Daniel, who was easing forward to the officer. 'Gabriela wanted some personal items. But we saw there was a police seal, so we left.'

'Yeah?' Kepler asked.

'That's right,' Gabriela said, looking around, as if Joseph was nearby, coolly observing this conversation.

Oh, and by the way, somebody'll be watching you. Every minute . . .

'Look, we have to go. I don't have time for this.'

Kepler continued, paying no attention to her protest, 'There was an officer in front of the building. Why didn't he see you go into the lobby?'

'I don't know,' Gabriela said stiffly. 'If he was supposed to be guarding the place, ask him.'

Kepler snapped, 'What the hell were you looking for?'

'Some *personal* things. You heard that. A checkbook, some bank statements of mine. Nothing you'd be interested in. Nothing having to do with Charles.'

'And you didn't break the crime scene seal?'

'Of course not.'

'It's a crime, you know,' Surani said.

'I assumed so. *That's* why we left.'

Kepler said ominously, 'I've got an officer going through the place now. Just to see if anything's missing.'

Daniel said, 'This's been a tough time for her. Couldn't you just give her a break?'

Kepler seemed to be practicing his skills at ignoring people. He looked Daniel up and down with what seemed to be contempt, then moved away, pulled out his cell phone and made and received several calls.

Surani stood nearby, less hostile, but at attention as if to grab them if they tried to escape.

She glanced at her watch. Daniel too looked down at it. 'The time,' she whispered. 'The deadline . . .' Her jaw was trembling. 'We have to get those files in my apartment!'

The deadline was forty-five minutes away.

'We really have to go!'

Kepler disconnected. 'Glad we ran into you,' he said, not sounding particularly glad at all. He nodded to his phone. 'The FBI's just found out something else. Those clients I was telling you about earlier today? A number of them are in the financial services area – the U.S., Europe and the Far East. Brazil, too. A lot of stock and bond traders. But at least one was a known arms dealer, specializing in explosives and chemical weapons. He's the only one we've been able to identify. Gunther. Probably that European guy you mentioned, the one from St Thomas. Thanks for that by the way. Don't know the first name. From Frankfurt originally. We think he has a safe house somewhere on the Upper East Side. That name ring any bells?'

'No. Charles never had a client named Gunther.'

'Well, he did,' Kepler snapped. 'I just told you that.'

'What I mean is I never heard of him.'

Suddenly Kepler glanced down at her purse and saw the corner of an envelope protruding. 'What's that?'

She eased away. 'Nothing.'

'Nothing? I'll bet it's more than nothing.'

'Just personal things.'

'What?'

'I'm not answering that. If you want 'em, get a fucking warrant.'

Kepler looked at Surani and said, 'What'd we learn in detective school?'

His partner said, 'Which part?'

'About when there's been suspicion of a felony – say, breaking and entering.'

'Oh, breaking and entering an office building?'

'Yeah, exactly. That means that we can search a suspect without a warrant, right? The Constitution lets us do that.'

Surani said, 'It *encourages* us to do that.'

'Don'tcha just love that Constitution?' Kepler mused, ripping the bag from her hands and lifting out the envelope.

CHAPTER
15

3:15 p.m., Saturday

1 hour, 35 minutes earlier

Moving cautiously, the couple continued down the damp, tree-lined street of Midtown in silence. Cautious of necessity. They knew the police had to be watching the Prescott office.

Gabriela eyed cars speeding along the cross street. Dark cars, pale cars, taxis, limos, trucks. Vehicles, as much as pedestrians, were part of the tapestry of Manhattan. But she noted nothing out of the ordinary, nobody paying particular attention to them.

Though seeing the unmarked police car at the curb, they paused near a ginkgo tree, encircled by a low, wrought-iron fence to keep marking dogs from the trunk. 'That's it,' she whispered, indicating a six-story office building about fifty feet east, on the same side of the street where they stood. On a sign beside the front door a half-dozen businesses were listed – therapists, a chiropractor, a graphic design company.

At the top: *Prescott Investments, LLC*.

'How're you holding up?' Daniel asked.

'I'm fine.' Dismissing the question.

Gabriela recalled that when she was a teen the Professor often comforted her by asking the very same or a similar question. 'You okay?' 'All right?' He'd sit close and look her over. She could smell tobacco and aftershave. She'd initially reply that she was fine, in this same tone as now, but he'd smile and persist. And he'd finally work out of her that she was sad or angry or stung about some incident at school or because somebody had laughed at her (even at thirteen she was tall and skinny as a post) or simply because the day was cold and overcast.

Gabriela had had mood problems all her life.

The Professor could usually trick the sadness away, for a time at least.

This memory she put away. With difficulty.

'There she is,' Gabriela said, nodding in the direction of her attractive Latina co-worker, Elena Rodriguez, across the street. The woman was walking toward the building from the opposite direction, her eyes down, face grim.

Elena Rodriguez looked up and saw them, then started across the street. Her gaze swiveled to the unmarked police car parked in front of the office building, manned by a single officer. She hesitated in the street, as if trying to avoid being seen, and stepped back. When a truck passed, she hurried across after it – straight toward an oncoming taxi. There came a wrenching scream and the screech of tires like a bird of prey's cry, followed by a loud thud. Daniel's and Gabriela's view was obscured but an instant later they saw Elena spiral to the curb.

'God,' Daniel whispered.

Immediately the officer sitting in the police car leapt out and ran to her aid. The cop looked around once then bent down toward the woman and pulled out his radio. The cabbie raced up, gesturing frantically with his hands.

'Jesus,' Daniel muttered. 'Is she all right?'

It did look bad, Gabriela realized, but she whispered, 'We can't worry about her. Let's go.'

She gripped Daniel's arm and pulled him forward. Taking her keys from her pocket, she hurried to the office building. As the cop was bending down over Elena and making a call they stepped into the lobby. Gabriela slipped the key into the inner door lock and in less than a minute they were on the second floor, at the door marked with another brass plaque: *Prescott Investments, LLC*.

The door was sealed with a yellow adhesive marker. *Crime Scene Do Not Enter*. The phone number to call in case one wished to access the office was at the bottom.

Daniel hesitated but Gabriela opened the door of the office and pushed inside, tearing the NYPD notice neatly in half with a loud, ripping sound.

Closing the door after them, she stopped, blinking, and looked around. 'My God, they took everything! The computers, shredders, hard drives, file cabinets, credenzas. They must've brought moving trucks!'

Daniel too examined the rooms, then glanced from the window. 'I can't tell how Elena is. The trees are blocking the view. I think she's still on the ground.'

'We can't worry about her. We have to search! The money and the October List. We need them!'

Her head swiveled as she regarded what few objects were inside.

Some bad artwork, photographs and diplomas and certificates up on the walls. Also, vases of fake flowers, office supplies, cups, mugs, wilted flowers, pictures of family, bottles of wine, boxes of coffee and snacks. On two coffee tables were professional journals, recent editions of the *New York Times* and *Wall Street Journal*, several books: *Debt Markets in BRIC Countries, Accounting Procedures* and *Tax Treatment of Oil and Gas Leasing Partnerships*.

In a corner were some storage boxes, missing lids but filled with papers.

Gabriela dropped to her knees and prowled through the cartons.

'Helpful?' Daniel asked as he began looking through drawers, which all appeared to be empty, except for office supplies.

She read through them quickly. 'No. These're just real estate records about the building. Nothing to do with Charles's business.'

She began rifling drawers and looking through closets while Daniel was prying up carpet and knocking on walls, searching, apparently, for hidden compartments.

A man's approach, Gabriela thought. Not necessarily a bad one.

They continued the search. But twenty minutes later Gabriela stood, stiffly, and looked around. She said in despair, 'Nothing.' She closed her eyes and sighed. Then she looked mournfully at the clock on the wall. 'He kept his own watch fast, ten minutes, Charles did, so he'd never be late, never miss an appointment or conference call.' Her eyes still on the timepiece, she said, 'We have two hours. Oh, Sarah.' She choked a sob. 'What're we going to do?'

Daniel peered out the window again, carefully. 'The cop's on the radio, looking at the building. He seems suspicious. Oh, hell.'

'What?'

'Somebody just came out of the building. Some woman. The cop called her over.' Daniel stepped back fast. 'He's looking up again. I think he's suspicious. We better get out.'

Which was when Gabriela cocked her head. 'Oil and gas.'

'What?'

She pointed to the reception area coffee table. 'That book?'

It was a textbook, thick and intimidating. *Tax Treatment of Oil and Gas Leasing Partnerships.*

She asked, 'We've never done any of that kind of work.' She picked up the tome. Flipped through it. 'Daniel, look.' The first hundred pages were dense text about accounting and tax procedures. In the middle, though, were a dozen pages bound into the book that had nothing to do with partnerships.

On the top of the first page were the words: *October List*.

Gabriela laughed. 'Yes!'

'He hid it in plain sight.'

'Smart of him. The list's actually bound in, like any other pages, so it doesn't bulge suspiciously. No one would think twice about it; and there wasn't much chance of anyone stealing a boring textbook on leases.'

Gabriela carefully tore the list out. 'Let's copy it.' She looked around. 'Wait. The copier's gone. The police took it. Why?'

Daniel shrugged. 'Maybe the memory chip. Fingerprints, I don't know.'

Gabriela glanced out the window again. 'Shit.' She stepped aside fast. 'Stay back.'

'What? The police?'

'No. Somebody else. I saw a man in the alley across the street, looking up at the window. It might've been Joseph. A dark coat, like his. I couldn't really tell.'

'How could he've followed us here? Why would he want to?'

'He said he'd be checking out if we went to the cops.' Gabriela glanced carefully out the window. 'I don't see anyone. I'm probably being paranoid.'

Daniel said, 'Maybe not. We don't exactly know what's in the list, but something tells me Joseph won't be the only one who wants it.'

She looked again out the window. 'The cop? He's on his radio. He knows something's up.'

'We have to get out of here.'

'This is the only copy of the list. We can't risk Joseph or the police or whoever's out there' – a nod at the street – 'stealing it. It's my only bargaining chip to get Sarah back.'

She examined the room fast and spotted on a credenza the bottles of wine. 'Gifts from clients,' she said. She nodded at a dark green box of Dom Pérignon champagne. 'Could you open that up?'

Daniel undid the clasp and lifted the top. She folded the pages of the October List very tightly and, when he lifted the bottle, slipped them under it. He sealed the box back up and put it into a plastic bag. With a black marker she wrote a note on a Post-it and added that to the bag.

'What are you doing with it?' Daniel asked.

'I'm going to have it delivered to my friend Frank.'

'Frank Walsh, Mr Complication,' Daniel said with a dry smile.

'Yeah. But a trustworthy complication.' She glanced at the window. 'What's the cop doing?'

Looking out, Daniel reported, 'Still on the radio, but he's glancing at the windows here. He suspects. Definitely.'

Gabriela returned to the desk on which the nameplate read *E. Rodriguez*. She took a blank letter-sized envelope and into it stuffed a dozen pieces of paper from her purse – receipts, discount cards, a few bills. She shoved the envelope into the Coach and left a corner protruding.

'Insurance policy,' she said. 'Just in case. Now let's get out of here.'

With Daniel carrying the champagne, they left the office and she closed the door. The sound of the elevator on the move filled the hallway. She looked around and nodded to the stairs. They climbed to the third floor, where they found a slim Latino man pushing a mop. 'Rafael!'

'Gabriela! I heard about Mr Prescott. It's not true, you think?'

'I'm sure it isn't. It has to be a big mistake.'

'I'm praying for him. My wife too.'

'Thank you, Rafael. This is Daniel.'

The men shook hands and then Gabriela asked, 'Could you do me a big favor, please?'

'Sure. What do you need?'

She took the bag containing the champagne and handed it to Rafael. 'I have to talk to lawyers now and get records together. I was supposed to take this to a friend of mine today, but I can't make it. It's real important to him. Can you please drop this off at his building in the Village?'

'Sure, sure, I do that.'

'He's at Three Eighty Greenwich Street. It's near Bethune. His name's Frank Walsh.' She jotted the address and name. He pocketed the slip of paper.

'Okay.'

'You're a lifesaver, Rafael.'

She fished in her purse and handed him four twenties.

'Oh, you don't have to do that.' He shook his head.

'No, no, I'm insisting.'

'Well, *gracias*.' He reluctantly pocketed the cash.

'*Nada*. If he's not there just leave the package with the doorman.'

Gabriela and Daniel headed to the stairwell again. She caught his eye, in which she detected a gaze of wry humor. 'Frank's only *sort of* a boyfriend. Really.'

'Hey,' he offered, 'how can I be jealous of somebody you're calling "the complication"? If you'd said "stud" or "lover boy," well, that'd be a different story.'

She flung her arms around him and kissed his neck. They fled down the stairs, exiting into the alley behind the building.

CHAPTER
14

2:50 p.m., Saturday

25 minutes earlier

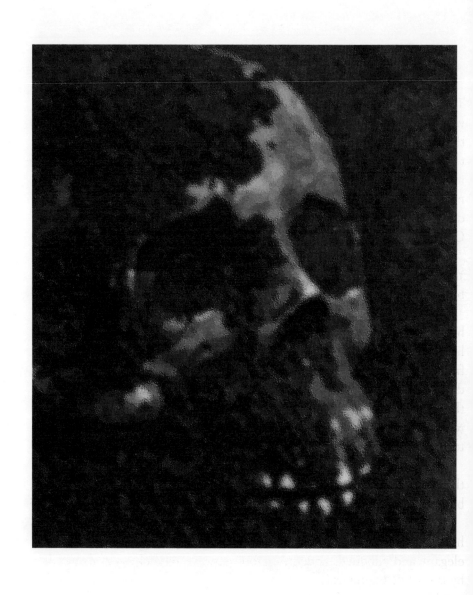

Turtle Bay, that portion of east Manhattan near the United Nations, was once one of the worst neighborhoods in the city. In the late 1800s the area was littered with unregulated businesses – tanneries, slaughterhouses, breweries, power plants and coal yards – where the rate of injuries and death among workers was horrific. Dark, overcrowded tenements were squalid and stank and were nearly as disease-ridden and dangerous as the blue-ribbon winner of depraved decay in the New York City of that era: Five Points, near where City Hall is now.

Gabriela knew this because the Professor's favorite topic was New York history. He knew the city the way some men know their favorite baseball team's stats.

The name, 'Turtle Bay,' he had told Gabriela years ago, as they sat in his cozy den one night, derived from the fact that the East River shoreline nearby was a small harbor, protecting cargo and passenger ships from the whims of the waterway, which was treacherous even on calm days and deadly in storms. Turtles would bask on the mud banks, in the reeds and on rocks, while herons and gulls dined on fish and fish remains in the narrow ledge of shallows before the river dropped steeply to its grim bottom.

He'd told her, 'The place was a dumping ground for bodies back then, the river was – true now but less so. After a bad rain, skulls and bones'd be uncovered. Kids'd play with the remains.'

The river may still have been a watery grave for the occasional Mafia hit victims but, my, how 125 years changed things. The area was now elegant and subdued, and the harbor gone completely – straightened by the FDR Expressway.

Gabriela was standing next to Daniel Reardon now in the residential heart of the Turtle Bay neighborhood, having snuck away from the shadows – in all senses of the word – of the Upper West Side, where they'd been the recipients of such bad news.

They peered down the quiet side street – and easily spotted an unmarked police car parked in front of a small office building that Gabriela pointed out as the home of Prescott Investments.

'You were right,' she whispered. 'They're watching the place. Looking for Charles. For me.'

The car with the cop inside was facing away from them but still they stepped back around the corner, onto Second Avenue, where they couldn't be seen. They were blinded by the deceptive sunlight; brilliant but useless against the chill.

'How many companies in your building?' Daniel asked.

'A dozen or so. Small ones generally. We're small too.' Just then Gabriela stiffened, looking up the street. Her eyes grew bright. 'Elena.'

Daniel followed her gaze.

The slim Latina, about thirty years of age, in jeans and a Fordham University windbreaker, strode toward them. Her hair was pulled back and it seemed damp, perhaps from a shower interrupted by Gabriela's call.

'Oh, Elena!' Gabriela hugged her.

'Isn't this awful? I'm sick. I'm just sick!' Her eyes were red, as if she'd only recently stopped crying.

Gabriela introduced Daniel as a 'friend.'

Looking the handsome man up and down, Elena Rodriguez shook his hand and winked to Gabriela, woman-to-woman, meaning, Well, *he's* a keeper. 'We work together, Gabriela and me.'

'I know. I heard.'

She puffed air from her cheeks. 'I guess I mean *worked* together. Not anymore.' To Gabriela, 'Have you heard anything else?'

'No, just what the police told me this morning.'

Elena's pretty face darkened. 'Did you talk to the same ones? Kepler and some Indian man. I didn't like them at all. Kepler, especially.'

'Yep.'

Elena looked wistful and nodded in the direction of the office building. In a soft voice: 'I walked this way to work hundreds of times and I've always been so happy. Now . . .' She shrugged. Then the woman sighed and asked, 'So what can I do? I'll do anything to help.'

'Daniel and I are going to try to find something in the office that'll prove Charles's innocent.'

'Find the asshole who's setting him up.'

Gabriela hesitated and then said, 'Exactly.'

Daniel glanced her way, undoubtedly thinking how guilty she felt for lying to her co-worker and friend.

'And we need your help.'

'Sure.'

'I have to tell you, Elena, it's kind of . . . extreme.'

'Hey, girl, did I say "anything"?'

'All right. I need you to get hit by a car.'

'*What?*'

'I don't really mean get hit. Just start to cross the street and *pretend* to get hit. When a cab or car goes by, slap it on the door or the side and fall down on the sidewalk. The cop guarding the building'll come to help you. When he does, Daniel and I'll slip inside and search the office. Just don't give him your real ID. Make something up – you left your purse at home. So you don't get in trouble after they find out the office got broken into.'

Daniel Reardon stared at Gabriela for a moment then gave a shallow laugh. 'You come up with pretty good plans,' he said.

'I was one hell of an office manager,' Gabriela replied.

'When I said "anything,"' the pretty woman muttered, 'I kind of meant stay up all night reading through files. But if you want me knocked on my ass, girl, you got yourself an accident. Hey, I get to scream?'

'As loud as you want.'

CHAPTER
13

12:30 p.m., Saturday

2 hours, 20 minutes earlier

'*Uhn, uhn, uhn . . .*'

'Jesus,' Detective Brad Kepler muttered. 'That's awful.' He was angry. And cold too, stiff, sore. They were on the roof of the building across from Gabriela's co-op apartment on the Upper West Side. Both men had earbuds in, one each. They were sharing.

'Uhn,' Surani said.

Kepler gave a harsh laugh. 'That supposed to be funny?'

Surani didn't get it.

'The noise you just made.'

'The . . . what noise?'

'The "uhn." You grunted. It's the same as *that*.' Grimacing, Kepler tapped his earbud. Then he stared back at the open but curtained window of Gabriela's living room.

'What noise?' Surani repeated. 'I grunted?'

'You grunted. You said, "uhn."'

'Oh. And? What're you upset about?' Surani asked, sounding pissed off that he'd been accused of something. Kepler didn't care; in this Saturday's pissed-off World Series, he was winning.

'So we just told her that her boss's booked on out of town, she's lost all her savings, she's outta work and what's she doing?'

Uhn, uhn, uhn . . .

'Fucking him. It's wrong. Just plain wrong.'

'He's pretty handsome. Give him that. Looks just like that actor.'

'No, he fucking doesn't.'

'But you know exactly the actor I mean, right? So therefore he does. And *I* think he's good looking.'

Kepler believed his partner said this to torture him a bit more.

Surani shrugged. 'It's not my business what she does in there. Yours either. It's our business to watch her. That's it. Nothing more than that.'

Gabriela and her boyfriend had surprised them by not remaining on the streets, but heading to her apartment. The detectives – prepared to follow her – had scrambled to set up the surveillance on a nearby building, sitting or kneeling on the cold, pebble-covered roof. Kepler and Surani started the recorder and trained the microphone at its target and waited.

Soon they'd heard voices. This was hot-shit electronics and they could make out a fair amount of conversation.

The discussion inside had initially been mostly about Prescott and the company and how Gabriela still had trouble believing the terrible things those 'assholes' had said, meaning of course Kepler and Surani. They had also caught a comment that she was shocked and angry about 'what had happened.'

All the dialogue got recorded. Nothing was helpful.

As for visuals, there hadn't been much to see at first – shadows, wafting curtains, reflections off shiny surfaces. Then, about twenty minutes ago, the cops had registered some soft whispers and Kepler blinked as he gazed through the window with the binoculars. He gripped Surani's shoulder, whispering, 'Jesus Christ.'

They both gaped at the sight of Gabriela taking off her sweater. In her bra and tight stretch pants, she walked to the window and pulled the curtain shut.

Je-sus . . .

Silence for a time, then the sounds of lust had floated through the airwaves.

And it was still going strong.

'Uhn, uhn, uhn,' punctuated by an occasional, 'Yeah, there. Don't stop!'

And the ever popular: 'Fuck me!'

'My knees hurt. Why do they have stones on the roof?'

'Drainage maybe.'

'Oh, the rain doesn't go through the pebbles?'

Surani said, 'You are in way too much of a bad mood. Oh, look at your pants.'

'What? Oh, Christ.' What seemed to be tar stains speckled his knees.

Kepler heard Gabriela being ordered to 'Get up on all fours. That's how you want it, right?'

She replied breathlessly that, yes, that was exactly how she wanted it.

And the *Uhn, uhn, uhn* started up again.

Surani laughed, which made Kepler all the angrier.

Then there came an extended *uhn*. Which meant, Kepler guessed, that the party was over with.

'Post-coital bliss,' whispered Surani. 'About time. I'm ready to get the hell off the roof. It's freezing up here.' He rose from his squat.

Kepler said, 'When she leaves, you better be ready for it. We stick on her like glue.'

'I'm ready,' Surani said. 'Do I look like I'm not ready? And "stick on her like glue"? Could you pick a worse cliché?'

Kepler ignored him.

But the pursuit didn't happen just then. From inside Gabriela's apartment, whispers arose. And the game began again.

Uhn, uhn, uhn . . .

'Fuck,' Surani muttered, sitting down once more.

Kepler stared. His partner rarely swore. The Charles Prescott Op was bringing out the worst in everybody.

CHAPTER
12

Noon, Saturday

30 minutes earlier

Gabriela pressed a tissue to her eyes as she and Daniel were back on the sidewalk, heading for Central Park, silent and digesting the stark news they'd received in the lobby of her building. They were on a sidewalk crosshatched by sharp shadows from the trees overhead. The September sun continued to radiate fierce power, though little heat, like a distant spotlight. Occasionally Daniel's arm brushed hers and she wondered if he would embrace her for solace.

He didn't.

'We'll go to the office,' she said, desperation in her voice. 'Maybe the police are finished with it now. I can try to find this October List.'

She caught a glimpse of herself reflected in a window. How like everyone else she looked, how normal – tan stretch pants, tight burgundy sweater, leather jacket, the purse over her shoulder, the Tiffany bag dangling from her hand, a handsome man at her side. On their way to a movie or a health club or brunch with friends.

How like everyone else.

Yet how different.

'That guy, Joseph,' Daniel replied. 'Jesus. You know, his giddiness was the most scary. His joking. It's just sick.'

'Part of me thinks I should go to the police anyway,' she said. Then looked at him. 'What do you think?'

Daniel considered this. 'Honestly, I think the consequences could be disastrous if he found out.'

'But they know how to handle these things!' Gabriela said fervently. 'They have kidnap specialists. I'm sure they do. Hostage negotiators.'

'This is different. It's not like Joseph's asking for money that you can agree to pay him – and the police'd back you up on that. If you go to them – even assuming Joseph doesn't find out about it – the October List is going to come up. And the cops're going to want it.'

After a moment she said, 'True.' Another dab of tissue to her eye.

'And we have to assume that Joseph's doing what he threatened: having somebody watch you to make sure you don't go near the police.'

'You don't deserve this, Daniel. You shouldn't have anything to do with it, with me. I didn't even know you twenty-four hours ago. You should just go home and forget all about me.'

Gabriela sensed his head swiveling.

He said, 'Not really interested in that.'

'In what?'

'Forgetting about you.' She gripped his arm and briefly rested her head against his solid biceps. She'd seen a movie starring the actor whom Daniel resembled, in which the man had removed his shirt, to the thrill of most women in the audience. Not only were their faces similar but their builds closely matched.

'My office is in Midtown, east. Let's get a cab. We should move fast. The deadline . . . six p.m. We have so much to do.' She turned to look for a taxi.

'Wait,' he said in a sharp whisper.

'What?'

'We're being followed,' Daniel said.

'Are you sure?' She sounded doubtful. But she looked behind and saw a van easing to the curb. 'Joseph?'

'I didn't see any vans before.'

'If it's police,' she said, panic in her voice, 'and Joseph sees, he'll think we called them! He'll kill Sarah!'

'We're not sure it's the cops. Maybe it's a coincidence.'

But the van wasn't happenstance; it was in fact occupied by the police. This was confirmed when they noticed a blue-and-white NYPD patrol car start toward them from Columbus Circle, then brake suddenly and make a U-turn.

She said, 'Somebody in the van just radioed the squadcar and told them to get the hell out of here. Yep, it's cops. They're hoping I'll lead them to Charles.'

'And look,' Daniel muttered.

She followed his eyes toward what was probably an unmarked police car – a gray sedan with several small antennas bristling on the roof.

'Goddamn it,' she snapped, furious. 'They're all over the place!'

'What should we do?'

After a moment of debate, she said, 'Let's go back to my apartment. Wait, walk over there, by the curb.'

'What?'

'Stay in the sunlight.'

Daniel frowned, uncertainly. Then he gave a smile. 'Ah, you *want* them to see us.'

'Exactly.'

In ten minutes they were back at her apartment building. They found no unwelcome assailants inside this time and stepped into the hesitant elevator for a ride to the second floor. In her unit, which faced south, she set the Tiffany bag he'd brought for her on an antique table by the door, her purse too. Shucked her jacket and slung it on a hook.

Daniel looked around the place, focused on the books, the pictures of a little blond girl.

'Sarah,' he said.

She didn't bother to nod. It wasn't a question anyway.

Daniel noted other pictures, mostly of Gabriela by herself. A few with her and her parents. One he studied for a long moment.

'You and your father?'

She looked his way. 'That's right.'

'He's a good-looking man. Do your parents live in the city?'

'He passed away,' she told him. 'Mom's in a home.'

'I'm sorry. What did he do for a living?'

'Worked for the power company. Con Ed. Manager.'

The picture had been taken a decade ago. It depicted a twenty-two-year-old Gabriela and her father, exactly thirty years older; they shared the same birthday, May 10. Taurus. She told Daniel this, then added wistfully, 'He used to say people who're Tauruses think astrology is a lot of bull.'

Daniel laughed. And he looked over the image of the tall man, with trim salt-and-pepper hair, once more.

She didn't tell him that the picture had been taken a week before his death.

They had the same expression on their faces, easy and humorous, unrehearsed. Her mother had been having a good day and she'd playfully snapped the picture.

Then Daniel noted a dozen framed artistic photographs, all in black and white. He walked close to examine them. They were mostly still lives and landscape but some portraits too.

He asked, 'So these are yours.'

She was gazing out the window, through a slit in a side curtain. 'What?'

'These photos. Yours?'

'Yes.'

'Well, I'm impressed.' He walked along the carpeted floor in front of them, bending close to examine each one.

'I used to paint but I decided I liked photography better. There's something seductive about taking reality and controlling it.' Her voice was enthusiastic, but that energy suddenly vanished and she fell silent, as she gazed at a framed crayon drawing of a heart. *I love you Mommy* was painstakingly written in the margin.

Now Daniel eased to the window.

'See the cops?' She turned away from the artwork.

'Not yet,' he replied looking out again.

They discussed what to do next, how to save Sarah – getting into the Prescott Investments office, trying to find the October List and the money.

She fell silent and sat heavily in a chair. 'It's overwhelming,' she said.

'Nothing's overwhelming if you take it step by step.' Scanning the street, he clicked his tongue. 'Yep. There they are. There's a playground across the street, a couple hanging out there, heads down. Only they're in business suits and there're no kids nearby. They might be talking into microphones in their sleeves. Oh, and then on the roof of the building facing yours? It looks like that duo from the street.'

'The roof?' she asked with a frown of disbelief. 'They're looking in?'

'No, they're just setting up equipment, it looks like. Microphone – a dish of some kind.'

Gabriela turned away and looked absently around the room.

'All right.'

Daniel looked at her inquiringly.

'Let me know when they're finished.'

She walked back and forth in front of the window, pacing anxiously.

Only a minute later he said, 'Okay, they're aiming some big phallic lens this way.'

She stepped close to him and whispered, 'Let's talk about Charles and the case, but don't say anything about Joseph.'

He nodded.

For five minutes they carried on an improvised, but credible conversation about Charles Prescott's alleged crimes and her desperate situation. At one point, though, real tears began cascading down her cheeks and she had to pause to compose herself.

Then, standing right in front of the window, she instructed, 'Come here.'

'What—?' Daniel asked.

'Come here,' she repeated firmly.

Frowning, curious at her tone, Daniel did as instructed. As a cool autumn breeze flowed into the room from the open window, she gripped him hard and kissed him on his mouth. Tentatively at first, then more firmly.

'Kiss me back,' she whispered.

He was startled but he did as ordered, firmly and with passion – his grip on her shoulders nearly hurt. She could sense his genuine desire. She felt a burst of longing within her.

Then Gabriela forced herself to tell him in a whisper, 'Step back, and look me over like you're enjoying what you're seeing.' She stripped her burgundy sweater off.

'I don't have to pretend about that,' Daniel mouthed.

In her pale blue bra and close-fitting stretch pants, she walked to the window, paused for a moment and slid the shade down. She then put the sweater back on.

'Bummer,' he whispered.

She held her fingers to her lips. She grabbed the TV remote and – muting the volume – turned the unit and the cable box on, then scrolled through pay-per-view channels until she found an adult movie. Two clicks and the bad film came to life *in medias res*, depicting a young couple going at it poolside in a very stressed lounger. The volume rose.

Uhn, uhn, uhn . . .

She nodded to the door then snagged the leather jacket from the rack in the hall. But her face grew somber as she looked at the garment on a neighboring hook: a child's faux-fur parka.

More tears flowed.

Daniel put his arm around her shoulder, gave an encouraging hug. Gabriela pulled on sunglasses. He did too and they stepped out the door into the hallway, which smelled of carpet and cleanser. In ten minutes they were slipping out of the service entrance in the back of the building, and heading once more for Central Park, free of prying eyes and ears.

CHAPTER
11

11:15 a.m., Saturday

45 minutes earlier

'I still can't believe it,' Gabriela whispered. 'If you ever met him, met Charles, you'd think it was impossible what those men were saying.'

She and Daniel continued walking in silence into the shadows of the Upper West Side. They were almost to her apartment. There, she'd explained, she'd call her co-worker Elena and Charles's lawyer and see if she could piece together what had happened.

She added, 'He was the nicest guy in the world. When I got divorced, he said anything I needed, just let him know. He found a lawyer for the divorce. One of the best in the city. He lent me ten thousand for expenses. But it wasn't a loan. I tried to pay him back but he wouldn't take a penny.' She took a tissue and pressed it to her eyes.

They turned down a canyon-like cross street to head west. In a moment they were at her building, a five-story brick structure a few blocks from Central Park, between Columbus and Amsterdam.

As they walked into the lobby a man, standing near the elevator, looked her up and down. 'Gabriela McKenzie?'

'Shit. Another cop?' she whispered to Daniel.

Then their eyes noted he carried a paper Whole Foods shopping bag.

'What's this?' she asked softly.

'You *are* Gabriela?' The man was six-two. He was solid, but not fat. Solid the way a bag of fertilizer's solid. His hair was a mass of curly blond ringlets.

'Yes. I'm sorry, who are you?'

A giddy laugh. 'Hey, there. How're you doing? Beautiful morning, isn't it? Gorgeous. Predicting overcast and temperatures plummeting later, but let's enjoy what we've got now, shall we?'

He strode up to them, moving in a lithe way for a large man. A faint grin. 'I'm Joseph.' He didn't extend his hand. 'Don't try to rack your brains. We've never met.' A nod at Daniel, who gazed into the man's dark eyes. Under an unbuttoned black overcoat, he wore a loose-fitting brown suit and a dress shirt with two slashes of crease across the belly. His teeth, curiously, had a slightly pinkish tint.

'And you . . . ?' She didn't complete the question but instead asked, 'How do you know me?'

'Oh, I don't yet. Not personally, that is. My loss, that. How you doing today? Not in the mood to chat? No worries. I've got something you'll be interested in.'

'What're you talking about? Leave us alone.'

'Wait. "Interested," I said. Aren't you curious exactly what?'

'No.'

'Oh, hey. I'll bet you will be. Betcha five bucks. Want to take me up?'

'Hey, fuck off, mister,' Daniel said, moving forward an inch or two.

Joseph held up a hand as if warding off a blow. Grinning, cringing. Playful. 'Just take a peek. Pretty please? I'm begging you.' He lifted the shopping bag.

Gabriela's head swiveled toward Daniel as Joseph reached into the bag and withdrew a windbreaker, black and blue like the water of New York Harbor at dusk. It was a child's size. He also displayed a plastic doll, similar to Barbie. But the dress had been removed from the toy. The beige flesh glowed in a band of sunlight.

Gabriela screamed.

Joseph frowned broadly. 'The ears. The ears!' He tapped his own. 'That was noisy.'

She raged, 'Where did you get those? That's Sarah's jacket! And her doll!' She stepped back and grabbed her cell phone.

Joseph said, 'Oh, about the phone. Just think about why I might not want you to make any calls. Is that too much of a stretch? I'll vote it isn't.'

'What the fuck is this?' Daniel barked.

Joseph wagged a finger his way but said nothing.

Her voice cracking, Gabriela repeated, 'Where did you get those? Where is she? Who are you?'

'So many, many questions . . . Let's take 'em one at a time. I got the jacket from Ms Sarah. That's a no-brainer. And *where* could she be? Where do you think? With some friends of mine. As for question number three, I'll hold off on that for the time being.'

Gabriela lunged, grabbing him by the lapels. This caught Joseph off-guard and he stumbled back, an angry frown replacing the smirk. Daniel restrained her.

Then the slick grin was back on Joseph's face. 'Re-lax! Little Sarah's fine.'

Daniel eased closer yet. Joseph opened his coat and jacket and displayed the butt of a pistol. 'More show-and-tell! So settle down there, Cowboy.'

Daniel, eyes wide, stepped back.

Gabriela gasped as she stared at the weapon.

Joseph looked Daniel up and down. 'And who exactly are *you*, Cowboy?'

'I'm a friend.'

'Friend. Okay. Let me see your wallet.'

Daniel hesitated, then dug into his pocket and handed him a wad of cash. Hundreds and fifties. Probably a thousand dollars.

'That's what goes *into* a wallet. That's not a wallet.'

'Take it.'

'I don't want it. I want your wallet.'

Gabriela shouted, 'Where's Sarah? What've you done?'

Joseph tapped his ears again. 'Let's not draw too much attention to ourselves. This' – he tapped the pistol – 'is even louder than your hysteria. Now, Cowboy, wallet.'

Daniel handed the supple leather over.

'No, no . . .' Gabriela was crying now.

As he flipped through the billfold, Joseph seemed to be memorizing various facts. He slipped out one of the business cards and examined it. 'The Norwalk Fund. Sounds lucrative.' He handed everything back. 'Here you go, Cowboy Dan, a resident of Eighty Five Franklin Street. Nice area. That's all I want for now. But if I ever do have need of a loan, glad to know you're sooo willing to part with your cash.' Then to Gabriela, 'Now, about Ms Sarah. The reason she's visiting my friends is because of your boss. Which maybe you figured out. Charles Prescott disappearing. Which troubled me mightily. You've heard from the police about that, I imagine?'

'Yes, but what does—'

A finger to his lips silenced her. 'Yes'll do just dandy. Don't say any more unless I ask. Okay?'

She nodded, her hands clenched.

'Now, if the fine constabulary of the city of New York calls you again, don't talk to them. If your phone rings and you don't recognize caller ID don't pick up. If they leave a message don't return their calls. If they stop you on the street and ask you anything, from the time of day to where to buy good donuts when they're on break to details about your boss's underwear preferences, tell 'em you're not saying anything until you see your lawyer. If I find out you've been talking to the police I won't be happy. And that means Ms Sarah won't be happy.'

'Stop it! Quit playing these fucking games!' Gabriela swallowed and stared at the windbreaker and doll. 'How do I know you have her? Maybe you stole them.'

Joseph carefully rolled the blue windbreaker up and slipped it into the bag, dropped the doll on top of it. 'Here's what's happened. Your ex-husband, Timothy, dropped your daughter off at her dance class this morning. Not long after that, an associate of mine who looks like Tim's father came to the school and signed her out. Grandpa's name and picture are on the assigned release list.'

'How did you know that?' Gabriela whispered in shock.

Joseph seemed not in the mood to answer. 'He said that there was a change of plans and he was supposed to take Sarah to some friends. You had an unexpected trip. Grandpa look-alike dropped her off with said friends. *I.e.*, me. That's how it worked. And pretty damn smooth if I do say so myself.'

'No! She wouldn't go away with a stranger!' Gabriela cried.

'The last time she saw her grandfather was two years ago. I learned that with a few mouse clicks. And I mean just a *few*. Tsk, tsk – all that social network stuff. People are *sooo* careless nowadays.'

Wiping her eyes with her fingertips, she whispered, 'I don't have much money. But I'll get you whatever you want. I'll borrow it. I'll—'

Joseph's amused eyes took in Daniel again. 'You're gettin' tense there, Cowboy; you're getting antsy. I can see it. Like you're thinking about playing hero. You want to take a pen and stab me in the eye? Well, first, I'd kill you before you got six inches toward me. But if you managed to grab a bat or have an RPG hidden on your person and you took me out, what do you think would happen to our Sarah? Be a little smarter, okay?'

Daniel said evenly, 'The police'll get you. And the FBI. Kidnapping's a federal crime.'

Joseph sighed. 'Oh, pul-ease . . .' His eyes swayed back to Gabriela. His voice was more reasonable now. 'Listen. She's fine. She's watching TV. She's got some toys. She thinks she's with some friends of yours she hasn't met. You had to go out of town for a day or two.'

'If you hurt her, I'll—'

'Movie dialogue alert . . . Let's not waste time, okay?'

'I want to talk to her. I want to see her.'

'In a minute.'

'Please.'

'In a *minute.*' Joseph looked around them. There were no observers. 'Now, listen to me carefully. Are you listening?'

'Yes, but—'

'Shhh. All I want is you to listen.'

'All right.' She looked down past her trembling hands.

'Have you heard from Charles Prescott today?'

'No, I swear. He left work early yesterday. I'd tell you if I'd heard from him. Please . . . What do you want?'

Joseph was nodding. Again he looked up and down the street through the front door. A few passersby but nobody was paying this group any attention. 'There's a list – with detailed information on some clients of Charles's. Thirty-two of them, to be exact.'

'Thirty-two?' she asked, looking quickly at Daniel.

'That's right. He called it the October List. These were *special* clients he did, let's say, some private work for.'

'I've never heard of it.'

'That's not really my concern, now, is it? Anyway, I'm one of those clients. And we were involved in an important project – which has been derailed thanks to your boss vanishing unexpectedly. I don't like derailings and now I need to be in touch with the others. Without him we're a rudderless ship. Did you catch that word, by the way? "Need" the list? And you're going to get it for me.'

'But how can I get you something I've never heard of?'

'You knew Charles better than most people. Even if you're telling the truth – I'm not exactly sure about that, by the way – but even if you are, you better than anybody can figure out where it is.'

Daniel said, 'But if it was that important, he wouldn't've kept it himself. He'd give it to somebody for safekeeping. His lawyer, his—'

'His lawyer doesn't have it. I checked.'

Gabriela asked, 'Mr Grosberg? You've talked to him?'

Joseph paused and his thick lips eased into what might have been a smile. 'We had a meeting. A . . . *discussion.* I'm convinced he doesn't have the list.'

'Meeting? You don't mean that at all. What the hell did you do to him?'

'Relax. He'll be okay in a month or two.'

'He's seventy years old! What did you do?'

'Gabriela, we on the same page here? I don't need you to be weird.

I need you to be focused, for Sarah's sake. Now, I heard about the list from a little bird – who's no longer with us, by the way.'

'*What?*'

Joseph wrinkled his nose, dismissing her shocked expression. 'This Tweetie Pie, I was saying, this little bird told me that Charles was so paranoid he didn't keep the list on computers. He said if the Mossad could be hacked, then he could be hacked. So he only had hard copies. And he kept one in New York. It's here somewhere. You get to find it.'

'How?'

Joseph held up a finger. 'Maybe you know more than you think you do.'

'I don't! Maybe some other employees heard of it, but—'

'Elena Rodriquez, his nod to Affirmative Action? The occasional temps? The bookkeeper? No, you were the only one worked that close to Mr Charles Prescott. He told me that. He said there was nobody like Gabriela. So you've got to be the little gal who can. I need you to find me the October List.'

He turned his eerie gaze at Gabriela probingly. 'And there's something else I want. The initial fee I paid Charles. I want it back. Four hundred thousand dollars.'

'Fee?' Gabriela asked. 'There is no upfront fee at Prescott. We get an annual percentage of the portfolio . . .' And then she nodded and added with disgust, 'But I get it: These're the *special* clients you're talking about. These thirty-two.'

'Exactly!'

'But if you're secret how would I know where any money for . . . *you* people is?'

'Oooo, that stung.' Joseph pretended to pout.

Daniel said, 'Listen, Joe. Be realistic. If her boss took off he'd take the cash with him.'

'"Joe"?' The man looked around broadly.

'Joseph.'

'Oh, *moi*.' He smiled. 'Charles left town pretty fast. According to my sources, when Prescott heard there was a warrant he bailed and didn't get all the money he could have. Maybe the police found some of it. But I'll bet there's a lot more. And I'm hoping for your sake – and Ms Sarah's – that you can hit the jackpot. Now, Gabriela, let's get some more ground rules set. First, like I said, no police. And a cone of silence with everybody else: Your ex-husband, your best friend, your hairdresser. Everybody.'

'You're despicable!'

Joseph said to Daniel, who looked like he was considering slugging the man, 'Sorry you walked into the middle of this. But you get the picture. You don't seem stupid. You keep your mouth shut too. You agree to that?'

'Yeah.'

Joseph laughed. 'If looks could kill.' To Gabriela he said, 'Now, it's nearly noon. I'll need the list by start of business Monday, so I'll give you – I'll *generously* give you – until six tomorrow to find it. Sunday. But about the money – that's a different story. In case everything falls apart and the police come knock, knock, knocking on my door, I'm going to need that cash in my hot little hand, so I can jump ship. That I want by six p.m. tonight.'

'*Tonight?* Impossible!' she said, gasping. 'Four hundred thousand dollars?'

'For Sarah's sake you better figure out how to make it *extremely* possible.'

Then, with an edge of resolve in her voice, Gabriela said, 'I'm not doing anything until you let me talk to my daughter.'

'You can't talk to her.' Joseph opened his phone and displayed a video. 'But . . .'

Daniel and Gabriela looked down. The cute blond girl was sitting watching TV cartoons. Oblivious to the shadowy forms of two adults in the background.

'How could you do this?' she raged once more.

Joseph sighed, looking bored, and put the phone away. 'Time for a pop quiz. Now, what's the most important ground rule?'

'No police.' The words sounded as if uttered underwater.

'Hooray, you get an A plus.' He picked up the bag containing the doll and the sweatshirt. 'Oh, and by the way, somebody'll be watching you. Every minute. You do believe me? No need to answer. See ya.' And he was gone.

CHAPTER 10

10:30 a.m., Saturday

45 minutes earlier

Light bore down on the foursome in Central Park. Stark light, painful.

Putting away his NYPD gold shield, Naresh Surani glanced at Daniel Reardon, ignored him and asked Gabriela, 'Have you heard from Charles Prescott today?' Even the brilliant sun couldn't warm the detective's gray complexion.

'My boss? No. My God, is he all right?' Her eyes eased toward Daniel. The other detective, Brad Kepler, had noted him too but was ignoring him as efficiently as his partner was.

'When was the last time you saw him?' tanned Brad Kepler asked.

'Yesterday, at work. In the morning. Then I went to a meeting and was out all day. Has there been an accident? Please. You have to tell me!'

They were regarding her with what seemed to be suspicion. Surani offered, 'Mr Prescott has disappeared . . . with, it seems, a lot of his clients' money.'

Gabriela barked a laugh. 'No, that's impossible. There's a mix-up.'

'I'm afraid not. Detective Surani and I are with the Financial Crimes Division of the police department. Mr Prescott's been under investigation for the past two months.'

'A different Charles Prescott. It has to be a different one.'

Surani had taken to doing most of the talking and he continued now, 'The SEC and the FBI were investigating cash flow into and out of suspicious stock trading accounts here and abroad. Some of those accounts were set up by Mr Prescott and it appears they were for the benefit of various clients. There were New York connections so we got involved. It's been going on for months.'

'It can't have!'

Surani continued, 'We were going to raid the office and arrest him at home this morning, but he must've gotten word about the investigation and fled late yesterday. There're teams going through the office and his houses now. He's vanished, cleaned out a half-dozen accounts in the U.S. and transferred the money into untraceable accounts overseas.'

She looked down. They were standing at a water main access panel in the sidewalk. The ironwork was from somewhere other than New York. It wasn't even American. She told them, 'He did say he was going to work late yesterday. I told you – I was at a meeting out of the office most of the day. I saw him for about an hour in the morning. We hardly said a dozen words. I assumed he worked late and then went home.'

'He didn't go home. We had it under surveillance.'

'He left? Oh, God.'

Kepler asked Daniel, 'You a friend of Ms McKenzie's?'

'That's right.'

'Do *you* know Charles Prescott?'

'No,' Gabriela said. 'He doesn't.'

Daniel explained, 'We just met last night. Gabriela and I.'

They lost interest in him, as if thinking it had been a pickup, a night of sex and breakfast this morning. Daniel didn't seem to care about their impression of him.

She continued, 'This just has to be a mistake. First of all Charles would never do anything illegal. It's not conceivable.' Her voice quivered. She cleared her throat. 'If he left unexpectedly, I'm sure it was an emergency. One of his clients had a problem. Charles's that way. He's more than an investment adviser. He's a friend—'

'A problem, yeah. A federal indictment.' Kepler added, 'Really, Ms McKenzie, there's no mistake.' He was unemotional, but you could also hear a fragment of irritation in his voice.

She was blurting now: 'I'm the office manager. How could he possibly do anything like that without my knowing? How could that be?'

Daniel stirred, his meaning probably: That might not be the wisest thing to say, suggesting she was complicit. She fell silent. Surani blinked through his none-too-effective shades and said, 'We don't have any evidence you were involved in the scheme.'

His tone, however, added the word 'yet' onto the end of that sentence.

'Who're the clients you were mentioning?' Gabriela demanded.

'We don't have any names yet. A fair number were from the Far East, South America and the Middle East, according to the FBI. They've been tracing the cash and stock purchases.'

Gabriela laughed, albeit a bit hysterically. 'It *is* a mistake! I've never heard of any clients there. And I know all of them.'

Surani countered, 'Well, our information is that he *did* have clients there. Thirty-two, apparently. And he was shuttling money into these accounts. Who knows why? Money laundering most likely. But we aren't sure.'

'My God.' A dismayed whisper. 'Thirty-two clients?'

'That was as of two days ago.'

Gabriela opened her mouth and then slowly pressed her lips together as if words failed her completely.

Surani: 'Ms McKenzie, you have to understand, Mr Prescott caught us by surprise. We knew he had a one-way ticket to Zurich on Columbus Day weekend, so we thought he'd be in the country until then.'

'One way?' Gabriela said. 'No. I make all his travel arrangements. He didn't have any plans to leave. Sure not one way.'

'Well, he did,' Kepler barked.

His partner continued, 'Prescott must've got word about the investigation and skipped early. But not to Switzerland. We don't know where. So we need to get the names and addresses of those thirty-two clients.'

'You didn't find anything at the office?'

Surani explained, 'We know he flew to St Maarten yesterday about six p.m. He disappeared after that. The authorities down there can't find him. Now we're hoping you'll cooperate. We need to know where he went.'

'Tell us what you know,' Kepler said emphatically, dark eyes narrow.

'I don't know anything!'

'You probably do, Gabriela,' Kepler said with a sardonic tone. 'For instance, did you know he had a house in Miami?'

'His beach house. Of course.'

'There! See? You did know something. And yet you didn't volunteer it. Let's keep going. How about other houses – overseas is what we're particularly interested in. Or any friends or romantic partners he might be staying with.'

She was looking down at the sharp shadows on the sidewalk, the sunlight falling stridently on leaves.

'Ms McKenzie?'

She looked up. 'What?'

Kepler asked more bluntly, 'Does Prescott have any homes outside of the country? Does he visit anyone in particular in any foreign countries?'

'He . . . no, not that I've ever heard of. He goes to the Caribbean a lot. I mean, he has clients *there*.'

The look on the cops' faces said, *We know he does.*

Some of them among the infamous Thirty-Two, of course.

'Come on, Gabriela, keep going. You're on a roll!'

Daniel said, 'Why don't you lighten up? You just delivered some pretty tough news. And I don't think you handled it very well.'

The cops ignored him yet again. It was Surani, the easier-going one, who continued, 'Think back, Ms McKenzie. Any references to trips he'd taken? People he was going to see?'

'Ah, ah,' Kepler said, 'looks like you're thinking of something. Share. Come on.'

Daniel glared at him. But the cop kept his eyes fixed on Gabriela's face.

She said, 'You mentioned St Maarten. When he was down there he sometimes flew to St Thomas. I don't know who he met with – maybe one of those thirty-two special clients you mentioned. All I know is that this man was from Europe and he lived in St Thomas nine months out of the year. And he had a big yacht, a huge one. I think "Island" or "Islands" was in the name of the boat.'

The cops looked at each other, as if they were intrigued by these crumbs.

'Okay, we'll check that out,' Surani said.

Kepler nodded. 'Good job, Gabriela. I knew you had it in you.'

Daniel seemed to want to slap the smirk off the detective's face.

She asked Surani, 'Have you talked to Elena Rodriguez? Charles's other assistant?'

'Yes, an hour ago,' Kepler answered. 'She wasn't any more helpful than you were.'

Surani handed her his card. 'If you can think of anything else, give us a call.'

She took it but then her hand dipped. And her face revealed yet more dismay. She stared at the policemen. 'But, my God. I just realized . . . I mean, my job? What am I going to do for money? My salary . . . And my retirement funds?'

Surani glanced at Kepler, who at last showed a façade of sympathy. 'I'm sorry to say, but Prescott cleaned out *all* the company accounts late last night. Payroll and retirement too. He moved close to twenty-five million into a bank in the Caymans and then it vanished. There's nothing left. Not a penny.'

CHAPTER
9

10:00 a.m., Saturday

30 minutes earlier

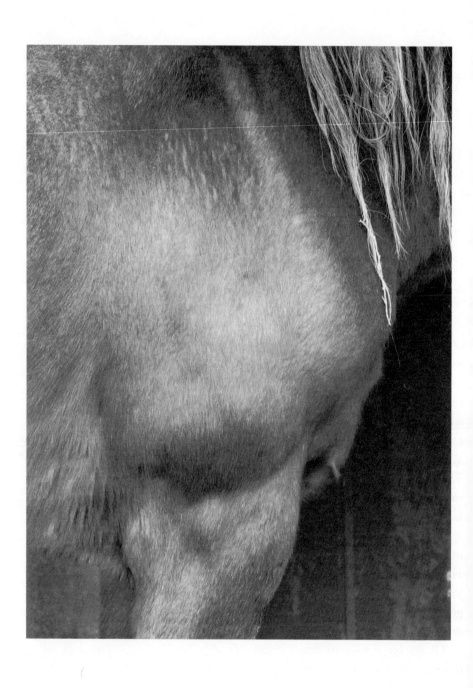

The two made their way past the Sheep Meadow in Central Park and under the bows of trees lit by unfiltered sun. The leaves still clung to branches and the configuration of tissue and vein was as busy and colorful as a Jackson Pollock painting, changing shade and glow constantly; the wind was persistent.

Her purse over her shoulder, Gabriela carried in one hand the Tiffany bag that Daniel had brought her, and in the other a paper sack containing a walnut cream cheese bagel for her daughter.

'Let's go that way,' she said, nodding.

Soon they were at the reservoir, walking wide of the path to stay clear of the many manic runners. A serious race walker, with his camel gait, overtook many of those jogging.

The conversation had turned substantive, typically morning-after-meeting, and Daniel asked about her history with Prescott Investments. She added with some passion, 'I love the work. I mean, really love it. I was one of those people who got good grades, graduated with honors, all that. But I didn't want to do anything practical. I was Ms Creative. That's what was important to me: writing, drawing, design, photography mostly. A headhunter sent me to Charles Prescott. He needed a free-lancer to take some photos for a brochure.'

Gabriela smiled. 'He was asking me about using Photoshop and some other software and right in the middle of the interview he stopped me. He said, "Forget it." I thought I was going to cry; I really needed the job. But he laughed and said, "I've seen your portfolio. The photos're great. You're an artist. But I can tell by talking to you your real talents are analysis and organization. Business."

'Of course, I thought he was just telling me to get lost, but then he offered me the job on the spot: office manager. Full-time, benefits, everything. At first I was insulted; I mean, I *knew* I was going to be a famous artist. But then I admitted maybe I didn't want that.'

Gabriela regarded Daniel with a smile. 'So have you learned not to ask me any questions? You get a whole Google-search of information. You going to flee?'

'Not yet. So far, this isn't the disaster last night turned out to be.' Then Daniel angled his head in that charming way of his and added with just the right amount of serious, 'But you didn't give up your photography.'

'Right. In fact, it was funny. I got *more* productive. Working full-time was liberating. I didn't have to worry about making a living with the pictures or designing, art, writing. I could take the images that moved me. And, it turned out, Charles was right. I had a head for business. Running the office, negotiating equipment leases, planning meetings, bookkeeping . . . everything. Meeting Charles saved my life. I was going through the divorce and I needed some direction, some validation, you know. He became my mentor . . . And guess what?'

'He never hit on you.'

'Not once. Always a gentleman. Kind, funny. Just a wonderful man. In a business where there are a lot of people who aren't so wonderful.'

'I know that all too well.'

They walked slowly over the pocked sidewalk. Their shoulders brushed several times. She felt an electric charge each time that happened. 'Funny, once or twice in your life you meet somebody who's a good person and it changes you forever. That's Charles.'

'And I assume,' Daniel said, 'that he knows the business. He makes money.'

'Oh, yeah. Charles's a genius. We've done well.'

'Maybe I'll give him a call. I'm always looking for outfits to do business with. Something to think about. And does he handle your investments? Your 401(k) or annuity?'

'He's put me in a couple good positions . . .' The words braked to a halt as she blinked, her mouth open.

Daniel was clearly struggling to keep a detached expression. Then he gave up and coughed a laugh.

'Shit,' she said, chuckling as well. 'He *suggested* some investment strategies. I won't become a millionaire, but when Sarah's ready for college there'll be money for that.'

'Does your ex contribute?'

Interesting change of tack, she observed. She kept her voice neutral as she said, 'Tim's trying to find himself. I used to joke – to myself – he should look under a rock. But he's doing the best he can, I think. It's just, if you have children, they're your priority. If you're not happy at your job, suck it up until they graduate. If you're depressed, deal with it for their sake. If the last thing in the world you feel like is another ballet recital, shut up and go.' Gabriela clicked her tongue. 'Okay. Nothing more from me on my ex. Now, tell me about *your* . . . kids.'

He laughed at the pregnant pause. 'Okay, Bryce and Steven. Fifteen and seventeen.' He described two handsome, all-American sorts of boys. He added that they were smart and never did anything worse than sneak a beer or get home an hour or so late. 'No drugs, no fights.'

Daniel explained that he had plans for them to go to good colleges but not Ivy League. He wanted them to get solid educations but at big, diverse schools.

'Finance? Business?'

'I wouldn't mind it. Capitalism's been good to me. It's exciting. I love it. But whatever they're happy with is the main thing. That's the only way to be a success. Who knows? Maybe they'll be artists, writers or *photographers* . . . Anyway, does anybody really know what they want to do until they're thirty?'

Not far away an elegant horse, ridden by an attractive young brunette in full gear, cantered along the bridle path.

He asked, 'You have your camera? You could take a picture for Sarah.'

'No, I don't carry it around generally. Besides, I've taken *lots* of horse pictures.'

They watched the beautiful creature disappear north, striding toward Harlem.

She was silent. Daniel frowned and glanced up the sidewalk.

'What?'

'Just thought I saw somebody looking our way.' The light grew fierce and he pulled on Ray-Bans.

She looked. 'I don't see anybody.'

'Imagination, maybe. Some man, I thought. In a dark overcoat.'

They continued their stroll to her apartment, looking over some of the vendor carts. Used books, CDs, food, of course. Always food.

Then Gabriela sensed Daniel's body language shift. He said, 'That complication you were telling me about at the restaurant? How much of a complication is he?' He glanced back once more, to the spot where he thought someone had been watching them.

'Frank Walsh isn't going to be following me.'

'No? Are you sure? Wait, is he bigger than me?'

She sized up Daniel's athletic shoulders, arms and chest. 'If it comes down to a fight, I think you'll win.'

He exhaled. 'Then I'll relax.'

'Seriously,' she said. 'Frank is a nice guy. He's dependable. He's . . . sweet.'

Daniel began to laugh hard at the telling word.

'I'm there.' She pointed to a nondescript building up a cross street, affordable only because of the bizarre but kind rent laws in New York City.

Daniel began to say something but at that moment two men in suits, which didn't fit particularly well, approached with obvious intent.

They didn't come from the place in the park where Daniel had believed he'd spotted their follower, Gabriela noted.

One of the men, Anglo and tanned, wore aviator shades; the other, of Indian – South Asian – extraction, wore those glasses that dimmed automatically in the sun. Gabriela blinked, looking down at their NYPD badges and ID cards.

'You're Gabriela McKenzie.'

'Yes. I . . . Yes, I am. Who are you?'

The one with the aviator sunglasses said briskly, 'I'm Detective Kepler, this is Detective Surani. Could we talk to you for a moment?'

CHAPTER
8

9:00 a.m., Saturday

1 hour earlier

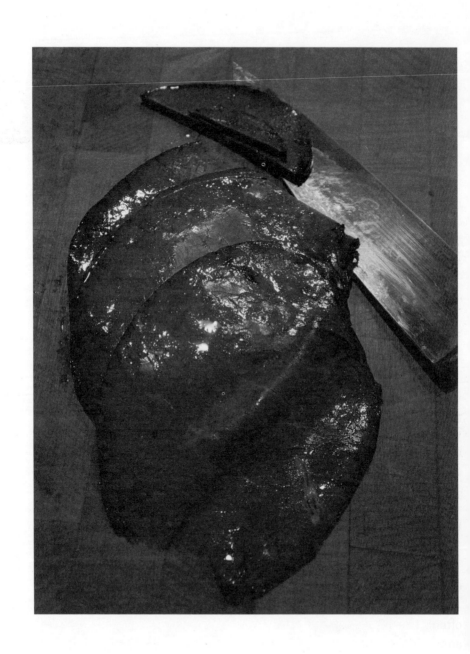

They sat across from each other in the spattered window of Irving's Deli, Upper West Side.

The restaurant, a mash of linoleum, dinged chrome and worn wood, was chaotic. The smells were of garlic, fish, bagel steam, toast, coffee. Mismatched perfume and aftershave, too, sprayed on in lieu of shower; on Saturday, why preen?

The day was beautiful, a bright Saturday in September, and people were swarming. Many locals were at tables and in the queues, but many 'interlopers,' too, as Gabriela said.

'You mean from my 'hood,' Daniel called over the ocean-roar of the patrons. 'The TriBeCa?'

'We're thinking of requiring passports for you people to cross Fourteenth Street,' she said.

'That's profiling,' Daniel said.

They returned to their food.

She thought it curious that Daniel wore a suit on the weekend – gray like yesterday, though a different cut and a dress shirt of blush pink. No tie. Had he planned to attend a meeting later? Or was he simply more comfortable not wearing casual clothes? Gabriela was in tan stretch pants, a burgundy sweater, pearls too. Ankle boots. He'd looked at her figure once – when he thought she wasn't paying attention. The sweater was tight.

The table was small and she adjusted the distinctive turquoise Tiffany bag on the corner. 'Thanks again for this.'

'The least I could do.'

Daniel asked where exactly she lived, relative to the deli, which was on Broadway, near 75th.

Gabriela grimaced. 'About four blocks away. I come here way too often. The hips I have, I have Irving's to thank for.' Her eyes swept around the counter, piled high with every imaginable taste. 'Kosher, I've learned, does not mean low calories.' She paused, frowning. 'I'm waiting.'

Daniel tapped his forehead with a palm. 'What hips?'

'Too little, too late.'

'But obviously you work out.'

'I'll give you a few points for that,' she said.

Daniel looked philosophical. 'You notice when men say to women, "Oh, you work out," it's a come-on line. When women ask it, they want to know if he's going to cuddle in bed on Sunday mornings or get up at dawn for a date with his Adidas.'

'I'd have to think about it. *Was* that a come-on line?'

Daniel asked, 'You want some jam?'

Breakfast was coffee, pumpernickel bagels and smoked salmon. No onions. 'Onions are a fourth- or fifth-date thing,' Gabriela announced.

'Is *this* a date?'

She was thinking about last night. Her response was, 'I don't know that we need to overthink it.'

'Fair enough. But you manage an investment house and I run a venture capital firm. We're professional overthinkers. No?'

'True,' she said.

'But it's not overthinking it to say we survived a completely excruciating last night.'

'No, that's accurate.'

He frowned. 'You're picking at your food. Can I have that piece of salmon? The lonesome one on the side?'

'Yours.'

He speared and ate it. 'What're your plans for today?'

'I pick Sarah up at one from dance class. And we spend the rest of the weekend together.'

'You two have a great time. I can tell.'

'Oh, we do.' Her eyes grew wide. 'We go to American Girl and FAO, naturally. But MOMA and the Met too. Sarah asks to go to the art museums. She's so smart. I have to keep reminding myself she's only six.'

'Smart. So she's got your genes.'

'She got my *temperament* genes. Ah, I think I just sniped at my ex again. I told myself I wasn't going to do that.'

They nodded to the young man server for coffee refills. And thanked him. Daniel looked her over with a coy smile. 'Is this where you tell me about the complication?'

Gabriela laughed hard. 'You make your clients a ton of money, I'll bet. With that kind of insight.'

'No engagement ring,' Daniel said, glancing toward her finger. 'You're beautiful – which by the way is less of a come-on line than "Wow, you totally work out." I just have a feeling there has to be a complication.'

'Okay. There's this tiny complication.'

'How tiny?'

'Stop it!' She laughed again. 'His name's Frank. Frank Walsh.'

'What an awful name,' Daniel said, wrinkling his perfect nose.

'Are you listening?'

'Tell me about Frank,' he said, thumping the last word with his lips. 'I'm dying to know about complicating Frank.'

'You're mean! We date some.'

'Are you going to marry him?'

After a pause: 'Fact is, he's a little more interested in me than I am in him.'

'Never heard of that happening before,' Daniel said sardonically. 'I actually got proposed to by a woman on a first date. She popped the question as soon as she heard I had a job. I'm not making that up. But I should add that there was some tequila involved.'

'Did you say yes?'

'To what?' Daniel asked with feigned innocence.

She continued, 'Frank's quirky – he's a computer nerd. And reclusive. But he knows movies – which I love – and he's funny and considerate. You don't find that a lot nowadays.'

'Here's my guideline,' Daniel said. 'The sweet factor.'

'Sweet?'

'If you describe your present love interest as infuriating and exasperating, then you're in love. If you say he's sweet, it's doomed and you need to ditch him pronto – for somebody who infuriates you.'

'I'm withholding all future adjectives about Frank for the time being.' She glanced at her watch. 'I don't have to be at the dance school for a while. Want to walk me back to my apartment?'

'Good idea,' he said, 'it'll help work some of that excess weight off your hips.'

'Nice try. But you're not infuriating me. Yet.' She took his fork, which contained his last piece of salmon, dunked the pink cube in sour cream and ate it fast.

CHAPTER
7

10:00 p.m., Friday

11 hours earlier

'You know, I have to be honest,' Gabriela told Daniel Reardon. 'This's been about as bizarre an evening as I can remember. Are you offended? I didn't mean to offend you.'

He made no comment about her assessment. Instead he asked, 'But was it a *date?*'

She thought for a moment. 'It was date-like.'

'Date-*lite?*'

'*Like,*' she corrected.

'Ah.'

They were walking north on Broadway from Battery Park through the cool September evening. A checkerboard of windows in the nearby office buildings. Many illuminated, some dark. The worlds of law and finance never rest, even Friday night. The streets were still busy with traffic if dwindling of pedestrians. Limos queued in front of the posher buildings.

'Bizarre,' he repeated quizzically. 'The restaurant, you mean?'

Well, that was part of it. They'd eaten in a dive of an Indian place, curry and tikka and Kingfisher beer. The air had been tropically humid and heavy with sandalwood, the canned sitar music corny and the food perhaps the best South Asian cuisine she'd ever had. The feature dominating the room was a massive saltwater aquarium, easily ten thousand gallons. Gabriela had been captivated by the colorful fish, which eased, or darted, throughout the tank. Shrimp was on the menu, she noted, but no other seafood was represented. ('Good thing,' she'd told him, nodding at the aquarium. 'Just wouldn't be right.')

'Mostly by "bizarre,"' Gabriela said, 'I was actually referring to what happened *before* dinner.'

'Oh. That.'

And thinking back to those hours, while there were many memories, most prominent was Daniel's touch as he lifted a silk handkerchief and wiped the moisture from her brow. Once again she now felt the tumbling within her, low, as she had then.

Silence for a time as they walked toward subways – her station first. Daniel finally asked, 'When you called your ex, I wasn't listening, but I noticed you didn't talk to your daughter for very long. Is everything okay?'

'Oh, she's fine. Sometimes, when her dad has her and he's nearby, she clams up. They get along fine. He's good with her. But you know how it is: exes.'

Daniel's wryly twisted smile said that he knew all too well.

A mid September breeze encircled them.

'You cold?'

'A little.'

'Take my jacket.'

'No.' She pulled her own light tweed around her more tightly. 'I'm fine.'

He didn't persist; he'd probably sensed that once she'd come to a decision it would remain made. Which was largely true of Gabriela.

She gave a grimace, pointing to a plaza near Wall Street they were just passing. Bankers' Square. 'See that building there?' She pointed to a squat structure situated next to the new stock exchange facility, still bustling with construction work, even at this hour. On the other side was a medical center – a branch of a major Uptown hospital.

'I have *that* to thank for my ruined weekend.'

'It doesn't look that intimidating.'

'If you only knew.'

In a few minutes they were at the subway station where she'd catch the train to the Upper West Side, the Eighth Avenue line. Daniel would walk home.

'Look,' he said and fell silent.

Gabriela turned to him. She stepped aside so that the beam from a streetlight was not in her eyes.

'Look?' she prompted.

Daniel spoke like a patient saved by an emergency room surgeon: 'I really owe you. For the Princeton Solution.'

'It would've worked out,' she said gravely.

'Not the way you handled it.'

'Did the best I could under . . . let's say, difficult circumstances.'

But the expression of gratitude was, of course, a prelude to the inevitable.

He said, 'Okay, I find you very attractive. But, that's only part of it. I like you. You're fun, you're artsy, you know business. So here's the thing: I'm not seeing anybody and I haven't been seeing anybody for a while. Can I call you?'

'Anybody can call anybody if they have the number,' Gabriela said. 'The question is, will I pick up?'

Daniel looked pensive. 'Remember the days before caller ID? That was life on the edge, wasn't it? Do I pick up or not?'

She filled in, 'Would it be a telemarketer, date, ex-boyfriend? A job offer?'

'Or a wrong number.'

'Or, God forbid, your mother.' Gabriela winced. 'We're soft nowadays.'

'Cowards.'

They stood three feet from each other. Businessmen scooted around them, cars shushed past.

It was time to part ways. They both knew it.

He leaned in for a cheek brush.

She felt heat, she felt a faint stubble. The residue of moisture from earlier, recalling his wiping it from their brows and cheeks. 'Night.' His word was spoken softly.

'Night.'

She turned and started down the stairs, digging for her Metro pass. Then stopped. She called, 'My shoes?'

'What?'

'That old Tiffany bag I had? With my grown-up shoes inside?' Earlier that evening she'd swapped her high heels for the Aldo flats she now wore. 'I left it at the restaurant.'

He grinned.

'No,' she said, stifling a laugh. 'Not on purpose.'

'You sure? Maybe for another chance to see me again?'

Gabriela said, 'Sorry. I wouldn't risk losing a pair of Stuart Weitzmans just to see a man again. Any man.'

Daniel said, 'How's this? We can avoid the phone call issue altogether. We'll commit now. The restaurant's on the way to my loft. I'll pick them up and deliver them tomorrow at breakfast. How's Irving's Deli, Broadway. Nine?'

She paused then said, 'I suppose.'

'I know,' he said, his face growing grave. 'You're thinking: Will break-fast be as dull as tonight?'

'Nothing could be as boring as the past three hours,' Gabriela replied and disappeared down the subway entrance.

CHAPTER
6

6:30 p.m., Friday

3 hours, 30 minutes earlier

The Aquariva Super cut an uncompromising swath through the dusk of New York Harbor, Daniel Reardon at the helm.

'How fast are we going?' Gabriela called over the sexy rumble of the engine, the wind, the waves.

'About forty.'

'Knots per hour?'

Daniel shouted, 'You don't say that. Knots include miles *and* hours. Forty knots. It's about forty-five miles an hour.'

Gabriela nodded, smiling at the speed. 'Feels faster.'

'Then you'd like the boat I keep in Connecticut. It'll do seventy.'

She didn't bother to ask knots or miles. Probably didn't matter at that velocity.

There was no passenger seat in the front of the beautiful Italian speedboat as such – just a leather U-shaped banquette encircling the rear of the open cockpit. Gabriela could have squeezed in next to Daniel on the driver's seat but she preferred to remain standing behind him, close, gripping his seat back, her head near his ear.

The thirty-three-footer, with her black hull and rich wood deck, plowed effortlessly through the temperate waves. The surface of the water was like dark linen and the cloudless sky over New Jersey glowed lava orange from the vanishing sun, the vista split by two purple exclamation marks of fume from distant smokestacks.

It was a photograph waiting to happen, though not to be shot by Gabriela. She worked exclusively in black and white, and this scene was about color only, without substance. Pretty didn't interest her.

She turned her attention back to Daniel. He was a superb driver – which is what pilots of boats like this were called, she'd learned. He anticipated the drift and power of each wave, as if it were an opposing player on a sports field. Sometimes he crashed over it, sometimes he eased up onto a crest and used the mound of water itself to speed the boat forward.

She found his handling of the wheel and chrome controls intensely sensual, and felt that low unfurling within her as she noted his firm grip, half smile, utter concentration. The blue eyes were focused on the water, the way a lion sights for prey.

Gabriela leaned closer yet and smelled past his aftershave to his hair and scalp and skin.

'What do you think?' he asked.

'I've been on rowboats in Central Park,' Gabriela told him. 'I'm not qualified to judge performance.'

The words might have been taken as flirt. He gave no response. She wondered how she felt about that.

She continued in a shout, 'But on the *surface* – so to speak—'

He laughed.

'Incredible.'

Daniel throttled back and for a time they cruised. They could speak without raising voices now. He said, with a grim expression, 'Well, hate to ruin the mood, but I don't have much time left. I really need your help.' A reminder of the conundrum he'd mentioned earlier.

He nodded at a thick binder sitting on the floor of the boat between them.

She said firmly, 'You have to go with the Princeton formula.'

'Princeton?' He frowned.

'Look on page thirty-eight. That's the answer.'

He balanced the binder on his lap and flipped through pages. At one he stopped and stared down. 'You're sure? Princeton?'

'Absolutely no doubt.'

'That's pretty risky, don't you think?'

'Which is why I suggested it.'

He seemed uncertain.

Gabriela said, 'But it's your decision.'

'No, no.' Daniel looked around him. 'Okay. I'll go with it.' He laughed. 'The Princeton Solution.' He added, 'You're a lifesaver.'

She blinked at the word. 'Could you pick another figure of speech? I mean, considering we're in the middle of New York Harbor and happen to be sailing toward that really big ship.'

He looked up. 'It's a mile away. That reminds me, I forgot to ask: Can you swim?'

'How bad a sailor are you?' she asked.

'I just mean I'll give you a PPD.'

'Pee-pee what?'

'Personal protection device. Or, your word: lifesaver.'

'I can swim,' she said.

'Hold on.' When he noted her firm grip on the handholds, he steered into an impressive wake, took it head-on. The boat nearly caught air and slammed into the water on the other side of the crest. Spray dashed onto their faces.

'Come here.' Daniel reached into his breast pocket and withdrew a white silk handkerchief. 'Decorative only,' he said, smiling. She leaned forward and he wiped the salt spray from her forehead and cheeks, then his own.

He now steered parallel to Manhattan. They took in the otherworldly sight of the lights of the city coming alive and growing brighter. In the deepening dusk, Gabriela was cold. She shivered and pulled her black-and-white jacket around her more tightly.

Daniel consulted his watch. Seven-forty. 'You still up for dinner?'

'Oh, by the way. I don't get seasick.'

He frowned. 'Should've asked too. Oops.'

'I would've told you. I just mean, in answer to your question, yes: I'm starving. And we should get back soon. On the nights I don't have Sarah, I call her before she goes to bed. I never miss it.'

'I try to do the same, with the boys.'

He turned south down the Hudson and back into the harbor proper. Daniel eased the throttle forward. He had a devilish smile. 'Fifteen minutes more?'

'Sure.'

He steered to the right, closer to the container ship she'd seen earlier, which was steaming at a good clip toward the Verrazano Narrows.

'God, it's huge.'

'That one's a post-Panamax. Means she won't fit through the Panama Canal.'

'How high is it?' She was staring up as they approached the massive hull, red and scabby, laden with containers of all colors.

'I don't know,' Daniel replied. 'Ten stories maybe. Probably more. They're classified by length and breadth, not height. She's probably a thousand feet long, a hundred twenty wide.'

'"She"? Are all boats girls?'

'No. They're women.' Without a millisecond of hesitation.

Got me there, she thought. And had to laugh. 'It's magnificent and it's ugly,' Gabriela called. '*She* is, I mean.' Then she tapped the dashboard. 'Your boat – what's her name? I didn't look at the back.'

'*Boat*.'

The wind gusted. She shouted: 'Right. What's her name?'

'No, *Boat*'s her name.'

'That's all you could come up with?'

'It's all I wanted.'

'And "Boat" wasn't taken?'

'It's not like you have to trademark names. But, no, I've never seen *Boat*. Most people are more creative.' He described and spelled some. '*Irritable Bow. A Crewed Interest. Charley's Tuition. Nauty Call*.'

She groaned.

'Hold on. Here comes the monster's wake.'

Impressive crests of water charged them.

She knelt, gripped more tightly yet, the backs of her hands pressed against his shoulders. It seemed that he settled back firmly against her knuckles. Daniel straightened the craft and expertly tricked the engine and wheel as they met the first wave.

Boat crashed into and over the swell. She felt her breath leave her lungs as they landed hard.

Another dozen collisions, each tamer than the one before.

The boat settled into a gentle rocking.

'Look,' he said with admiration bordering on awe in his voice. If the Chinese sea monster was impressive, the ship they saw to their right was breathtaking.

'It's as big as a city,' she called. 'What's *that* one?'

'A VLCC. Very large crude carrier. A tanker. And see how high she's riding? She's in ballast – no oil on board. She off-loaded in Jersey.'

'Going to the Panama Canal?'

'She's not going to fit either. She's headed to the Mediterranean or all the way around the Horn.'

'*Titanic*.'

He laughed. '*Titanic* was *half* her size' – nodding at the supertanker.

'How fast is she going?'

'Even full they can do eighteen knots. Empty, twenty-five, I'd guess. If I was alone I'd race her to that buoy.'

'Why?'

Daniel shrugged. 'Because it'd be fun.'

'No, I mean why only if you were alone?' When he hesitated she added, 'Go ahead. Do it.'

'Race?'

'Sure.'

'I don't know.'

She whispered, 'You have me to thank for the Princeton Solution, remember? You owe me.'

Daniel steered toward the buoy and throttled back, as if giving the VLCC, which must've outweighed *Boat* by a hundred thousand tons, a head start. The speedboat's exhaust bubbled, the wind hissed and behind them gulls shrieked a plea for chum.

'Ready?'

She cried, 'Go!'

Daniel rammed the throttles forward and *Boat* sprang away, her needle-shaped bow lifting high as they sprinted for the buoy.

Boat and the massive tanker were on intersecting forty-five-degree courses. Every second it grew bigger and darker as they wedged toward each other. Soon the VLCC was an otherworldly thing, visible only in outline and running lights and occasional amber dots of windows. An unstoppable shape, absorbing the entire sky, yet still growing, growing.

'It'll be close,' Daniel shouted. They both glanced to their right at the crude carrier, then ahead to the buoy, which was three hundred yards away.

Then two hundred.

One . . .

'Close!' Daniel repeated in a ragged shout. 'It'll be close. I can stop. You want me to stop?'

Her heart pounding, a primitive drum, electrified by the speed, by the looming nearness of the massive vessel, by the presence of the man at the wheel, inches from her, Gabriela leaned closer and put her head against his. 'Win,' she whispered. 'I want you to win.'

CHAPTER
5

5:00 p.m., Friday

1 hour, 30 minutes earlier

Limoncello's was not busy.

Perhaps it would be, *probably* would, since the restaurant was in the heart of Wall Street and it was Friday. And the place overlooked pictur-esque New York Harbor, offering a view of boats and endless waves, rising and falling like a metronome. This was just the spot for traders and brokers, who'd toyed with millions of other people's dollars in the last eight hours, to celebrate their good decisions, to forget the bad.

But now, late afternoon, the bar was half empty. Those business folks who'd arrive later were still at their desks or writing up tickets on the floors of the closed exchanges or at health clubs and on jogs through Battery Park.

Here particularly, near the water, you could smell autumn in the air.

Gabriela wove through the brass- and oak-accented room, returning from the toilet and sat in the high chair at the bar, which she'd occupied for the past half hour. She slipped her black-and-white-checked jacket off, hung it over the back of the stool. A white silk blouse was tucked primly into a knee-length pleated gray skirt. She wore black hose and mottled burgundy-and-black high heels; she would change into her black flats – her walking-to-work shoes – later; that comfy pair were on the floor, in the faded Tiffany bag she used for footwear transport.

She resumed editing documents she'd been poring over since she'd arrived. The top one was headed *Open Items for Accountant*. Several entries she crossed through completely. Others she marked with precise asterisks, each line of the sunburst an equal length. Beneath these were a half-dozen sheets headed with the names of companies and below that *Balance Sheet and P & L*. There wasn't a single sheet that listed assets below $250 million. Another said, *CP Personal Accounts*.

She then turned to another contract, headed *Short-term Commercial Lease*. But there was nothing brief about the contents. Twenty pages of dense type. She sighed and started through it again, pausing once to note herself in the mirror. Her hair was pulled back severely and pinned, which made the auburn shade lighter, for some reason.

She edited the lease some then looked out the tall windows, sipped wine and caught a glimpse of City Pier A. The structure wasn't as large as other piers farther north, in Greenwich Village and in Midtown, but this one had more history. The Professor had been particularly interested in the sagas of Downtown Manhattan and would spend hours reeling off stories to her. Built in the 1880s for the Department of Docks and the Harbor Police, Pier A had been witness to the relentless expansion of the city. She noted the seven-story clock tower, which had been built in 1919. The elaborate timepiece was a memorial to the U.S. soldiers killed in the First World War. This was particularly poignant, considering that the original pier had been built by the son of a famous Union general in the Civil War.

She could listen to the Professor for hours.

As Gabriela returned to the lease, the man beside her set his drink down and continued to speak into his mobile phone.

Gabriela stiffened and blurted, 'Oh. Hey.' When he didn't respond she spoke more forcefully. 'Excuse me.'

He finally realized that he was the object of the comment. He turned, frowning.

She was displaying her sleeve, which was stained brown. 'Look.'

His square handsome face, eerily resembling that of a well-known actor, beneath close-cropped, black hair, studied the sleeve and then her face. His eyes followed hers to his glass of scotch. His brows rose. 'Oh, hell.' Into the phone, 'I'll call you back, Andrew.' He disconnected. 'Did I do that? I'm sorry.'

Gabriela said, 'When you put your glass down, yeah. Just now. On the phone, you were talking, and you turned. It spilled.'

'Sorry,' he repeated. It sounded genuine, not defensive.

His eyes migrated from the stain to her white blouse, all of the blouse, beneath which a trace of bra was visible. It was pale blue. Then his gaze settled back on the stain. 'Silk?'

'Yes, it is.'

'I know what to do,' he explained. And took charge, summoning the bartender, a young man who seemed to be covering tats on his neck with makeup; this was a Wall Street, not an East Village, bar.

'Soda water and a towel, no, not the green one. The white one. The white towel. And salt.'

'Salt?'

'Salt.'

The remedies arrived. He didn't apply the water and seasoning himself but let her do it. She'd heard the trick too – from her mother, as he had from his grandmother, he told her.

'Careful with the salt,' he said. 'I don't know how well it works on silk. You might hurt the cloth if you rub too hard.'

The magic trick did a pretty good job. Just the faintest discoloration remained.

She examined him with eyes beneath furrowed brows, then: 'Why don't you drink Martinis like everybody else here?'

'I don't like Martinis. I'd probably have a strawberry Cosmo, and if that was the case, the stain would *never* come out. I'll pay for the cleaning.'

'If I were a man would you make that offer?'

'I don't make *any* offers to a man wearing a silk blouse.'

She kept a straight face for a moment then laughed. 'No, thanks. It'd have to go to the laundry anyway.'

'Well, I apologize again.'

She lifted her palms. 'Accepted.'

With détente achieved, she returned to the lease and he to his mobile. But when the last page of the document was marked up and when his call disconnected, the silence prodded them to glance toward each other – in the mirror at first – and conversation resumed.

'I'm sending you back home stinking of whisky. What's your husband going to say?'

'He probably won't find out. Since he lives thirty miles away from me.'

'Ah, you're in that club too. I'm Daniel Reardon.'

'Gabriela McKenzie.'

They shook hands.

Conversation meandered for a bit, both of them testing the waters, and then found true north, which included the question you can never avoid in New York: What do you do for a living?

Daniel worked as a venture capitalist, private equity, he told her. 'The Norwalk Fund.' He nodded. 'We're a few blocks from here. On Broad.'

Gabriela glanced at the documents. 'I'm office manager for a financial adviser. Prescott Investments.'

'Don't think I know them.' He glanced down at the documents before her, then away quickly, as if looking at confidential client details was tantamount to glancing through an inadvertently left-open bathroom door.

'It's a small outfit. He was with Merrill years ago but opened his own shop. He's a lot happier.'

'Your office is near here?'

'No, Midtown, east. Turtle Bay.' She sighed. 'My boss – he's a great guy – but he dumped this in my lap this morning. He wants to lease a warehouse on Bankers' Square – near Wall Street – and the deal fell through. I got elected to check out some new space. . . and go over a forty page lease. We need to sign it up in two weeks.'

'Two *weeks*?'

'Yep. And you know Banker's Square? It took hours even to get inside and look the place over. All that construction.'

'Oh, the new stock market annex. Supposed to finished by now.'

'Anyway, I came here to jot some notes and unwind.'

'And get a drink spilled on you.'

'It sounded like you were working too, a business call.' She nodded at the two mobiles that sat in front of him. An iPhone and a Motorola Droid.

'I was doing a project with a partnership in Aruba. It just closed today. I've been banging out the details since nine.'

'Congratulations. And my sympathies.'

'Thanks.' Daniel laughed and sipped the scotch. 'I went for a swim at my health club and came over here . . . to unwind.'

She smiled at the echo.

The talk veered slowly from the professional. Personal stats were recited. They both lived in Manhattan. He told her that he had two sons, living with his ex in Nyack.

'My husband and I have joint custody.' Gabriela tugged her phone from her Coach purse. She scrolled and displayed a picture. 'This's Sarah. She's six.'

'Adorable.'

'She's into ballet and gymnastics. But she just discovered horses. Oh, does she want a horse.'

'Where are you in the city?'

'Upper West. Two bedroom, a thousand square feet. We could probably fit a horse in, but I don't think they do well in elevators.'

'And Sarah's dad?'

She said, 'No. He's okay in elevators.'

'You're pretty funny.' Spoken as if Daniel didn't date women who were.

'Tim lives on Long Island,' Gabriela continued. 'But not in the horse stabling neighborhood.'

Daniel gestured to the bartender, who responded immediately. 'Another for me. And the same for her.'

'No, really,' Gabriela protested.

'Cheaper than buying you a new Neiman Marcus blouse.'

'It's Macy's. But I didn't mean no to the drink. I mean no to *what* I'm drinking. I'll upgrade to the Merry Edwards pinot noir. Since he's buying.'

Daniel lifted an eyebrow, impressed at her choice.

A moment later the drinks appeared. She wondered what tats the bartender was hiding with the makeup.

Occupy! Down with the One Percent!

Or maybe something simple: *Fuck Capitalism.*

She thought about saying this to Daniel but, while he'd probably laugh, she decided not to.

When the new glasses arrived, they tapped and talked about the agony and ecstasy of living in the city. About Ground Zero, which was visible from Limoncello's. The Trade Towers would forever cast indelible shadows over the city.

Then a dozen subjects arose in easy conversation: restaurants, traveling, parents, politics – the last in a safely glancing fashion, though their views seemed similar.

When they were close to finishing their drinks, Daniel looked at his watch. Didn't sneak a glance, just lifted the heavy Rolex and noted the time.

She nodded. 'Dinner plans, sure.'

'Actually, no. I have a meeting.' Daniel's eyes circled, her hair, her face, her eyes. 'You have to get back to your daughter?'

She sniffed subtext. 'I'll pick her up tomorrow. She's at her father's tonight.'

'Don't know if you're interested, but that meeting? You have any interest in helping me out?'

'Doing what?'

'Actually, I'm meeting an interior designer to pick out upholstery.'

She shook her head. 'That's not a good come-on line.'

'I'm having new leather installed in my speedboat.'

'That's a better one.'

He opened the backpack he used for a briefcase and took out a booklet of leather samples. She flipped through the pages, which were organized by color. Her favorites were the rich oranges, the sort she imagined as the color of seats in brash sports cars. The names were words like 'carrot,' 'pumpkin,' 'amber,' 'tomato.'

But her favorite was called 'Princeton,' presumably after the school colors of the New Jersey university. It was the boldest offered by the company.

'I do have a preference,' Gabriela said slowly. 'But how can I say for sure without seeing the boat?'

'We can fix that.'

CHAPTER
4

1:30 p.m., Friday

3 hours, 30 minutes earlier

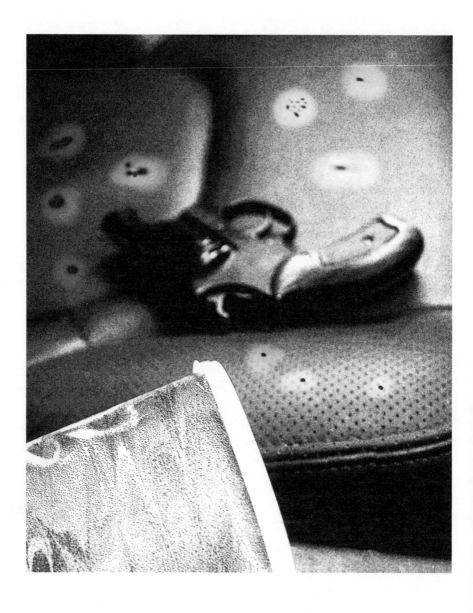

The Prius, tinted in Toyota's wan, innocuous light blue, eased through the winding streets of Bronxville, New York, past mansions nestled in spacious yards of yellowing grass, waning gardens, banks of damp September leaves.

Accustomed to driving his Maserati, Daniel Reardon didn't much care for the car, though he hadn't expected power. It was mostly the quiet of the engine he objected to. He'd heard there were some cars that now added sound sexy engine noises through speakers. This was a cheat and he thought it ridiculous. Daniel liked authenticity, for good or bad. The Maserati's Tubi exhausts, for instance, resonated at a high pitch that could, in the upper gear ranges, threaten to pierce your eardrums.

He loved that.

Faint classical music was on the radio but it dimmed when an incoming call announced itself. Daniel answered and spoke to his client in the awkward language of business that is at the same time vague and precise. Finally, some technical legal and financial decisions made, he offered a pleasant farewell to the man who'd earned The Norwalk Fund close to two hundred thousand dollars last year. He disconnected. The classical music rose once more. Mozart. The clarinet concerto. An odd instrument and very difficult, he knew, to play well. He'd dated a girl once who'd been a cellist in a symphony orchestra. She'd explained that the reeds had taken her the most time to master. 'You've got to negotiate the sound from them.'

Daniel had liked that expression quite a lot, which was why he remembered the sentence, while the image of the girl had all but vanished years ago.

In his gray Canali suit, Daniel was certainly dressed for this area. He seemed like any other businessman returning home early from his White Plains law firm or investment bank.

He drove carefully. The streets were slick with colorful layers; wind and rain had conspired to thin the canopy of oak and maple, decimating the foliage (almost literally, removing about every tenth leaf or so – Daniel grew irritated when people used the verb incorrectly).

He steered onto Henderson Lane, presently deserted of traffic, and continued past houses less opulent than the mansions but just as quiet. The windows of the structures were dark, mostly, and he spotted not a single person on the clean sidewalks. At a four-way intersection, he braked to a stop and let a Grand Cherokee, dark red, precede him, turning into Henderson. Daniel accelerated slowly and fell in behind the vehicle.

Several blocks away, when the SUV eased up to a stop sign, Daniel stabbed the brake pedal. The Prius skidded on the leaves and tapped the bumper of the Jeep gently.

He frowned and glanced forward. He saw the eyes of the occupants of the Jeep: the driver's in the mirror and his college-aged passenger's directly; the girl turned to gaze with some generic hostility.

Daniel winced and climbed out. He joined the driver, standing by the Jeep's open door. He shook his head. 'I am so sorry!'

The stocky man in a navy sport coat, tan slacks and blue shirt grinned ruefully. 'Not like you were doing a hundred miles an hour.'

'I didn't think the leaves'd be that slick. Man, it was like ice. I just kept going.' Daniel looked into the front seat. He said to the girl, clearly his daughter, 'Sorry, you okay?'

'Like, yeah. I guess.' The blond girl returned to her iPod. The day was warm but she wore a stocking cap pulled down tight over her long hair and the sleeves of her thick sweatshirt extended nearly to her fingers.

The two men walked to the back of the SUV and regarded the vehicle. The Cherokee driver said, 'They make 'em tough. I was going to say American cars, but, hell, I don't really know where these babies're built. Could be Tokyo.' A nod at the Prius. 'And that could've been made in Arkansas. Parts of it anyway.'

Daniel looked around the immaculate neighborhood. All was still deserted. 'Thomas, listen carefully. Are you listening?'

The driver kept grinning. Waiting for an explanation. When there was none, he asked. 'Do I know you?'

'No, you don't. Now, I want the name of the bank in Aruba your investment partnership uses. And the main investment account number and the PIN.'

'Wait. What is this?'

Daniel unbuttoned his jacket and displayed the narrow grip of an old Smith & Wesson revolver. A .38 special.

'Oh, my God.' His eyes went to his daughter, lost in the elixir of music.

'Just give me the information and you'll be fine. She will too.'

'Who are you . . . ?' His voice rose into a filament of sound, not unlike a note from a reed instrument.

'Hold on, hold on,' Daniel said, keeping a smile on his face, just in case anybody *did* happen to be behind one of those black windows. 'Don't panic. You don't want to do that. This is just business. All I want is that information. I'll verify it and then you go on your way. You'll be out twenty million dollars but no one will get hurt. Besides, you didn't exactly get that through socially minded investments, did you?'

'You're insane,' he whispered. Panic was gone, anger had taken its place. And fast. 'You fucker. You do this in front of my daughter? Who are you working for?'

'Thomas, you don't have much time. I'll shoot your daughter first, because I need you alive to give me—'

'All right. Don't even mention that! Don't even say it! All right, I'll give it to you.'

Daniel placed a call.

'Hello?' came the low, melodious answering voice.

'Andrew.' He handed the phone to Thomas and instructed, 'Give him the information.'

'I don't have it memorized!'

'She gets shot first and—'

'I just mean it's in my phone! It's encrypted. It'll take a minute.'

Daniel said into the phone, 'He's got to decrypt it.'

Andrew Faraday said through the tinny speaker, 'Okay. But hurry.'

Daniel glanced into the Jeep. The girl seemed irritated that she couldn't find a song on her playlist.

With Daniel watching, to make sure that Thomas didn't hit 911, the businessman began typing on his mobile. He lost his place. He took a deep breath. Daniel told him, 'Stay calm. Take your time.'

'He said hurry!'

'Calm,' Daniel said.

Thomas started over. He nodded at the screen and took the phone from Daniel's hand. He began reciting numbers.

Daniel took back the iPhone. 'Well?' he asked Andrew.

He heard keyboard taps. A delay. 'It's good.' The phone disconnected.

The whole incident from car tap to confirmation had taken four minutes, just the time for two drivers to good-naturedly swap insurance info and agree there'd be no point in calling the police.

'Now get in your car and drive home. It's okay. You gave us what we wanted. It's all over with now. Just go home.'

Thomas turned and reached for the Jeep's door with shaking hands. When he'd opened it, Daniel took a paper towel from his pocket and, wrapping it around the grip of the gun, drew the weapon and shot the businessman twice in the back of the head. He leaned down and looked in the passenger compartment, where blood flecked the dashboard and the windshield and the face and hat of his daughter, who was screaming as she stared at her father's twitching body. She was clawing frantically at the door handle.

Daniel held up a reassuring hand. She froze, uncertain about the gesture, he imagined, and turned slightly toward him. He shot her once in the center of the chest. As she slumped back, staring up, he shot her twice more, in the mouth. For the brain stem. This emptied the five-round cylinder.

Daniel dropped the gun on the seat and pocketed the paper towel. He returned to the Prius and pulled around the Cherokee slowly. He drove out of the neighborhood, occasionally checking the rearview mirror, but saw no lights, no emergency vehicles. He noted only a few SUVs, two, coincidentally, with nearly identical infant seats affixed in the backseat.

He took a direct route to the parkway and then headed into the city. Eventually he ended up in the South Bronx. GPS sent him to an intersection, near one of the better – or at least cleaner – housing projects. He drove to where a Taurus sat idling in a parking space. He eased up behind it and flashed his lights, though the driver had already seen him, he'd observed. When the Ford had pulled out of the space, Daniel parallel parked, wiped the interior for fingerprints, then climbed out and dropped the keys on the floor of the car, leaving it unlocked. He got into the Taurus's passenger seat.

Daniel nodded to bald, fit Sam Easton, behind the wheel, and Sam lifted his foot off the brake and sped down the street.

'Heard it went good. Andrew called.'

'Fine. And no tail,' Daniel said. 'I'm ninety-nine percent sure.'

Sam nodded, though – as Daniel would have done – he continued to check the rearview mirror more frequently than a prudent driver might.

Before the Ford turned onto the street that would take them into Manhattan, Daniel glanced back and noted two young men slow as they walked past the Prius, looking around, then easing closer, like coyotes sniffing out wounded prey.

Daniel read a text. The cash had been drained from the Aruba account and was already laundered, scrubbed clean.

'You want to go home?' Sam asked. 'Or drop you at the usual place?'

'Downtown. The club.'

Daniel invariably spent Friday afternoons swimming at his health club in Battery Park, then would have a drink or two at Limoncello's and take his boat out for a sunset ride in New York Harbor.

After that some Indian or Thai food and back home, where he'd summon one of the girls from the outcall service he used. Whom to pick? he wondered. Daniel was in a particular mood after the shooting – he found himself picturing the outstretched bloody body of the target's daughter. This memory was persistent and alluring.

He decided he'd ask for one of the girls who allowed her customers to practice rough trade. Still, he reminded himself that he'd have to exercise a bit more restraint than several weeks ago when Alice – or was it Alina? – ended up in the emergency room.

CHAPTER
3

12:20 p.m., Friday

1 hour, 10 minutes earlier

Gabby!'

She turned to see the pudgy redheaded man approaching through the aisles of the electronics superstore, near City Hall.

She thought again of her initial impression from a month or so ago, when they'd met. The round thirty-something had *farm boy* written all over him. A look you didn't see much in Manhattan. Not that there was anything wrong with this image intrinsically (anything but the hipster look, Gabriela felt); the problem was just that it was too easy to picture him in overalls.

She smiled. 'Hi!'

'What're you doing here?' Frank Walsh asked her, as he beamed, smiling.

He wore a tan Polo shirt, which matched everybody else's here. His name tag reported, *F. Walsh, Computer Fix-It Dept. Manager*.

She took his hand, which he turned into a hug.

Gabriela said, 'Have a meeting downtown. Thought I'd say hi.'

His face seemed to glow. 'No kidding! I was just thinking about you. Wow, Tiffany's.'

She glanced down at the bag. 'Just my comfy shoes.'

'I like the ones you're wearing,' he whispered, noting the spiky high heels, which elevated her to his height. Stuart Weitzmans. They cost the same as one of the computers on sale at a nearby end cap.

'Try walking to work in them sometime,' she said with a laugh.

On the far wall scores of the same Geico commercial flickered from TV screens large and small.

Frank glanced at his watch. 'You free for lunch?'

'No, I have to get back to that meeting. Got time for coffee, though.'

'Deal.'

They went to a Starbucks next door, collected their drinks – she a black coffee, Frank a frothy latte. They sat and chatted, amid the muted grind of blenders and the hiss of the steam device.

Despite appearances, Frank was about as far removed from the farm as could be. 'Nerd' was a better descriptive, a word that she would have avoided but he'd said it about himself once or twice so maybe it was politically correct. Computers consumed him. His job here, of course. And he seemed to be an avid participant in online role-playing games; she deduced this from the way he had coyly asked her if she knew certain titles (she'd never played one in her life). Then, looking a bit disappointed, he'd changed the subject and didn't bring the topic up again, probably embarrassed.

Frank Walsh was a film buff, too; he went to the movies twice a week. This they had in common.

They sipped coffee and chatted. Then he confided with a grimace, 'I've got the weekend off . . . but I've got to visit my mother.'

'Congratulations. And all my sympathies.'

He laughed.

'She's on Long Island?' Gabriela recalled.

'Syosset. But I'm back about noon Sunday. There's a noir festival at the SoHo that starts then. You interested? Sterling Hayden, Ida Lupino, Dan Duryea. The best of the best.'

'Oh, sorry, Frank. Have plans Sunday.'

'Sure.' He didn't seem particularly disappointed. 'Hey, I'm making a mix tape with those songs you liked. Well, mix *download*. Mention "tape" to a new clerk here and they're like, "Huh?"'

'Wow, thanks, Frank.' Though she wondered: Which songs were those? She didn't listen to much modern music, no pop at all. A lot of classical and jazz. Many old-time crooners and cabaret singers. Sinatra, Count Basie, Nat King Cole, Rosemary Clooney, Denise Darcel. She'd inherited a massive collection of marvelous albums. Hundreds of them, embraced by their beautiful, rich-smelling cardboard jackets. She'd bought a Michell Gyro Dec turntable a few years ago, a beautiful machine. When she cranked up the volume in her apartment, the sounds it sent to the amplifier were completely pure. Arresting. They stole your soul.

She may have mentioned this to Frank in passing and he'd remembered.

Conversation meandered: to De Niro's latest film, to Frank's mother's health, to Gabriela's plans to redecorate her Upper West Side apartment.

Then: 'Funny you show up today.' Uttered in a certain tone.

'How's that?'

'I was going to call you later. But here you are. So.'

Gabriela sipped the strong coffee. She lifted an eyebrow toward him pleasantly. Meaning, *Go on*.

'Ask you something?'

'You bet.'

'Any chance of us?' He swallowed. Nerves.

'Us . . . ?' Gabriela wondered if that pronoun was the end of the sentence, though she suspected it was.

Frank filled in anyway: 'Dating, more seriously. Oh, hey, I'm not talking about marriage. God. I don't even think that makes financial sense nowadays. But every time we've been out, it's clicked. I know it's only a few times. But still.' He took a breath and plunged forward. 'Look, I'm not a Ryan Gosling. But I'm working at losing a few pounds, I really am.'

He looked down into his coffee. He'd made a show of using Equal, not sugar, and ordered with 2 percent milk, though Gabriela knew those were not the tools for fighting weight.

She told him, 'Women like men for a lot of reasons, not just their looks. And I went out with somebody who was a dead ringer for Ryan Gosling once and he was a complete dick.'

'Yeah?'

'Hey, I like you, Frank. I really do. And, there could be an "us." I just want to take things real slow. I've had some problems in the past. You have too, right?'

'Hey-ay, I've been a mistake magnet.' He elaborated on what he'd told her a few weeks ago, about a difficult breakup. She couldn't quite tell who was the dumpee and who the dumper.

As she listened, she counted sixteen freckles on his face.

'I respect that,' he said seriously.

'What?' Had she missed something?

'That you're being reasonable. Taking time, thinking about things. And that you didn't get all weird and run out of here.'

'How can I run? I'm wearing killer high heels.'

'Which're pretty nice.'

And now that Frank had raised a Serious Topic and the matter had been debated, he dropped it, for which she was infinitely grateful. He rose, pulled three sugar packets out of the tray and returned, spilling the contents into his coffee, then stirring up a whirlpool. Before he sat, though, he whipped his Samsung phone out of its holster.

'Smile.'

'What?'

He aimed the camera lens at her and shot a few pictures, full length, from head to shoe, as she grinned.

Finally he sat, reviewed the pictures. 'Some keepers.' Frank then sipped more coffee and looked up at her. 'You know, that film festival's going on all week.'

'Really? I'm free Tuesday if you like.'

'I'm working then—'

'Well—'

'No, if Tuesday works for you, I'll swap shifts.'

'Really?'

'For you, yeah.'

'That's really sweet, Frank. Really sweet.' She gave him a breezy smile.

CHAPTER
2

11:00 a.m., Friday

1 hour, 20 minutes earlier

Brad Kepler and Naresh Surani waited in an NYPD conference room that featured a single speckled window that overlooked a building that, Kepler believed, overlooked New York Harbor. This was as good as most views got – at least for detectives third – in One Police Plaza. At least when they were involved in an operation that had no name, that nobody knew about, and because of that, that could presumably fuck a career as much as make one.

Kepler admired his arm, less muscular than when he'd joined the force but more robustly tanned. He then regarded Surani, who had a nearly gray complexion, which stayed gray no matter how much sun he got. Both men were more or less mid-thirties and more or less fit, though Kepler's physique reflected the reality of life as a detective: sedentary, with walking the most strenuous exercise on the job. He'd chased somebody a month ago, and caught him, but his hip still hurt.

Fucker.

'This guy the shit he seems to be?' He tapped a file on the table in front of him.

'Dunno,' Surani answered his partner. 'Never heard of him. What's this room for? I didn't know it was even here.'

The office, near their division, Major Cases, was scuffed and dim and populated with a lopsided table, six chairs, three of them unmatched, a filing cabinet, and dozens of boxes labeled *Discard*.

And the fucking useless view. But at least it was a view, unlike his cubicle, five or six or a thousand floors away, where the only thing he could feast his eyes on was the ass of Detective Laikisha Towne. Which was a lot to see. And that image appealed not in the least.

Kepler now regarded the boxes and decided it was amusing, the labels. The boxes looked like they'd been here for months. So why hadn't somebody just *discarded* them, per instructions?

Welcome to the NYPD.

The time was just after 11:00 a.m. You could smell old oil, garlic, fish – like you could in much of the building from time to time, depending on prevailing winds and humidity, given the proximity, and the relentless encroachment, of Chinatown. As for Little Italy: *Arrivederci!*

'I'm hungry,' Kepler said.

'I am too. But.'

'Where is everybody?'

Surani didn't know. So they took phone calls, they made phone calls.

'Because,' said Kepler, on his Droid, explaining to a perp he'd busted, now out on bond, 'they wouldn't knock it down any farther. It's the best they'll do, which means it's the best *you* can do. Eighteen months. You can serve that standing on your head.'

'Shit, man' came Devon's voice from the other end of the line.

'Okay. Gotta go.' Kepler disconnected, snuck a look at his warm brown arm once more. He didn't tell anybody its source was the lamps of the Larchmont tanning salon, fifteen miles from home. He told people he jogged every day, he played golf, he swam.

'That was Devon?' Surani asked.

'Yeah.'

'Eighteen months? Standing on his head? No way. He's fucked.'

'I know that. You know that. Devon *will* know it. Too bad but he shouldn'ta drove the getaway car.'

'Which it wasn't,' Surani said.

'What?'

'The car. Nobody got away.'

Kepler gave a laugh. 'Captain's late. They're both late. And I'm hungry. You fucking ruled at trial yesterday.'

Surani said with some modesty, 'Yeah, that went good. I was happy. Good jury. I like good juries.'

The two detectives bickered more than they complimented each other, and were sometimes downright insulting – but all forms of repartee were based on a similar affection. 'Infuriating' was a word that often arose.

He and Surani had been lovers for the past seven years, and partners – in the professional sense – for four. Someday soon, one or the other would propose marriage. Kepler was pretty close to popping the question.

And God save anybody on the force who made a single comment about it, lifted a single eyebrow, exhaled a single sigh.

Kepler examined his phone again, to order takeaway. At the beginning of his address book on the Galaxy were three folders, *!breakfast, !dinner, !lunch*, the punctuation mark added so the files would stay first in line, before people. He was debating between the first and third – he was sort of in a pancake mood – when the brass finally cruised into the room.

The promise of sausages and waffles went away, along with the phone itself, when the harried man, in a suit, strode inside. Wrinkled of face, boasting multiple chins, Captain Paul Barkley was in his late fifties. He carried the round belly of somebody who ate when it was convenient for him, not when the long hours and necessities of a case required him to grab breakfast to go when it was really lunchtime, or vice versa.

Still, the man had a rep as righteous as Kepler's tan – and far more genuine. Everybody knew Barkley had paid his dues and he carried bullet scars to prove it, according to legend. So none of the detectives griped, at least not too much, and definitely not to his face.

'Gentlemen.'

'Captain,' Surani said. A nod from Kepler.

'Busy day,' Barkley muttered and looked at his iPhone to prove it. Read a text. Sent a text, ignoring the men.

Kepler's stomach protested. Waffles. He wanted waffles. Or maybe a club sandwich.

Barkley snapped, 'So, what's this about? Request for an undercover op?'

'Right,' Kepler said.

'Where's Detective McNamara?'

'On the way,' Kepler said.

'Well, get started.' Barkley raised an intimidating eyebrow. Impatience ruled.

'Well, you know, sir, we're not sure. We didn't put it together.'

'It was—' Surani stopped speaking and looked behind the captain, into the doorway. 'Here's the mastermind of the op. She can give you all the details. Hey, Gabby!'

The beautiful but severe woman stepped into the room. Unsmiling, typically, she looked over all three men, nodding a greeting to the captain.

Kepler, with his proclivities, wasn't the least interested in Detective Gabby for her body. But, man, she dressed well. He appreciated that. A thin white blouse beneath the black-and-white-checked jacket. What was that cloth called again? There was some word for it, that pattern. A gray skirt.

And those were great dark stockings. Nice high heels too.

He and Surani weren't into cross-dressing, but if they had been, there were worse people to mimic than Detective Gabby.

She was a bit of a legend herself. Daughter of a detective working Organized Crime, she'd joined the force right out of college, working Crime Scene. When her father was killed in the line of duty, she became a detective and moved up to Major Cases, often working OC detail, like her old man had, specializing in the ultra-violent Eastern European gangs based in Brooklyn and Queens.

Known for her undercover work, she had a shining arrest record. And – more important – her conviction rate was off the charts. Anybody could collar anybody; having the brains and balls to make sure the fuckers went away for a long period of time was something else altogether.

Gabby pushed an ornery strand of auburn hair off her forehead.

The captain asked her, 'So you want to run an undercover op?'

'Sounds like a TV show,' Kepler quipped, trying to get her to smile. Everyone ignored him and he decided to stop being cute.

'That's right,' she told them.

'What's the deal?'

'I heard from a CI of mine there's a player who's surfaced. Guy named Daniel Reardon.'

'Never heard of him. Organized crime?'

'No connection with any of the crews I could find,' Gabby reported. 'According to my informant, he runs a small operation out of a Wall Street front. He's got two partners he works with. Have first names only. Andy or Andrew, and Sam.'

'Or "Samuel"?' Kepler inquired.

She turned her eyes on him; usually they were green, today they were more yellowish, eerie. 'Only "Sam."' Spoken briskly, as if: Wouldn't I have mentioned the longer name if that was what I'd heard? 'Don't know anything else about them. But my CI heard it's an eight-figure operation.'

'Jesus. Who's your informant?'

'Guy connected with the Sedutto crew.'

With some reverence, Kepler asked, 'Your guy's a confidential informant embedded with *Sedutto*? And he's still alive?'

As if irritated at the interruption, she said curtly, 'He's very good. And I pay him a lot of money to be good.'

The captain asked, 'What're Reardon and his crew into?'

'It's serious shit, Paul. Mostly cleaning money, some drugs, some guns. Offshore stuff. But the worst is he's hit at least a half-dozen people. A couple witnesses and some rivals. And one of the witnesses? Apparently the guy's family was with him. Killed them too.'

'Oh, man,' Surani said, shaking his head. He and Kepler were exploring adopting.

'Multimillion operation and hits,' the captain mused. He did not sound at all dismayed. Good press material, he'd be thinking. This was cynical but Kepler knew you had to consider image in this business. White Knight shit mattered at budget time, it mattered at promotion time. This was a game everybody learned and nobody felt guilty about playing.

'What do you have in mind for the set?' Barkley asked.

'It's going to be tricky. Reardon's smart. And suspicious as hell, according to my CI. I need to set up a fake office somewhere in Manhattan.'

'Office? What does that mean?' Barkley asked bluntly.

Her voice matched his: 'A company. A business, an *office*. Probably an investment firm. I don't need much. A couple of rooms, furniture. Some phony files I'll gin up myself. Decorations, props. The office'll be deserted – and half empty, like it was raided. That's part of my plan.'

'We're not Abscam, we don't have a lot of money.'

'What's Abscam?' Surani asked.

No one answered. Kepler reminded himself to explain to his partner that it was one of the biggest stings in U.S. history.

Gabby said, 'Won't cost us much. I was thinking we could use that place Narcotics closed up last month. It's just sitting empty. Midtown. Turtle Bay. Oh, and I'll need an unoccupied town house somewhere on the Upper East Side. Just for the exterior. The whole thing'll probably come in under a couple G's.'

Barkley grumbled, 'That's probably do-able.'

'I'll have IT put together a fake website for the company. I'll make it look like it was just raided. And I'll do a Facebook page for my cover identity. Simple stuff. But good enough to fool Reardon if he checks. Which he will.'

Barkley grunted once more. 'Hold up. You gotta convince me, Detective. Tell me more about Reardon.'

'Don't have a lot. I've datamined him. He's rich, lives fast. Owns a Maserati, but it's slower than his Porsche. He's got a fancy boat in Connecticut and another one in lower Manhattan.'

'Well, well,' said Surani. 'We're going after a whole new class of perps. Moving up in the world.'

'Or down,' Gabby corrected, frost in her voice. 'He kills families, remember?'

At least Kepler wasn't the only one she tapped with her whip.

'Reardon's single. Never married, though my CI tells me he sometimes claims he's divorced and sometimes he's a widower. He's got a loft in TriBeCa worth three million and a company on Wall Street. It's legit – he's involved in venture capital work. The Norwalk Fund. But he only made one point two million last year, according to his taxes. His lifestyle's five times that. So the investing's a cover for the money washing, arms sales and other things he does.'

'Maybe he just lies to the IRS about how much his legit company makes,' Kepler suggested.

'Not about his cover business. Why would he do that? Who'd do that? It's suicide. He's not stupid, Brad.'

Ouch.

Surani asked, 'And the partners? Andrew and Sam? They're connected to The Norwalk Fund?'

'I checked out the company, of course, trying to find their full names. And, no, they're not.'

Of course . . .

'So whatta you want to have happen out of this?' Barkley asked. He was known for his love of the big picture.

'I'll get close to Reardon, then lay out some bait, give him and Andrew and Sam the chance to hook up with my CI informant in something big. I'll be an innocent, so they'll have to take me out.'

'Nail them on criminal conspiracy,' Barkley said.

'Exactly. My CI, his name's Joseph'll be wired. As soon as they meet with him and mention the kill word, we can move in. And get warrants for their offices and houses. If we're lucky we can find something linking him to the earlier hits – weapons, records, cash transfers.'

'Seems like you've thought this through – like you always do, Detective. Tell me how you want to run it.'

She explained, 'My cover for the set will be Gabriela McKenzie, manager for the phony business I mentioned. I'm calling it Prescott Investments. It'll look like my boss – Charles Prescott – has been doing some kind of illegal stock trades. And you two have been investigating him for that. It's time for the bust, but he's disappeared. You come up to Reardon and me

n the street. You break the news about Prescott. That'll get Reardon's
attention. Then, after you leave, my Joseph comes up too. He'll tell me
that he was doing some illegal deals with Prescott and he's pissed he skipped
own. He'll ask me to hand over this mysterious list that's worth millions.'

Barkley asked. 'What's in the list?'

A good question, Kepler reflected.

'Doesn't matter,' she said dismissingly.

Or maybe not.

'It's a MacGuffin,' Gabby continued. 'Could be anything. But I've
decided to make it *seem* to Reardon like it's a list of underworld kingpins
involved in a plot to take down the stock exchange for a day or two and
clean up in a big way. I'll drop some clues for him to figure out. Like,
one of Prescott's clients is a German terrorist/arms dealer. I'm calling
him Gunther. The others are brokers or traders, mostly overseas. And
'm working on a lease that has to be signed up in the next few weeks
- for that property on Bankers' Square in Manhattan, where the stock
exchange is putting in a new communications system. Reardon may figure
it out from that, but to be on the safe side I'm going to hide this memo
in some files that I give him to examine, like I didn't know it was there.'

She slapped another document on the table.

From: Charles Prescott
To: Investment Syndicate
Re: Updated Timetable

2nd *of the month: New York Stock Exchange Technology Center, on
Bankers' Square in Lower Manhattan opens.*

4th *of the month: The lease for warehouse at 7 Bankers' Square is effec-
tive. Our 'engineers' arrive, with appropriate equipment to disable Technology
Center's fiber optic system, directly below warehouse.*

6th *of the month: U.S.-based investors exit jurisdiction to safe havens.
Recommended: Switzerland, Cayman, St Kitts, St Thomas.*

8th *of the month, 11 a.m.: The event occurs at warehouse. NYSE suspends
trading.*

$8^{th} - 9^{th}$: *Completion of short sales transactions made throughout the
year, distribution of profits to investors.*

'The target date's around Columbus Day, so I'm calling it the October
List – the people in the syndicate Prescott put together.'

'Love it,' Kepler said. He was truly impressed. If he played for the other team, he could easily fall in love with Gabriela.

She continued, 'Joseph's also going to demand back the deposit he paid Prescott. Four hundred thousand dollars, something like that.'

'Whoa, hold on – I can't come up with buy money like that,' the captain said quickly.

'No. I won't need actual cash. It's enough for Reardon to know the stakes are high. If the deposit's four hundred K, then the operation's dealing with serious cash. It'll seal the deal.'

Barkley asked, 'Why use your CI for the part? Why not an undercover detective?'

'Credibility. If Reardon checks around, he'll find Joseph's connected with the Seduttos. But, like I said, I *will* need at least a couple other officers, in addition to Brad and Naresh. I want Elena Rodriguez from Narcotics.'

'I'll try to swing it,' Barkley said.

Gabby said firmly, 'Make it work out. I need her. She's good.'

'What's her role in the set?' Barkley asked.

'She'll be a fellow employee of mine at Prescott.'

Surani: 'You said threaten you. How's Joseph going to pressure you into giving him the list?'

'He'll kidnap my daughter.'

Kepler blinked at this, surprised. She has a daughter? Gabby was the least maternal person he could think of.

She continued, 'Reardon'll stay close to me while I run around town trying to find the October List and the four hundred K. I'm sure he'll call in Andrew and Sam – they'll pretend they're helping me get my girl back. But what they'll really do is cut a deal with Joseph to sell him the list or go into business with him.'

'What if Reardon doesn't bite?' Kepler asked.

'Then you've wasted a day or two when you could be playing golf.'

'He doesn't play golf,' Surani said. 'He *watches* golf.'

Kepler gave him the finger. Subtly. And an affectionate glance.

'And I'm out two grand for the set,' Barkley grumbled.

She looked at him as if he were a husband making an extremely petty remark about starch in his shirts.

Only Gabby McNamara, of the thirty thousand cops in the NYPD, could nail brass with a look like that.

'So, Paul, can we go forward?'

Or use their first names.

He debated a moment. 'You got three days tops. We roll it up on Monday, whatever you find, or don't find.'

'Deal. Thanks.' Her gratitude extinguished fast. 'Now, a lot of the work's going to be convincing Reardon this's legitimate.' As if she were saying she had to drop her laundry off, Gabby said, 'I need to shoot a cop.'

Did she glance my way when she said that? Kepler wondered.

Barkley said firmly, 'No weapons discharges on the set. Can't happen.'

'I need to,' she said, and the words were all the more forceful because she was so blasé. 'If Reardon has any doubts, that'll put them to rest. We'll rig a gun with blanks or training rounds.' She steamrolled ahead. 'We'll get some youngster from Patrol. He'll be jazzed.'

Kepler said, 'No.'

Everyone turned to him, Gabby most piercingly. He said, 'You can't have Reardon next to you. The patrolman or witnesses would see him and he'd become a suspect. He'd go to ground or back off.'

'Good point. I hadn't thought of that. I'll make sure he's at a distance.'

Barkley pointed out, 'The press, the public, everybody'll go ape shit, a cop gets shot. Suddenly it's front-page *New York Post*. People're going to ask questions about him.'

She said, 'It'll happen on a deserted street. Upper East Side. That'll minimize witnesses. And we'll give the cop a fake name. I've checked and there's nobody on the force named Fred Stanford Chapman. My date to the high school prom. We'll get a fake name tag and have a phony press release ready. Tell the head of the Patrolman's union it's part of a set.'

She fixed Captain Barkley with a sniper rifle gaze. And she kept mum. He said reluctantly, 'I guess it'll work.'

'I've got the whole set orchestrated.' Gabby dug through her purse. Kepler noticed a roll of yarn, blue and green. He remembered she relaxed by knitting. It seemed strange at first but he wasted time on Angry Birds and Sudoku and, yes, *watching* golf. She extracted a single sheet of paper and put it on the table in front of them. 'This's the script, day by day, starting this afternoon. Memorize it now. It gets shredded before I leave. There'll be variations and improvisations but I'll text you as plans change.'

The three men eased forward and read.

Undercover Operation 2340-42
(Code Name: 'Charles Prescott Op')

Friday

— Det. McNamara, AKA Gabriela McKenzie, makes contact with Subject Daniel Reardon.

Saturday

— Dets. Kepler and Surani contact Det. McNamara and Subject Reardon re: Charles Prescott fleeing city.

— Confidential Informant Joseph contacts Det. McNamara and Subject Reardon about kidnapping of daughter (Sarah), extorting Det. McNamara to provide 'October List' and $.

— McNamara and Reardon attempt to find October List and $.

— With assistance of Det. Elena Rodriguez, Det. McNamara and Subject Reardon obtain access to Manhattan set location, 'Prescott Investments.' Locate October List.

— At said location, Det. McNamara and Subject Reardon are confronted by Dets. Kepler and Surani but manage to smuggle October List out of Prescott Investments. Adds to credibility of its importance. Clues given to Subject Reardon about possible financial scam.

— Det. McNamara and Subject Reardon remain undercover, attempting to find $, while appearing to negotiate with C.I. Joseph, as the 'kidnapper.'

Sunday

— Det. McNamara and Subject Reardon attempt to find money at townhouse of Charles Prescott's lover, Upper East Side. Intercepted by Dets. Kepler and Surani and Patrol Officer using fictional name Fred Stanford Chapman. Stage shooting of Chapman. Det. McNamara and Subject Reardon flee. Det. McNamara feigns injury in escape.

— If he hasn't done so already, Subject Reardon will probably contact partners, Andrew and Sam, under guise of helping Det. McNamara secure release of daughter.

— Subject Reardon and either/or Andrew and Sam meet with CI Joseph, with intent to engage in conspiracy to defraud and murder Detective McNamara. CI or site of meeting will be wired. CI will relay location information to Det. McNamara.

— Tactical takedown of Reardon, Andrew and Sam by Emergency Service.

Barkley was obviously impressed, though he tried not to show it. 'Man. It *is* a script.'

She said matter-of-factly, 'With people like Reardon, you don't improvise.'

He kills families . . .

Kepler asked, 'You're sure Reardon'll run with you?'

'He'll come along. I'll make sure of it.'

'How're you going to snag him?'

'Every Friday afternoon he swims at Battery Park Health Club—'

'Or plays racquetball or tennis,' Kepler pointed out fast.

She swiveled toward him. 'The only reason to join that particular club is for tennis or the pool. My datamining shows he's never paid for court time or bought balls. *Ergo*, he swims.'

I stand corrected. And she speaks Greek. Or was it Latin? What a woman. The other team was looking more and more interesting.

'After that he goes to Limoncello's for drinks.'

'What's Limoncello's?'

'Restaurant on the harbor.' Gabby was getting pretty proficient at talking to Kepler while not looking at him. She continued to Barkley, 'He generally has scotch or red wine. I'll have some small bottles of each with me. I'll see what he's drinking and go to the ladies' room, spill some on my sleeve. Make him think he's stained my blouse. I'll take it from there.'

On reflection, Kepler was thinking, Gabby might *not* be the best woman in the world to date.

'What do you mean that you "feign injury"?' Surani asked, tapping the script.

'I'll have to seem vulnerable. To make Reardon believe I'm no threat. I'll probably fall then bite the inside of my cheek – to make it look like I'm bleeding from a broken rib and ruptured lung. Also, it seems Reardon's a bit of a sadist. My being in pain'll be a turn-on.'

'You'd be armed?' Surani asked.

'How can I be? I'm an office manager of an investment company.' A glance at the script she'd written.

'A wire then,' Kepler offered.

Gabby said, 'No.' Frowning as if infinitely perplexed he didn't get it.

Surani said, 'We've got some good gadgets from the tech department, Gabriela, surveillance gear, I mean. We've got a GPS and mike in a cigarette lighter—'

'You'd give me a cigarette lighter when I don't smoke? What's Reardon going to do with that?'

'I'm just saying. Something.'

'No. No wires. And no third-party surveillance either. You two and everybody . . . keep your distance. I can't take any chances that Reardon'll tip to the set. That's the biggest danger. He hasn't survived this long by being careless. Now, read the script until you've got it memorized.'

She pushed the pages forward and, like students in front of a stern teacher, Surani and Kepler did as she instructed. When they'd nodded, Gabby swept it up and walked to a shredder. She plugged the unit in and made confetti. Then she slung her purse over her shoulder. She said to the detectives, 'I'll email you more details tonight. Intercept us on the corner near my apartment around ten or eleven.'

Surani recited, '"Detectives Kepler and Surani contact Detective McNamara and Subject Reardon re: Charles Prescott fleeing city."'

Her first and only smile. 'Good.'

Kepler said, 'One thing?'

Gabby regarded him seriously. 'Yes?'

'Your CI, this Joseph. You trust him?'

'Pretty much I do.'

'Pretty much,' Kepler echoed. 'Okay, Joseph's boss? Sedutto? He's trouble; you know that. Is there any chance Joseph's running *you*? I mean, maybe he's thinking that Reardon's a source for some big money. And he'll take you out too when he gets what he needs.'

The best confidential informants were morally always just an inch away from the perps they were embedded with.

Would Gabby be pissed off that he'd questioned her judgment in trusting this Joseph?

But she said only, 'I appreciate that, Brad. But I've assessed the risk and it's acceptable. Not much we can do about that.'

Then she was gone.

'Well, that's one hell of a gal,' Barkley said.

A noun that neither Kepler nor his partner wanted to go anywhere near.

The captain then said, 'I want eyes and ears on her.'

'But,' Surani pointed out, 'she said no surveillance.'

'I don't care what she said. I want to know everything she says and where she goes and who she sees. Twenty-four/seven. This's too dangerous to leave her spinning in the wind. Get on that now.'

CHAPTER
1

8:20 a.m., Friday

2 hours, 40 minutes earlier

'I'm going to tell you what I need. I need someone dead. Someone who's bad and who's been troublesome and has caused me and other people a great deal of pain. It's a simple goal – a killing – but there are complications. A lot of complications.'

Peter Karpankov paused, as if these words were too dramatic. Or perhaps not dramatic enough, ineffectual in conveying the magnitude of the sins he wanted justice for. Today his weathered skin was more wan than normal and he seemed sixty years of age, not his actual fifty. The man's bullet-shaped head, dusted with short, thinning hair, was looking out the window of Karpankov Transportation, Inc., a medium-sized company, which he had run for years, inherited from his father. The building, unimpressive and scuffed, squatted in Midtown, near the Hudson River. He had enough money to build a large, modern facility, but he kept the company's original building. The same way he lived in the same two-thousand-square-foot red-brick detached house in Brighton Beach, Brooklyn, that had been in his family for nearly a hundred years.

His eyes still averted, Karpankov continued speaking. 'I didn't know where else to turn for help – because of the complications, you understand. And because I would have a clear motive for this man's death. I'd be a suspect. That's why I need you. You can make sure that the motives aren't what they seem to be. You're good at that. No, not good. You're the best.'

He finally turned and his eyes met those of the woman across the desk. Gabriela McNamara looked back easily, taking all this in. 'Go on, Peter.'

'Oh, and for this job, I'll double your fee. Plus all expenses, of course.'

Karpankov didn't need to mention the latter. He always paid for her expenses when she did a job for him. A murder or anything else.

Gabriela's green eyes focused on his, which were, curiously, two shades of gray.

The mob boss continued with a raw anger in his voice, 'I wish I could kill him myself. Oh, I do wish that. But . . .'

Gabriela knew Karpankov had not killed anyone in a long time. Still, the lean-faced man with the two-tone eyes, and matching gray stubble on his scalp, looked fully capable of murder at the moment.

She felt warm breath on her hand. She looked down; Karpankov's huge dog, Gunther, had ambled from his bed in the corner to lick her palm. She scratched the spiky gray and black fur between his ears. Gabriela knew animals; she'd hunted with bird dogs from when she was a teenager. She and the Russian's dog had bonded when he was a puppy. He was huge now. A month ago Gunther had killed a hired assassin who'd lunged at Karpankov on a walk in Brooklyn. Lightning-fast, the dog had snatched the assailant by the throat and shaken the life from the screaming attacker. Murdering the man who'd hired him – a Jamaican drug lord – had been Gabriela's most recent job for Karpankov.

The dog licked her fingers again, nuzzled and returned to his bed.

'What's his name, the man you want dead?'

'Daniel Reardon.'

'I don't know him.'

Now it was Gabriela who looked at the Hudson River through the window, which was free of curtains. The putty in the frame was curling and needed replacing. She felt an urge to strip out the old wads and replace them and paint. She did a lot of the repair work herself, in her apartment in the city and at her hunting lodge upstate, in the Adirondacks, where she frequently hunted – both with her Nikon camera and with her Winchester .270.

Karpankov now touched his cheek, then the fingers settled on the chin. Rubbed it as if searching for stray bristles he'd neglected to smooth off that morning, though the skin seemed perfectly planed to Gabriela. He muttered words in Russian. 'Hui blyad cyka.'

Gabriela was adept at languages. Since she worked frequently in Brooklyngrad and the other Eastern European immigrant areas of New York, she'd learned Russian. She understood 'cocksucker.'

She asked, 'What's Reardon's story?'

'You know Carole?'

'Carole? The daughter of your assistant, Henry?'

'That's right.'

'Pretty girl. Teenager?'

'Twenty.'

'Henry's been with you a long time.' Gabriela had noted, upon arriving, that Henry had not been at his desk in the anteoffice and he was not here at the moment. Usually he was a constant shadow.

'Eighteen years. He's like a brother to me.'

Karpankov's tone – more than his earlier words – explained that this would be a hard story to tell.

He turned and poured some Stolichnaya into a glass. He offered it to her. She shook her head. He tossed down the whole glass then began the story. 'Reardon picked Carole up in a bar. Took her back to an apartment his company keeps for clients. The Norwalk Fund. Somewhere on the East Side, in the Fifties. He seduced her, though it was really rape. He drugged her. He took pictures of her. Disgusting pictures. He tied her down on an iron coffee table. He used these tight knots he knows because he sails boats. It was like a game with him. She couldn't move. Then he beat her with a riding crop.' His voice choked. 'The pain was terrible . . . the pain.'

After another shot of vodka and a dozen slow breaths: 'Then he and another man, they took turns . . . well, you understand. That was filmed too. Her face was visible, not theirs. Reardon threatened to put the videos out on the Internet. My God, Carole was in college, she taught at Sunday school! That would destroy her life.'

Gabriela took this information in with a faint nod. Her heart-shaped face revealed no reaction. To her these were just facts. Though she knew and liked Henry, she felt no personal interest in the matter whatsoever.

The ease of making this separation was part of her gift.

If gift it was.

Karpankov continued, 'Reardon used the pictures to force Henry to divulge information about my operation. Computer files, passwords. Reardon and his associates broke into our system and stole nearly four hundred thousand dollars before we shut down the servers. Henry tried to kill himself. He took pills. I went to the hospital and he confessed what had happened.' After a pause. 'I forgave him.'

'Carole?'

'What can I say? She'll never be the same.'

Gabriela nodded.

On his large desk were papers and files and printouts and a large collection of model cars. Expensive ones. Metal. You could open the doors and hoods and look inside. They were really quite some works of art. Aside from the phonograph records the Professor had given her, Gabriela didn't collect anything. There were no trophies in the upstate house; she hunted for the meat. And weapons? They were simply tools of the trade, to be discarded or swapped if a more efficient one came along.

'So. Reardon? He's after your company?'

Karpankov Transport didn't transport much except laundered money, weapons and prostitutes – though, despite such limited specialties, it made a great deal of money.

'I think what happened with Carole was opportunistic. Reardon struck up a conversation with her, learned her father worked for a profitable company and he took advantage of that.'

'He and this other man? It's just the two of them?'

'No, there are three who work together. One is Andrew. There's an enforcer too, first name Sam.' Karpankov added solemnly, 'I think Sam was the second man with Carole.'

'That's their modus operandi? Finding innocents and exploiting them?'

Karpankov laughed. '"Modus operandi." You studied Latin, I remember. Your father told me that. He was very proud of his schoolgirl.'

Her father had gone to the police academy right out of high school, but he appreciated education and had indeed been proud that his only child had graduated with honors from Fordham. He himself had taken continuing education courses, specializing in history, and would spend hours talking about New York's past with Gabriela and her mother. They'd good-naturedly dubbed him 'the Professor,' and the nickname had stuck.

'It's *one* of his MOs,' Karpankov now said. His voice trembled; the sentiment of a moment ago was gone. 'They come up with a lot of different schemes – extortion, blackmail, kidnapping, outright murder. Sometimes they masquerade as business consultants or insurance experts. They get close to executives, find inside information, learn their weaknesses.'

'Businessmen, insurance?' Gabriela mused. She found this an interesting strategy. She filed the fact away for her plans, which were already forming. 'So you want Reardon dead, you want me to find out who Andrew and Sam are. And them dead too. And your money back?'

'That's right.' Karpankov pulled a model car closer to him. She thought it was a Jaguar. She didn't know much about autos. In the Adirondacks, she kept a thousand-cc Honda motorcycle.

The mob boss continued, 'I don't care about the money but—'

'Respect.'

'Exactly. Respect and revenge. You see what I mean by complicated?'

It was, yes.

But Gabriela lived for complications. She straightened her jacket, small white and black checks, houndstooth. And smoothed her skirt, which was gray as the Hudson's unsettled water this morning. From her orange leather Coach bag Gabriela took a roll of knitting, blue and green yarn, and began absently working the needles.

Click click click competed with the sound of trucks from outside Karpankov's window. He said nothing.

'Tell me what you know about Reardon,' she asked, matter-of-factly, which was her way of saying, Yes, I'll take on the job. Of course I will.

'He's in his late thirties. Good looking. Here.' He displayed a picture of a dark-haired businessman.

Good looking enough, yes, she decided. Broad shoulders. Gabriela felt a stirring, though only partly because of his physique and curious resemblance to the George Clooney of ten years ago. The attraction was primarily due to his narrow eyes. Cruel, they seemed. Savvy. Predatory.

'Ink?'

'Apparently no tattoos,' Karpankov said. 'But he has a scar – on his chest and shoulder. He set a bomb in an arson scam and it went off prematurely. Apparently he claims he got it saving two children from a car crash, or when somebody saved *him* from a crash. He changes the story to suit the scenario.

'He has a degree in business from an Ivy League university. And he has a legitimate investment company he runs as a cover. The Norwalk Fund I mentioned. Makes a lot of money and spends it. Cars and boats. But he's also a sociopath. Last spring Andrew and he killed a man who threatened to be a witness against him. Reardon could have shot the man when he was alone. But he killed the family too. I have to believe part of him killed them that way because he enjoyed it. The wife was tortured and raped. Sadist, I was saying – like with Carole.'

Gabriela, knitting.

She closed her eyes, letting thoughts churn. Karpankov remained silent; she'd worked for him for years and he knew how her mind spun, when to speak, when to demur. For several minutes she was in a very different place. Making order out of tangle. And he said not a word.

When she surfaced she was for a split second actually surprised that she wasn't alone. She re-centered herself. 'I have some ideas. I'll need somebody else to help. Muscle. Not afraid of dirty hands. Better if he didn't have too much of a connection to you.'

Karpankov thought for a moment. 'There's somebody I use on a free-lance basis. He's good. Very smart.'

'And he has no problem with?'

The sentence didn't need to be finished.

'None at all. He's done a dozen jobs for me. He's here now, as a matter of fact. Downstairs,' Karpankov said.

'Let's talk to him.' Her eyes settled on Gunther again. He looked back. His tail thumped with pleasure.

Karpankov made a call, politely asking the man to join them. Then disconnected. 'What are you making?' A nod toward the yarn. Green and blue.

Reminding of a song she liked. James Taylor.

She said, 'It's going to be a shawl.' She gazed at the tips of the needles. Ideas were coming quickly.

Five minutes later there was a knock on the door and Karpankov called, 'Come in.'

A large man with blond hair, thick and curly, and a square-jawed face, stepped into the room and shook Karpankov's hand. 'Peter.' His eyes were confident and he glanced at Gabriela without curiosity or lust or condescension.

'This is Gabriela McNamara.'

'Joseph Astor.' The man's face was a mask as he regarded her. He apparently didn't know who she was, or care. That was good. Reputations were useless. Like praise and insults and high school sports trophies.

Hands were shaken. His skin was rough. She detected a faint scent she identified as shave cream, not aftershave. He sat in the other office chair. It groaned. Joseph wasn't fat but he was solid, built like a supporting column.

'You go by "Gabriela"?'

'Yes, I hate nicknames.' To her, 'Gabby' was a particular gnat. The only nickname she'd ever liked was her father's. To him she was Mac. As he was the Professor to her.

'And,' Karpankov said, 'I hate it when people call me "Pete."'

The other of the triumvirate here said nothing but she sensed 'Joe' was not a felicitous option.

The dark red needles tapped their dull tips. Karpankov explained the situation about Reardon to Joseph, much as he'd explained it to her. Then he added, 'Gabriela is taking on the job of finding these men and eliminating them. She's asked for an associate to help.'

Joseph said, 'Sure. Whatever I can do.'

Silence, save for the clicking of the needles. Finally she said to Joseph, 'What I'll be doing is putting together a set. You know the word "set"?'

'Police talk for undercover operation. Like a play, sort of.'

'I still have to think out the details – I'll do that over the next few hours. But in essence I'll get some people at my regular job to put together an operation, a sting, to catch Reardon and his associates. It'll seem like some police officers're after me, so that Reardon'll believe I've got access to a lot of money and some secrets or something like that. With the cops after me, he'll be inclined to believe it's legitimate. I can talk my captain into it, I'm sure.'

'Police?' Joseph said, confusion hazing his face. 'Your captain?'

Gabriela said, 'I'm a police officer.'

'You're . . .'

'I'll call and set up a meeting with them, my captain and a couple of other detectives in a few hours.'

'The police?' Joseph repeated, though with less uncertainty than before.

Karpankov filled in, 'Gabriela's a decorated NYPD detective. That job has been . . . helpful to us. As you can imagine.'

Joseph gave no reaction other than a time-delayed nod. He then lifted an eyebrow. 'How did you happen to end up there?'

'My father was NYPD too,' she said calmly. 'I followed in his footsteps. I was interested in photography—'

'She's good,' Karpankov broke in. 'Real good.' He gestured to a black-and-white landscape on his wall. 'That's one of hers.'

Joseph reviewed the image without reaction and looked back.

Gabriela continued. 'I took a job with the Crime Scene unit as a photographer. One day we got a call in Queens. A shootout. Nobody checked my last name, and it turned out that my father was the victim.'

'Well.' Joseph's brows dipped.

'There wasn't any mystery; he was killed by friendly fire. Two junior detectives just emptied their guns at a kid they thought was an armed rapist – he wasn't either of those, by the way. The investigators screwed up and had the wrong man. The supposed suspect was wounded superficially. My father – he was backing them up – was hit six times and died instantly.

'When the lead detective realized who I was they took me off the case – conflict of interest, of course – but I shot plenty of pictures anyway. I wanted to record who the killers were, his fellow cops.'

'They went to jail?' Joseph inquired.

'No. My father's death was deemed accidental. They were suspended for two weeks – with pay. Then returned to duty. Like nothing had happened.'

'They're still on the force?'

'They're no longer with us,' she said quietly. Then she looked at Joseph. 'But aren't you really asking how I ended up *here*, working with Peter?'

'Yeah, I guess I am.'

'After Dad's death, my mother fell apart. She was sick, emotionally sick, even before it happened. His death destroyed her. The department and the city didn't do anything for her. It was like they couldn't admit they'd screwed up. But Peter showed up on our doorstep. He saved her life, got her into a hospital. His wife took care of her too. It turned out that Dad had worked for Peter all along. I decided I was going to do the same.'

'I didn't want her to at first,' Karpankov said. 'But she was persistent. I'm glad she was. Ralph McNamara was helpful getting my organization inside information about investigations and the like. Gabriela's been helpful with that . . . and with other skills.'

Gabriela didn't tell Joseph that her father's nature was ingrained within her. She could recall dozens of incidents at school where she'd ended up in the principal's office, often along with security or even the police, after she'd lost it – madly attacking a girl or boy who'd bullied her or another student. The Professor's status as a respected detective protected her from the juvenile system and he helped her learn to control her urges toward violence.

But control only, never eliminate.

Now Gabriela disposed of family history with a click of knitting needles. 'So, with Reardon, we'll have the NYPD help us.' Ideas were continuing to come fast. This was how it always worked. The mind is an inventive and fertile creature. Some thoughts she discarded, some she wrestled into shape, some she let stand as perfectly formed components of her scheme. Her palms were damp with sweat and her heart beat a fast, visceral rhythm.

Joseph asked, 'What can I do?'

'I'll explain to my captain and the police that you're a confidential informant working for me. That'll let me keep you anonymous. We'll use only your first name. I'll be Gabriela . . . *McKenzie*.' Her eyes had taken in the brand name on the label of a bottle of whisky sitting on the credenza behind Karpankov. 'Gabriela McKenzie, a businesswoman of some sort, and you'll be extorting me for a lot of money.' A faint thud as an idea emerged. It was gold. 'We'll pretend you've kidnapped my daughter.'

'You have a daughter?'

'No. I don't have any children. But you come up to me when I'm with Reardon and tell me that you've kidnapped her and you'll kill Sarah if I don't get you what you want.'

'Your daughter's going to be Sarah?'

'That's right. It's the name of my horse. A filly I stable upstate and ride on weekends. But we'll download some pictures of a six year old. Videos, too.'

Joseph nodded. 'People're idiots, how much they post online.'

'Isn't that the truth.'

'What am I going to want from you that's worth kidnapping a little girl?'

Another idea occurred. Sometimes they fell like snow. 'A document. A secret list. Very valuable. A list that everybody wants – which means Reardon'll want it too.'

'A MacGuffin,' Joseph said.

'What's that?' Peter Karpankov asked.

Gabriela said, 'Hitchcock.' She was surprised Joseph knew the term. Not because he seemed ignorant – just the opposite – but he was only in his forties and the film director had coined the term more than a half century ago. She explained to Peter Karpankov, 'A MacGuffin's a thing, an *object* that everybody's chasing after in a suspense movie. The treasure of Sierra Madre, the lost ark, the NOC list of secret agents. Doesn't matter that it doesn't even exist. It's what drives the story forward. I'll come up with some bomb plot or something equally ridiculous. Blow up a bank. Or take out the stock market for a few hours. The implication is that the people on the list stand to make a fortune when that happens. Short selling stock maybe.'

Joseph said, 'What about we call this list something mysterious? Give it a name.'

Karpankov suggested, 'I have an idea. How about the October List?'

Gabriela nodded. 'Good, I like it. But why that?'

'The wife and I went to the Hofbrau last night, Third Avenue Thursday's Oktoberfest night. The best Wiener Schnitzel and Sauerbrater in the city. Oktoberfest . . . October List. Just occurred to me.'

'Perfect. It's mid September; I'll drop clues that whatever's going to happen'll happen next month. Now, Joseph, you want this mysterious list. And some money too. Reardon stole four hundred thousand from Peter. But let's go for five – interest payment.'

The Russian nodded.

'How will you get the cash from them?' Joseph asked.

She considered this for a moment. 'Ah, Reardon'll come up with it for me to pay as the ransom. He'll hit one of his accounts and cough up the money. Of course, what he'll really use it for is to pay you – as an incentive to do business with them. Only you can tell them how to best use the October List. They'll need you for that.'

Joseph too had a thought. 'Let's start out with four hundred thousand but to add believability, maybe you could miss a deadline and I up the ante to five hundred thousand.'

'Yes, I like that.' Her eyes shone. 'And when I miss that deadline, you send me something of my daughter's to show you mean business.' She happened to glance down at her fingernails, which were dark red. 'Maybe . . . I know, a bloody finger.'

'What?' Karpankov blurted.

She gave a smile. 'Just from a mannequin or a doll. Get some fake blood. Or buy a bloody steak.'

Joseph nodded, as if this were the most logical idea in the world.

She continued to him, 'We'll play it out till Sunday night. You pick a target zone – a safe house somewhere – and arrange to meet them When they show up, you kill them.'

Joseph considered this. 'I've got a warehouse in SoHo I'm just about finished with. I'll use that. They think I've kidnapped your daughter right? The place has a room in the back. I'll put on some kids' video in there. When they go to check it out and open the door, I'll take care of them from behind.' Then he frowned. 'But what'll you tell your captain? If it's an undercover sting, won't they be expecting to get evidence, from a wire or something?'

It was a good point but she'd thought that through. 'I'll tell them that you – my CI – went rogue, killed Reardon and the others and stole the money. Then vanished. Nobody trusts CIs anyway. It won't look too great – a failed operation – but the fact is, my captain won't be very pissed off. After Reardon's dead, we'll search his houses and office; we should be able to close a half-dozen cases he and his crew were behind. And they'll've saved the expense of trial.'

'Brilliant, Gabriela,' Karpankov said reverently.

Tap, tap.

Gabriela added a lengthy row to the shawl she was knitting. She had another thought. 'You know, Peter, it would be helpful if it looked like there was someone *else* after me. It'll draw Reardon into the set more if he feels there's another player after the October List too. Make it seem that much more valuable. Any thoughts?'

Now Karpankov, sitting back, was the one scanning the ceiling with his gray-and-gray eyes. 'Would it make sense if this person died?'

'Interesting idea,' she replied. 'It *could* work. Why?'

'I'm aware of something.'

'Yes?'

'There's someone . . . this piss-ant from Brooklyn. Thinks he's the Godfather. Hal Dixon. Do you know him?'

'I think I've heard the name.'

'He's been talking about moving into Manhattan and Jersey. I've been thinking about taking him out. This could be the chance.'

Gabriela smoothed her skirt as she considered the additional player. She said to Karpankov, 'You could meet with Dixon. Tell him you've heard that there's this October List and that I have it. Give him the job to get it. When he comes after me, I'll make sure nobody can see me and take him out. Afterward, I'll tell my captain it was Reardon who did it.'

This brought up another thought, and the yarn ended up in her lap. 'There's a personal situation *I* need to deal with too.'

She squinted slightly as she explained, 'I've been having some trouble with someone. It goes back a month or so. I'd finished a job and had taken care of the body, but the police were closer than I thought. I ducked into a movie theater and picked up this guy, so we could leave like a couple. It worked. But the problem is, he didn't go away. It cost me a couple of dates. He's turned into a bit of a stalker. He spies on me, shows up outside my apartment. He could eventually make the connection that I work for Peter. He's even taken pictures of me when he thinks I don't know.' Her lips tugged into a grimace. 'He's pretty sick – he's got a shoe thing. He starts salivating when he sees me in high heels. Takes pictures of me with his mobile, and always makes sure he gets my shoes in the frame. Damn pervert.' She shrugged. 'It would be helpful if he died too.'

Joseph asked, 'What's his name?'

'Frank Walsh.' She described him and added, 'Let's frame Reardon for his murder too.' She resumed knitting. The men looked at the aluminum needles. She got the impression they'd be wondering if she'd ever killed anyone with them. She never had. 'I know what would work. After Reardon and I find the list, I'll arrange to get it to Frank for safe-keeping, maybe have it delivered to him. I'll make sure Reardon's prints are on the envelope or box or whatever I put it in. Peter, could you arrange for one of your men to be in the building we use for the set? Pretend to be a janitor. I'll have him deliver it to Frank.'

'Sure. How about Rafael?'

'Yeah, he's good.' Then she said to Joseph, 'After the package is delivered – on Sunday – you go to Frank's, shoot him and get whatever evidence has Reardon's prints or DNA on it. So it'll be at the target zone when you take Reardon and his associates out. But get Frank's mobile and wipe his hard drive. He'll have pictures of me on it.'

Joseph nodded. Then he said, 'Your associates – the detectives, your captain – they'll want to run surveillance on you. That could be a problem.'

She grimaced. 'I know. Even after I tell them not to, they'll try to put some eyes on me. I'll just have to keep it in mind and make sure I lose any tails or electronic snooping.'

Putting down the knitting, Gabriela sat forward. She was pleased with Joseph, liked that he was smart and that he looked back into her eyes so easily, without challenge or timidity or flirt. 'Now, before we go any farther, I want to say something: Obviously you're familiar with movies. You know what method acting is?'

'I've heard about it. Don't really know exactly.'

'It's when actors mentally and emotionally become the characters they're playing. For this to work, to fool Reardon and make sure you and I both survive, I'm going to *be* the office manager and single mother I've created. Gabriela McKenzie. Gabriela *McNamara* will cease to exist.'

She didn't share with Joseph or Karpankov that this would be an all-consuming transformation. She'd move into a different place entirely. She'd repeat the name of her fictional daughter over and over again – aloud and to herself – until the girl came alive. She'd come to believe that if she didn't deliver the October List and the cash, she'd never see her beloved Sarah again. She'd feel regret at the death of Hal Dixon. At Frank Walsh's too, even though he was in reality an irritating complication in her life. She'd feel genuine fear the police were after her. And she'd form a real attraction to Reardon, as if they'd mutually picked up each other in the bar, a spark igniting what might turn into a real relationship. She might even fuck him.

And after Joseph shot Reardon dead, she'd go through a period of mourning.

Gabriela was good at what she did precisely because she tricked herself as smoothly as she did her victims.

She looked levelly at Joseph. 'You understand?'

'Yes.'

'I need you to do the same thing.'

'I get it.' Joseph looked off for a moment. 'You know, talking about acting. What do you think about this? I could be like that actor who died, the one in that *Batman* movie a few years ago. Heath Ledger, the Joker. Taunting, unpredictable, eerie.'

'I like that. And what was his philosophy?' she reflected, thinking back to the film. 'The only good is what furthers my interest. That'll be your driving force.'

Joseph cocked his head. '"The only good is what furthers my interest." I'll remember that. I like it.' Then he asked, 'One question, at the kill zone? You'll be there too?'

She considered this. 'No, they won't want me there. Reardon and one of the others will want to meet with you alone. They'll leave me with a babysitter, probably Sam – a safe house somewhere.' A look at Karpankov. 'Most likely the same place they took Carole, that apartment in Midtown, the one his company keeps.' Then she said to Joseph, 'I'll text you the exact location when I know.'

'You'll have a weapon with you?' Joseph asked.

'No. I can't. But I'm sure Sam will.' She thought back to Reardon's pattern. 'Reardon will probably be planning on coming back to the safe house after he cuts a deal with you – probably to finish me off himself. And, considering what he did to Carole, I imagine he and Sam may have other plans for me first. More rope and knots.

'So after you kill Reardon and Andrew, get the key to the safe house and come over there. If there's a chain or security bar on the door, I'll take it off. You text me when you're close and I'll distract Sam or Andrew or whoever my babysitter is. I'll tell him I've figured out the mystery of the

October List, or something like that. You let yourself in. Whoever's there probably will think it's the other two returning and not be too suspicious.

'But we should be careful. When I hear the door open I'll say one of two things. If I say "Is my daughter all right?" that'll mean Sam doesn't have a weapon out. He doesn't suspect anything. It's safe to just walk in and shoot him. But if I say, "Daniel, what happened?" then that means he *is* suspicious and has his weapon. Get back into the hall. It'll be a firefight. I'll take cover and do what I can from inside.'

Joseph nodded. '"Is my daughter all right?" means I'm green-lighted to shoot. "Daniel, what happened?" means take cover.'

'That's right.'

'Got it.'

'Good.' Gabriela slipped the yarn and the half-finished shawl back into her bag. She glanced affectionately at Gunther, who wagged his tail once more. She rose, shook Karpankov's hand then Joseph's. 'So. Let's get to work.'

Foreword

We have Stephen Sondheim to thank for this book. Several years ago I was listening to a National Public Radio interview by the inimitable Terry Gross, on her *Fresh Air* program, with Sondheim, one of my favorite musical theater composers and lyricists. One of the plays he discussed was *Merrily We Roll Along*, which happened to be perhaps the only play of his I had not seen. I was fascinated by the fact that it began in the present and moved back in time. Of particular interest was his comment about a song that meant one thing in the present and meant something different when first (well, later) introduced.

I happen to love the concept of a fractured time line. Look at Stanley Kubrick's second best film, *The Killing* (*Strangelove* – not *2001* – is my number one), or *Pulp Fiction, Memento, Back to the Future*. And, of course, the classic *Seinfeld* episode 'The Betrayal,' which was an homage to Harold Pinter's own reverse-chronology play, *Betrayal*.

I began wondering if it was possible for a thriller writer to pull off a backward-told story that was filled with the cliffhangers, surprises and twists and turns that are, to me, the epitome of good crime fiction. The task, of course, is to present the twist (the 'reveal' as they say in Hollywoodspeak) *before* giving the facts that led up to it and still make the surprise thrilling. It's like telling a joke's punch line first, then giving the set-up itself – and yet still making the audience laugh just as hard as if they'd heard the gag in proper order. It *can* be done:

The bartender says, 'We don't serve time travelers in here.'

A time traveler walks into a bar.

Many, many Post-it notes later I plotted out and wrote *The October List* – a novel that begins with the last chapter and then moves backward in time, over the course of about two days, to the first chapter. Though it's a bit shorter than most of my novels, I can say that it was more challenging, byte for byte, than anything I've previously written.

Because of my heroine's passion for photography, I thought I would include images throughout the book, at the beginning of each chapter. Some are merely illustrative. But some are clues as to mysteries the book holds, and some are twists in themselves. As Gabriela has said, 'There's something seductive about taking reality and controlling it. Sometimes I make a literal image, sometimes I start there and manipulate it. Sometimes the end result is obscure, abstract; only I know the truth.'

I couldn't agree more.

Rather than give the titles to the pictures where they appear in the book, I thought it was best to include them in the table of contents. That surprise thing, again.

– J.D., Chapel Hill, NC

Acknowledgments

With special thanks for taking a chance on this one (and helping me get as backward as was humanly possible) to Mitch Hoffman and Carolyn Mays. Thanks too to Jamie Hodder-Williams, Michael Pietsch, Jamie Raab, Lindsey Rose, Katy Rouse and David Young. And I really appreciate all the juggling my regular crew did to keep this book on track and me more or less sane: Madelyn Warcholik, Julie Deaver, Deborah Schneider, Cathy Gleason, Vivienne Schuster, Betsy Robbins, Sophie Baker, Jane Davis, Will and Tina Anderson and Hazel Orme.

About the Author

A former journalist, folksinger and attorney, Jeffery Deaver is an international number-one bestselling author. His novels have appeared on bestseller lists around the world, including the *New York Times*, the *Times* of London, Italy's *Corriere della Sera*, the *Sydney Morning Herald* and the *Los Angeles Times*. His books are sold in 150 countries and translated into twenty-five languages.

The author of thirty novels, two collections of short stories and a nonfiction law book, he's received or been shortlisted for a number of awards around the world. His *The Bodies Left Behind* was named Novel of the Year by the International Thriller Writers Association, and his Lincoln Rhyme thriller *The Broken Window* and a stand-alone, *Edge*, were also nominated for that prize. He has been awarded the Steel Dagger and the Short Story Dagger from the British Crime Writers' Association and the Nero Wolfe Award, and he is a three-time recipient of the Ellery Queen Readers Award for Best Short Story of the Year and a winner of the British Thumping Good Read Award. *The Cold Moon* was recently named the Book of the Year by the Mystery Writers Association of Japan, as well as by *Kono Mystery Wa Sugoi* magazine. In addition, the Japanese Adventure Fiction Association awarded *The Cold Moon* and *Carte Blanche* their annual Grand Prix award.

He contributed to the anthology *Books To Die For*, which won the Agatha Award this year.

His most recent novels are *The Kill Room*, featuring Lincoln Rhyme, *XO*, a Kathryn Dance thriller, for which he wrote an album of country-western songs, available on iTunes and as a CD, and before that,

Carte Blanche, the latest James Bond continuation novel, a number-one international bestseller.

Deaver has been nominated for seven Edgar Awards from the Mystery Writers of America, an Anthony Award and a Gumshoe Award. He was recently shortlisted for the ITV3 Crime Thriller Award for Best International Author.

His book *A Maiden's Grave* was made into an HBO movie starring James Garner and Marlee Matlin, and his novel *The Bone Collector* was a feature release from Universal Pictures, starring Denzel Washington and Angelina Jolie. And, yes, the rumors are true; he did appear as a corrupt reporter on his favorite soap opera, *As the World Turns*. He was born outside Chicago and has a bachelor of journalism degree from the University of Missouri and a law degree from Fordham University.

Readers can visit his website at www.jefferydeaver.com.

Contents

And Titles of Photographs

To Frank, Maureen and Caitlyn Jewett

First published in the United States of America in 2013 by Grand Central Publishing

First published in Great Britain in 2013 by Hodder & Stoughton
An Hachette UK company

1

Text and photographs copyright © Gunner Publications, LLC 2013

A CIP catalogue record for this title is available from the British Library

Hardback ISBN 978 1 444 78043 7
Trade paperback ISBN 978 1 444 78044 4
Ebook ISBN 978 1 444 78045 1

Typeset in Fairfield LH by Palimpsest Book Production Ltd, Falkirk, Stirlingshire

Printed and bound by Clays Ltd, St Ives plc

Hodder & Stoughton policy is to use papers that are natural, renewable and recyclable
products and made from wood grown in sustainable forests. The logging and
manufacturing processes are expected to conform to the environmental regulations of the
country of origin.

Hodder & Stoughton Ltd
338 Euston Road
London NW1 3BH

www.hodder.co.uk

Also by Jeffery Deaver

Mistress of Justice
The Lesson of Her Death
Praying for Sleep
Speaking in Tongues
A Maiden's Grave
The Devil's Teardrop
The Blue Nowhere
Garden of Beasts
The Bodies Left Behind
Edge

The Rune Series
Manhattan is My Beat
Death of a Blue Movie Star
Hard News

The Location Scout Series
Shallow Graves
Bloody River Blues
Hell's Kitchen

The Lincoln Rhyme Thrillers
The Bone Collector
The Coffin Dancer
The Empty Chair
The Stone Monkey
The Vanished Man
The Twelfth Card
The Cold Moon
The Broken Window
The Burning Wire
The Kill Room

The Kathryn Dance Thrillers
The Sleeping Doll
Roadside Crosses
XO

A James Bond Novel
Carte Blanche

Short Stories
Twisted
More Twisted

JEFFERY
DEAVER

THE
OCTOBER LIST

HODDER &
STOUGHTON